BEYOND THE MASK

The First Wave

Ellen Matzer, RN, CCRN and
Valery Hughes, FNP, RN

Edited by Elizabeth Grobel
Cover designs by Joshua Altmann

Fulton Books, Inc.
Meadville, PA

Published by Fulton Books 2021

ISBN 978-1-63860-715-1 (paperback)
ISBN 978-1-63860-716-8 (digital)

Printed in the United States of America

I'm afraid all this talk about nurses as heroes is priming the public to accept our deaths as casualties of war rather than as a public health failure.

—Author unknown

Acknowledgments for Valery Hughes

First and always, I want to acknowledge Mary Arzilli, my wife. Without her, there is nothing.

I also want to thank all those people at Weill Cornell Medicine and New York Presbyterian Hospital who stepped up with the fastest opening of a study I ever saw. Kristen Marks and her team from ID—especially Britta—were a brilliant force in getting the answer to the efficacy of remdesivir, and Dr. Marks and her team at Cornell Clinical Trials Unit got the Moderna study up and running with remarkable speed. To all who did the heavy lifting—Caroline, Celine, Mia, Sarah, Caique, Gianna, MaryAnn, Brian, Minkyung, Monique, Todd, Wayne, Patrice, Rebecca, Shaun, Catherine, Nadi, Jessenia, Tahera, Jiamin, Grant, Noah, Roxanne, Liz, Sophia, and the staff at the CTSC Core Lab—I acknowledge your hard work, your dedication to the research process and to the safety of the participants.

To Teresa Evering and Jonathan Berardi who opened the most complicated therapeutics study for early COVID-19 treatment, I acknowledge that monumental task.

For the rest of those at Cornell Clinical Trials Unit who kept the fires burning for our real work—HIV treatment, prevention, and cure—because of what you did for COVID-19, the work can continue. Thank you to Trip, Marshall, Tim, Genessi, Kinge-Ann, Meredith, and Christina.

Finally, I want to acknowledge all participants in the therapeutics and vaccine research. You have helped the world get through this pandemic.

Acknowledgments for Ellen Matzer

This book is dedicated to lives well lived and unfinished.

To my husband, Kenneth, my life, my heart, my partner, thank you for supporting me in everything I do, including your story. Thank you for being on the front line.

To my mom, Adele, the strongest woman I know, eighty-nine and as strong and resilient as ever.

To Amy, my daughter, PA and frontline worker, the people whose lives you touched will stay with you forever.

To Joshua, my son, frontline worker, your support work during the pandemic made a profound impact on many lives.

Faye Malonas, LPN, and Oliver Foley, LPN, your stories were awe-inspiring and will be forever remembered.

To Valery Hughes, FNP, RN, our friendship over four decades will never fade. Thank you for coauthoring with me.

To the many nurses and frontline workers whose stories we got to tell, I thank you, Michelle A., RN; K. B., RN; T. B., RN; Chloe A., RN; Marjorie H., RN; Elizabeth B., RN; Nick M., RN; M. A., J. RN.

To Caitlyn M, RN, thank you for becoming part of our family. AND thank you for your tireless advocacy for your patients and your family.

To Dr. Hugh Cassiere, voice of reason during the pandemic, thank you for your insight and knowledge.

To my dad, Dr. Alan T. Schechter (1934–1980), your impact on my life will never fade.

Chapter 1

Janet Madison was in her early fifties but could easily pass for forty. She kept herself slim with vigorous exercise and was rigid about skin care. She did not even go out in the rain without sunblock all over her face and neck. She was on her way for her usual every-six-week session with her hairdresser on February 19, having left work early to nab the last appointment before he left for vacation. She never let anyone else cut or color her hair. While in the waiting room, she ran into the woman who had recommended her to the stylist, so they sat and chatted for a while. Janet was happy to catch up with Marie. Marie was a former client and still referred a lot of work Janet's way. Marie was in the middle of a nice gossipy story when she started to cough.

"Let me get you some water," Janet said and went to the water dispenser that the salon had so conveniently put out.

They used the nice paper cups too, Janet thought, *instead of all that plastic.*

She went to her friend who was still coughing into a wad of tissues. Her eyes were watering, and she really looked distressed. She pulled down the tissues to drink, and Janet saw they were unsoiled.

After a bit, the coughing subsided, and Marie said, "I'm getting punished for telling tales!" and she laughed.

"Are you okay?" asked Janet. She took the tissues and threw them in the wastebasket and refilled Marie's water.

"I'm fine! Thanks!" She looked a bit embarrassed. "I'd better go before I talk your ear off." She put on her coat. "I think it's the coldest winter ever though! I cannot seem to warm up!" The two women hugged and promised to catch up another time.

Janet mused about how Marie looked. She should have been at her best right after having her hair done, but she looked off somehow. If Janet had been of a more observant type, she might have noted the bluish tinge of Marie's lips, or noted how fast she was breathing especially while she was talking. If she had any understanding of germs, she might have gone to the ladies' room to wash her hands after discarding Marie's tissues. However, by then, the salon was crawling with a particular virus—all over the doorknobs, sink faucets, light switches, chair arms, the pen they used to sign the credit card pad, just everything that people touched multiple times a day.

A week later while sitting with her husband watching the news, she started to cough.

"Are you okay?" Robert, her husband, asked.

"I'm fine. Must have swallowed wrong." Janet hoped she was not coming down with a cold.

In the lower part of the screen came the breaking news, *Coronavirus Hits the US*, Robert always commented on whatever news was being broadcasted. "It's another flu. What is everyone so excited about? People get a sniffle, and it makes the news."

Janet said, "Honey, I'm tired. I think I'll go to bed."

"Okay, I'll be in soon."

As Janet was lying in bed, her chest began to feel tight. She felt anxious. *Stop being so worried*, she thought. Janet drifted off to sleep, thinking she should have called their daughter Emma, who was away in her third year of college.

She woke up in the middle of the night freezing. *I must be coming down with something*, she thought. Janet got out of bed to get some Tylenol, the only medication she ever took. Robert was snoring and had pushed off all the covers. Janet saw a throw on the chair by her bedside and put it on the bed on top of the duvet. She had some water and went back to sleep.

Janet woke up the next morning feeling somewhat better but not quite right.

"I must have a little cold." She folded the extra throw and made the bed before having her morning shower. After dressing, she looked out the window. They were lucky with a view of Gramercy Park. But it was a cold and cloudy February day, and all the trees and flowers were dormant.

"Good morning, honey," said Robert. "How're you feeling this morning?" He handed her coffee.

"I think I'm probably coming down with a cold. I'll be fine in a day." Janet thought about taking the day off from work but thought better of it. "I have so much to get done this week." She sat with her coffee for a few minutes more.

Robert was off to work. "See you later, honey." He kissed her goodbye.

Janet got dressed and went into the office. She made sure to carry cough drops and tissues with her. She had a few meetings to attend.

What Janet did not know was that the SARS-CoV-2 she had been exposed to at the hair salon was starting to ravage her body. She didn't know this because she was healthy, took good care of herself, and never gave it a second thought. She was a lawyer, not a nurse or physician, and she tended to dismiss what she thought of as minor complaints. She couldn't know that her body was going to be starving for oxygen very soon, that the virus she was exposed to was now replicating in her upper respiratory tract and on its way down to the lower respiratory tract to cause even more damage. She had received a huge inoculum of the virus when her friend coughed it into the air and into Janet's airways. She could not know the virus generates a secondary viremia—where the virus journeys via the blood and then targets the heart, kidney, gastrointestinal tract, blood vessels, and potentially other parts of the body. She had become a factory for the virus, and she spread it wherever she went.

Her body was going to try to fight the virus and produce an inflammatory reaction the medical communities were starting to call a cytokine storm, a response of pro-inflammatory substances that might be as dangerous as the virus itself. She was oblivious that soon her blood's ability to clot properly was going to be impaired.

Janet's body would soon be out of control. Hemoglobin, the part of blood that carries oxygen and carbon dioxide, would be circulating with significantly less oxygen since the red blood cells would not be able to pick it up from the lungs efficiently. This hypoxemia—low blood oxygen—would lead to cell death all over her body.

What Janet did not know was that she should have called Emma before she died of respiratory failure caused by COVID-19 (Cao, W. Li, T., "COVID-19: Towards Understanding of Pathogenesis," May 2020).

Chapter 2

Critical Care
January 2020

Maureen walked into the unit at the start of her shift at 0650. She was always a few minutes early. She was in her twenty-eighth year working in this ICU. She looked at the assignment board and sighed. "Another day, another dollar." Another eighty-five-year-old patient waiting to die of multi-organ dysfunction syndrome. She was assigned only two patients today, a relief from the three she had been assigned on her last two shifts. The beds never stayed empty for long.

Her first patient, an eighty-eight-year-old postman who had coronary artery bypass graft with four arteries grafted, still on a ventilator, no future of getting off the ventilator in sight. He was on the usual drips, Levophed to maintain blood pressure, insulin to maintain a normal blood sugar, Protonix to prevent gastrointestinal ulcers, as well as the sedative Precedex to maintain comfort.

Her second patient, a woman in her seventies, was awake and ready to progress to a regular bed. She had the same surgery two days earlier, was weaned off the ventilator within four hours, out of bed in twelve, eating regular food in twenty-four hours. Today her chest tube[1] was coming out. She would be walked around the unit again and sent out. Maureen wondered whom she would get next.

She logged on to the computer to begin the day's charting. *First, the transfer*, she thought. Neurological status normal—check; cardiovascular status normal sinus rhythm—check; blood pressure

---

[1]   A chest tube helps to remove fluid and excess air in the intrapleural space—the space between the two linings of the lungs—after chest surgery.

normal—check. Gastrointestinal, last bowel movement last night, intake progressing.

She filled out the nursing care plan. *Knowledge deficit related to postoperative complications. That ought to be good enough*, she thought. *Let me see, interventions now—educate patient and family regarding coughing and deep breathing, ambulating, wound care.* Maureen went into the room to explain all these things to Mrs. Huang and her family. They were already calling for the bed for another admission.

She looked around at the unit. It had gone through several reconstructions in her thirty-five years here. She was a veteran, having grown up in this hospital. She started as a nursing assistant and then went to nursing school. Next, she was hired on a surgical floor for the first year after graduation. She always knew she wanted to work in critical care. After working in medical ICU for five years she transferred to the CTICU (cardiothoracic ICU) where she had been for the last twenty-eight years. Now there were all private rooms. It used to be two patients to a room, and in the center in rooms 254 and 256, the divider opened so it could be a four-bed room. There used to be only two rooms set aside for isolation. Now they could all accommodate a patient on isolation.

The unit seemed as large as a football field. Ten patients on one side separated by a large nurses' station and the long hallway at the end of which was the entrance to the OR and the elevators. The other side held the other ten patients. It was so large that you never knew who was working on the other side on the same shift.

Maureen looked around at all the newer nurses. *All you young ones don't get it yet.* She witnessed them calling the PA or attending physician for every little abnormality. She looked at Sandy, a perky twenty-five-year-old nurse talking earnestly with the young PA Keith. "His potassium is 3.4," she was saying.

"So—don't you guys have a protocol for this?" he said with annoyance.

"Not on the third day," said Sandy, "It ends on day two."

"I'll get to it."

Maureen just shook her head. She knew what to do. She walked over to Keith and said, "I'm gonna put in an order for 20 mEq PO for you."

"Thanks, Mo," he said.

After several years here, Maureen was affectionately referred to as just Mo. Maureen liked having a nickname. It seemed to her a sign of respect and friendship.

Sandy said, "I didn't know we could do that."

Maureen stopped herself from a snarky reply. Sandy was just young and inexperienced, after all. She just nodded and said, "We know what to do, you just have to tell them you'll put in the order." Maureen thought, *I used to be like that a long time ago. I was young, excited, and scared. Now I'm just an old know-it-all jaded nurse, and this is just a job.*

She reviewed some of the things she was unhappy about in her work. *What we have to tolerate from administration.* She knew she could think of many things that she now hated about her once passionate feel for nursing. *I wish I could just retire.*

Maureen thought back on her life as she sat in the swivel chair in front of one of the desktop computers, pretending to chart. Legs crossed, one foot swinging back and forth, furtively watching the activity on the unit, and pretending not to see things so someone else would take care of it. Call bells always ringing. Patients calling out for things like water, ice, close the lights, open the lights, close the curtain, open the curtain. Maureen pretended to be busy or not to notice. She continued to swing her foot back and forth.

She thought, *Why should I have to do it, I've done enough for a lifetime.* She also needed a cigarette.

Unfortunately, Maureen was one of those who could not kick the habit although she had tried several times.

I guess I'm just destined to have this habit, she thought. *It's not so bad, I don't really drink or do drugs or go out much. I can smoke if I want to—in fact, I think I'll go out now, I could use a cigarette.*

She motioned over to Sandy indicating with her hands the motion of smoking. Sandy nodded back. Mo went outside out to the curbside employee smoking area.

They used to have a smoking area on the property, she thought. *Now I have to go down to the street. I must look like an idiot, like I'm waiting for a bus.* She wished she had worn a jacket so she wasn't seen in scrubs. After all, she was supposed to be a role model of health. *Fuck it.* Maureen took a long drag on the first of her two cigarettes she would have. She looked at the smoke whirling around her as she exhaled. She looked at the line of cars coming into the hospital visitors parking lot. *More visitors coming in to let us know their Google thoughts on health care. I'm just sick of it.* Maureen stamped out her last cigarette butt, looked at her watch, and sighed. *I'd better get back.*

When she came back in, she went into the employee bathroom to use some mouthwash. *No sense in having bad breath*, she thought. But she knew that the smell of cigarette smoke was already on her uniform.

Maureen looked in the mirror. *Ugh, my gray roots are really showing now.*

She remembered when she used to have her hair professionally colored. Not anymore. She used a box from the drugstore once every six weeks or so. She wore her long brown hair in a messy ponytail.

What the hell do I have to look good for? she thought.

Maureen was a tall slender woman nearing sixty, with signs of once having been a beauty. Now she looked worn and haggard.

She had been married and divorced at an early age. She had a daughter immediately after marrying the man she thought was the love of her life. Sadly, she wasn't the love of his life. He left her for a younger woman. Since then, she lived with her daughter and her elderly mother in the same house she grew up in. After the huge betrayal, she never dated and never had another relationship.

She came out of the locker room onto the unit. She checked in with Sandy.

"Anything?"

"Nope," said Sandy, "all good."

Ethan came over. "Mo, Mrs. Huang needs some attention." Mrs. Huang was due to have her chest tube removed later today. Maureen sighed.

"Tube out today," Maureen said.

Mrs. Huang looked at her with a perplexed look and lifted the chest tube.

"*No*, leave down," Maureen said.

"Oh, okay—down."

"Yes." Maureen nodded. "Down."

She knew if she went out of the room, Mrs. Huang would summon her back to go through the same conversation with the Foley catheter and then again with the central line.

Maureen looked up at the monitor. She saw several premature beats that she had not noticed before.

She knew what that meant. Mrs. Huang was about to go into A-fib.

Maureen thought, *I wonder if I will be the only one to notice… again.*

She walked slowly to the medication room and got out an amiodarone bolus and drip and a Cardizem drip. She knew the PA would want one or the other to control this arrhythmia.

Maureen sauntered over to Jan, the charge nurse for the day.

"Think we'd better hold off on Huang's transfer, she's gonna go into A-fib."

Jan came over to the monitor to look, as she would have to explain the holdup on the transfer. "Yup, she's throwing those APCs. Maybe we should let her attending know, maybe he wants to start something PO now." PO is short for "per os," a Latin phrase for "orally."

"I'll call," said Maureen.

I wish I wasn't so smart, thought Maureen. *Now I will have to deal with Mrs. Huang for a few more hours.*

"Sandy, come over here and look at this."

Sandy got up quickly and came over to Mrs. Huang's room.

"Look at her monitor."

"Okay," Sandy said, feeling tested. "Uh, she's having some APCs.

"Good," Maureen said, "now what?"

"Well, APCs are usually benign," Sandy said with trepidation.

"Yes, they are," replied Maureen, "but what surgery did she just have?"

Sandy stared at the monitor, the central line with pacing wires attached, the chest tube, the Foley catheter, trying to think of the answer. She knew she was being tested.

It hit her. "She had a valve replacement. Do you think she is going to go into atrial fibrillation?"

"Good girl," said Maureen, "now you're thinking."

Sandy looked at the bedside table and saw that Maureen had already gotten amiodarone and Cardizem ready.

"How do you know what they're gonna order?" she said.

"I don't, it will be the drug de jour. But there are only a few choices."

"Thanks for sharing that with me," Sandy said. She knew she would never forget that moment.

Sandy went back to her computer terminal WOW (workstation on wheels). *I should have known that a K of 3.4 could wait*, she thought. *Now Keith will think I am an idiot.* She felt that sting of fear in the pit of her stomach, a feeling that she might never be good enough for this work. *I wonder how Maureen does it? She just tells them what to do. I hope I get to be like that soon.* She was happy that Maureen had taught her something today too. She knew she wouldn't forget it. *Valve. APCs. A-fib. Cardizem. Amiodarone. Check.* She felt more confident already.

Suddenly, an alarm sounded in the background.

Sandy rushed over to the central station to see what was ringing. Alarms often sounded, but most of the time it was the patient moving or being disconnected from the monitor.

She was startled to see the saw-toothed pattern that was a real reason for concern.

She thought, *Is that V-tach?* and rushed into the room. Before she could get into the room, Maureen was already there, a dose of amiodarone[2] in her hand, shaking the patient. "John, wake up! *John!* Are you okay?"

---

[2] A drug used to treat serious heart rhythm abnormalities.

John slowly woke up and said, "What happened?" Maryanne looked at Sandy.

"Your heartbeat was a bit irregular for a few seconds. We think it has something to do with your potassium."

"Am I gonna be okay?"

"Of course, you are!" Sandy said.

Maureen leaned into Sandy. "Sandy, don't go to the central monitor, go to the patient," she said in a whisper. It was a novice mistake to "nurse the monitor" rather than evaluate the patient.

Maureen took a strip from the bedside monitor, looked at it for a few seconds, and handed it to Sandy.

"Yep, he had a run. Is this the guy with the low K?" Sandy nodded. Maureen was using shorthand to confirm the patient had a run—several beats—of a potentially lethal arrhythmia called ventricular tachycardia, or V-tach for short. She called potassium K which is the way potassium is listed on the periodic table of the elements.

"You might want to get Keith. Some post-op patients have a low threshold for V-tach and need a higher K level. Maybe he won't be such a smart-ass to you now." Maureen decided to let Sandy take the lead on this one.

Sandy wondered if Keith treated everyone the same way or he was just being short with her. She thought, *I know I am a new nurse and have a lot to learn, but he's so mean.* She went to talk to Maureen. "Is Keith this mean with everyone, or is it just me?"

"No, these young PAs think they know a shit ton about everything and will try to intimidate you. Just don't let them. You have to know what you're doing to survive around here. We all went through it. It's like a sort of hazing, don't let it get to you."

Sandy wondered if she was cut out for this type of nursing with all these strong personalities.

She said to herself, *Just learn your stuff, then they will have to respect you, just like Maureen.*

Sandy had been a nurse just over two years now. She took a year off after high school to travel for cheerleading competitions throughout the United States. She had been a champion in high school, someone who was looked up to and respected. Being a nurse was a constant reminder of her inadequacies, and she found it slightly oppressive. Sandy let her thoughts wander back to competition and how it made her feel to be so proficient.

She thought back to a routine where she was thrown into the air by two of her teammates, how thrilling it was to be up in the air, doing a somersault and twist to impress the audience. She always landed perfectly on the shoulders of Roy, one of the stronger guys in the competition.

A monitor alarm brought her back to the current reality. She wasn't flying in the air, she was responsible for lives now, and she needed to focus. She was determined to become respected in this arena too.

She wanted to be a nurse ever since her grandmother Edna died of cancer seven years ago. She wanted to help people get better, be with them when they were at their worst, sit with them if they were dying as she did with Grandma. Edna chose to be in hospice for the last weeks of her life. She had fought a long battle with colon cancer, having had surgery and chemotherapy. After three long years, the cancer had come back and spread to her liver. Sandy wanted so much to relieve her pain.

"Grandma, I am going to be a nurse and make you proud," Sandy said, crying.

"You already do." Grandma patted her hand.

Sandy watched the expert nurses convince Edna to take her pain medication, putting it in Jell-O so she could swallow. She watched as Edna became less responsive and the nurses injected pain medication into her infuse-a-port.[3]

Sandy thought, as she watched the hospice nurse expertly inject Dilaudid into the port. "How did she know to give that now?"

She noticed that Grandma's breathing had eased and thought, *Okay, so they watched her breathing, and they gave her the medication.*

I'm going to be the one that makes that important decision some-day, she thought. Grandma Edna left this world with Sandy and her

---

[3] This is an access port to a person's blood vessels and avoids the need for repeated needlesticks for intravenous infusions, and for obtaining blood.

mom by her side, Sandy's cell phone YouTube set to her grandma's favorite song "Somewhere over the Rainbow" playing softly. They used to sing it together when Sandy was a little girl, and they would watch Dorothy sing it in *The Wizard of Oz*. "Somewhere, over the rainbow, way up high…"

Sandy remembered every moment of those times, being afraid of the Wicked Witch, watching Glinda the Good Witch of the North say "Be gone, you have no power here." Sometimes, when she needed comfort, those memories popped into her mind.

Her last words to Grandma were "Grandma, I'm going to be the best nurse, I promise."

Grandma said," I know, my little Sand-girl, I know."

Sandy graduated at the top of her class in nursing school. She excelled at her clinical rotations and got the first position to which she applied.

Her parents were pleased she chose this field. When she started her first nursing job, reality set in. On the surgical floor, she had up to seven patients. Of those, it was common to have four fresh post-ops (people who had just had surgery that day), plus two discharges or transfer out. The physical care was one thing, but the charting was detailed and extensive. The bed never stayed empty long enough to catch up, and then there would be an admission requiring another load of detailed charting in addition to the physical assessments and care.

She almost never took a lunch break and often stayed late to finish her charting. After a year on surgery, she wanted to go to critical care. She had seen those nurses when they came down for a code[4] or RRT[5] and thought, *I want to be one of them.*

She applied for the transfer and got it.

---

[4] A code is shorthand for cardiac arrest. In most hospitals, the overhead announcements are coded so as not to alarm other patients or visitors. A code blue might be used to mobilize the cardiac arrest team. A code red might mean a fire in some part of the hospital.

[5] RRT—rapid response team. This is a team that comes quickly to assess and treat a patient who has taken a sudden turn for the worse.

Sandy's first case ever by herself was a fifty-four-year-old man who had an uncomplicated coronary artery bypass graft, often called a CABG (pronounced "cabbage"). Sandy remembered being nervous. She had support from her preceptor Maureen, but the preceptor always had her own patients and was just there for backup. *I hope I don't have to call her for much*, Sandy thought. When a patient came out from the operating room after open-heart surgery, they were really fragile and often unstable. After about six months, Sandy stopped feeling like she was going to vomit every time she was up for a fresh heart.

Mrs. Ruth Nissenbaum, eighty-six years old, was in room 251. She had a complicated hospital course.

She had been in the CTICU for over three weeks now. She had an aortic valve replacement called a TAVR (transfemoral aortic valve replacement).

Ruth was one of the patients in whom the surgery did *not* go well. She came out of the operating room agitated and confused. She tried to pull out her temporary pacemaker. She required medication to sedate her and keep her calm and safe. This eventually resulted in respiratory compromise and intubation—something the TAVR procedure hopes to avoid. After two weeks of intubation, the family was consulted about a tracheostomy as she was unable to be weaned from the ventilator. They agreed to the procedure.

When Dr. Henderson tried to shut off the temporary pacemaker, Ruth no longer had her own heart rhythm resulting in a permanent pacemaker being implanted. The family agreed. Since she couldn't have proper nutrition, the family then agreed to a PEG (a feeding tube placed through the wall of the stomach) placement. She then developed aspiration pneumonia, so she was placed on a course of antibiotics.

This resulted in C. difficile diarrhea.

Ruth's daughter Leah could not understand how this all happened so fast.

Dr. Henderson explained, "Unfortunately, this is often the case with elderly patients undergoing any type of heart surgery. Sometimes the body just doesn't respond well postoperatively, and complications like this occur."

"But you said she would be just fine," Leah said with desperation.

Leah had started spending day and night by Ruth's bedside. She started questioning the moves of every nurse, aide, respiratory therapist, and consultant on the case. She desperately sought answers.

As the days went on, Ruth became less responsive.

*****

"Hey, Ethan, can you help me turn in 251?"

"Sure!" said Ethan. "Meet ya right there in a sec."

Ethan was one of two nursing assistants that worked the day shift on the unit. He had been there a few months when Sandy first started, and they struck up an immediate friendship. Ethan was currently in nursing school and extremely interested in learning all he could while he was on duty. He took an interest in all the nuances of being a critical-care nurse. He watched as drips were titrated, as patients were extubated, and he held patients' hands as their chest tubes were being removed. He was a real team player, and Sandy was glad when they were on together. Ethan worked only part-time now since he was in school full-time. He always asked questions when he wanted to understand something fully. Some of the nurses found it annoying, but Sandy loved to share her newfound knowledge.

Sandy and Ethan entered the room. Leah was sitting by her mother's bedside.

"We're just going to turn her," Sandy said gently.

"Can I ask you a few questions?" said Leah. "Of course."

Sandy and Ethan knew what was coming next, a barrage of questions Leah asked of every health-care provider that walked in the room. Leah even questioned the housekeeper about putting two plastic bags in the garbage can, and she also watched as the employee mopped and pointed out missed areas.

"So did Mom have a chest x-ray today?"

Sandy replied gently, "No, she did not."

"Why?"

"Well, often a change in a chest x-ray is not seen immediately, so there is no reason to have a daily one."

"Okay, I see her tube feeding is on hold, doesn't she need all her food?"

"Yes, she does," replied Sandy, "it is just that we have to lay her flat in order to turn her, so we have to turn it off briefly."

"But will you make it up, I want her to get every calorie to get better."

"Yes, we have a system to increase the feedings every six hours to make up for times when the tube feedings must be shut off."

"Her tube feedings are *shut off?*"

"No, Leah, they are only put on hold for a short duration when we have to lay your mom flat."

Sandy's patience was starting to wear. She smiled sweetly and said, "Leah, we really don't want your mom to be on one side for too long, so if you could just step out for a few moments, we can get done and you can come back in."

"Just one more question, I promise," said Leah

"Don't you think you should open the curtains on the window. I read that vitamin D in sunlight is especially important for healing, and I want mom to get some."

Rather than going through an entire explanation of the window's capacity to block sunlight, Sandy said, "Of course, we can open the curtains, that's a great idea!" Sandy was well aware that people needed control of some part of an uncontrollable situation, and she felt it couldn't hurt to give Leah some say in her mother's care.

"I am going to put on some music for her," said Ethan as he took out his phone.

"Ruth likes this song." He pulled up YouTube and pressed play. The song started to play. "She also likes it when we sing along with her," Ethan said cheerfully.

It's the song I used to sing with my grandma Edna," Sandy said gently to Leah.

"Somewhere over the rainbow, way up high…," both Ethan and Sandy started to sing.

"I didn't know Mom liked that song," said Leah.

"Look at her," Ethan said, "she seems like she's smiling."

"Why don't you take a short break, get a cup of tea?" Sandy said. Leah went outside to the cafeteria.

With "Over the Rainbow" playing in the background, Ethan and Sandy began the arduous process of turning Ruth on her side.

"I'll take these pillows out," Sandy said as Ethan pulled the bedsheets toward him. "It smells like we need a linen change," he reported. He removed his blue plastic gown and gloves, washed his hands, and went outside to collect the necessary supplies.

Sandy stayed behind to perform her assessments required every four hours. She removed her stethoscope from underneath her gown and listened to Ruth's lungs. *Not too bad today*, she thought. She started talking to her, explaining what she was doing.

"Just cleaning out your breathing tube—you're going to cough now." She suctioned Mrs. Nissenbaum's endotracheal tube, using the in-line catheter attached to the ventilator. She noted secretions were thick but not purulent (not containing pus).

Next, she removed a swab stick from the sterile pouch containing chlorhexidine, a topical antibacterial, and began to clean Ruth's mouth. She spoke to her softly.

"It's okay, Ruth, it's okay—just cleaning your mouth."

She looked at the Foley catheter[6] and emptied the top chamber into the bottom to record the output. Next, she checked the PEG site and changed the dressing. She put the tube feeding on hold so she could lay Ruth flat. It was safer not to have the tube feeding going in when a person was flat to decrease the possibility of vomiting.

Ethan came back gowned and ready to bathe Ruth.

"You hold her over, and I'll wipe," said Sandy. "Okay, we're going to turn you now and wash your back," she said soothingly.

Ethan gently pulled on the sheets to roll Ruth to her side. Sandy tucked the dirty sheets halfway underneath Ruth's back. She took the first washcloth and gently wiped away Ruth's buttocks and anal area. "Looks like C. diff again," Ethan said.

---

[6] An indwelling urinary catheter.

"She's still on vanco… I don't understand why it's not working," said Sandy.

Sandy had made a bed roll using a new sheet and chux (waterproof pads) and rolled it underneath the soiled one. She then gently turned Ruth back over the new and soiled sheets.

The clean sheets are under the soiled sheets and so stay clean.

"It's okay, Ruth, just going over the big bump."

Ethan rolled out the sheets from the other side, careful to keep the contents contained. The linen hamper was in the room as was the case with all patients with C. diff diarrhea.

He put everything into the hamper. He wrinkled up his nose, wishing for deodorant spray. They carefully positioned Ruth on her right side, placing two pillows behind her back, one under her right arm, and pulled the pillow under her head down underneath her shoulder. She looked clean and comfortable. All that had taken them almost forty-five minutes.

"Ethan, where are you?" another nurse was calling. "Need help in fifty-six."

"Gotta go," Ethan said. "Duty calls," he said with a wink. "See ya later for a repeat, I'm sure."

"Don't forget your phone," said Sandy. "Maybe the guy in fifty-six needs to hear 'Over the Rainbow.'" Ethan removed his gown and gloves, washed his hands, and took his phone out of the plastic wrap that had contained the gown. Off he went into 256.

At 12:00 p.m., Ethan went into the break room for lunch. A vegetarian, he was having Ensure and vegetables with hummus.

Ethan thought, *Six more months of school and hopefully I'll be doing this. Then no more bulk buying at Costco."*

Ethan, twenty-five, had not had an easy childhood. His father, a construction worker, had been injured on the job when Ethan was ten years old and had become addicted to prescription narcotics.

His mother, a professional athlete, had developed psychosis from usage of amphetamines and had been in and out of the hospital. He wondered how she was doing now in her new assisted living apartment. He had not seen her for years.

Ethan, an only child, was left with the burden of taking care of both parents until his mother left them. Ethan was thirteen. He cleaned the house, he walked the dog, he mowed the lawn. He had watched his mother diet down for competitions. Ethan considered her a role model with her discipline around food and exercise.

Ethan thought back then, *I could have this kind of discipline too.*

So he consciously limited his food intake to see how far he could go. Mom was taken to the hospital for severe malnutrition and overdosage of over-the-counter antihistamines (Pseudofed). She was never the same. She never came home. Ethan continued to limit his food intake. One day his father walked in and saw him with his shirt off.

"What's wrong with you? You look like you just came out of Auschwitz!" He looked shocked. "I am calling your doctor!"

"Dad, I'm fine! I'm just getting in shape."

Things were never the same after that. His father kept to himself. They only spoke when his father would complain about there being dishes in the sink or the bathroom toilet was clogged.

Otherwise, there was silence.

Ethan thought now, *How stupid was that?*

Ethan had been the object of much bullying throughout middle and high school. He was singled out for being different—with his slight frame, effeminate qualities, and deliberate tone. He remembers coming home after being beaten up only to have his Dad ask, "What happened? Did they kick you around again?" He barely looked at Ethan. He never called the school or even the police to report this. Ethan never felt as though he was ever seen, much less understood.

He was thankful he had his grandma, Mary, to support him. His uncle, whom he never even met, had died of AIDS in 1990. He wondered about him. "What was he like? Would we have been close?"

Grandma Mary always said, "Ethan, you remind me so much of your uncle, I know you would have been close."

He wondered what it was like to have been a nurse during the AIDS epidemic.

I think I would have fit right in with those nurses, he thought Ethan was grateful he was able to finally come through the other side of his own demons, anorexia/bulimia and drug use. He wondered if he would ever have enough nerve to share all of this with Sandy or anyone for that matter. His mind wandered back to his admission to an eating disorder unit.

"You sit there until your tray is finished," said the technician assigned to monitor the food intake of the patients. He wasn't unkind, but he was immovable.

Ethan finished his lunch.

"Done," he said. "I have to go to the bathroom, you gonna follow me?"

"Yup," said the attendant abruptly. In they walked to the bathroom where Ethan was watched as he used the toilet.

"I know, I know, don't flush until you look."

"Right on that, kid."

He got out after a week and went on an even bigger eating and purging binge.

Dad used to give him $10 a day for food. He remembers going to the grocery store and buying every sugary snack that $10 could buy. He came home, ate all of it, broke the lock on his father's door, and took all the snacks his dad had hidden there.

Then into the bathroom he went.

He had been hospitalized several times for this eating disorder in his short twenty-five years. He remembers the multiple fights with his father over this and the multiple admissions to rehab for treatment, all not working.

Then came the drugs. One addiction turned in for another. Crack, cocaine, heroin, ketamine, anything that he could get his hands on was fair game. He was dazed all the time. His dad just thought he was deep in thought. They hadn't really talked that much anyway. Each was absorbed in their own toxic life.

One day he just decided to stop. He lay on the sofa for two weeks' detoxing, sweating, vomiting, feverish. Dad thought it was the flu.

Then it occurred to Ethan, *I need a way out of this mess.*

What he needed was to figure out his goal in life. And with nursing, he seemed to have found it. At twenty-one, he moved into the basement apartment of his childhood home, got a job as a nurse's aide after completing his certification course, and supported himself through nursing school. It was tough. He kept himself on a tight budget. He bought most of his food in bulk at Costco, such as cases of Ensure and vats of hummus. He had to save for tuition and the rest for rent. He wished his father wouldn't insist on charging him rent for a house that was paid off. On the other hand, he was grateful for a place to live.

It was a great basement. *A pretty cool space*, Ethan thought. Calling it affectionately his hobbit hole, he had to walk down ten steps from the outside into the basement. He had it set up just the way he liked it, what he called quirky-modern. There was a big bedroom space with his bed, a desk, and laptop computer and an even larger screen hooked up to watch YouTube videos—mostly clinical scenarios on what he was learning in school at the moment. He had a large white erasable marker board to write notes for school, his exercise routines, draw diagrams, and for meaningful quotes he used for inspiration.

There was a nice-sized kitchen with a table and chairs. The finishes were all vintage 1975, but he kept it well organized and scrupulously clean. There was another space for his futon sofa. His favorite space was a room for his arts and crafts projects. Ethan loved to make soap, sew, and play the guitar and ukulele. He sang a little, too, although not that well. He really enjoyed his space. He had a big bookcase with pictures of charts of anatomy, a replica of the human body to take apart to learn, and his prized possession, a shadow box full of his grandfather's surgical instruments.

He wondered how his ex-boyfriend was doing. They had recently separated when Ethan found out that Danny was using amphetamines. He had known that Danny was a bit of a party guy but did not realize how bad the addiction had become. Ethan had to worry about way too much to take care of Danny right now. He was working at a job he loved, and he was going to be a nurse.

He came back from his break with a smile. Time to go help my nurses, time to learn more things, time to use my life experiences to help others.

Ethan loved his job, but as Ethan was leaving the break room, he looked down at his phone. There was a text from Danny. His heart skipped a beat. "Hey baby, going to be in New York for a few, can I crash with you?" Ethan tried to take his mind off Danny as he went back to work. He pictured Danny's face, something he was trying to avoid since the breakup. *Damn, but he was so cute.* He came back onto the unit and was quickly summoned by Sandy to turn and clean Mrs. Nissenbaum again. Ethan wasn't upset that this was the third time this shift. He felt badly for this woman who was so fragile, unable to do anything for herself anymore, and her daughter who was so immersed in saving her mother, she couldn't see past the fact that Ruth no longer had any quality of life. Still, he went in with a smile ready to put on music, turn, and bathe her again. He tried to keep the text from Danny away from his thoughts, but Sandy picked up on it.

"Waz up, beb," Sandy mimicked his favorite saying. "Got a text from Danny." Sandy's expression turned stonelike.

"What does that lowlife want now?"

"Coming to NY, wants to crash with me."

"Don't do it, you know what happened the last time," Sandy said with a bit of anger.

"Yeah, you're right."

"Remember you are out $2,500. He's only gonna take advantage of your weak spot for him again and get money out of you."

"I know, Sandy, but with work and school, I have no social life."

"Well, if you consider Danny, the one who took your money and broke your heart a social life, I have nothing to say." Sandy and Ethan finished cleaning and turning Ruth, music playing in the background. They disposed of the linens, washed up, doffed their gowns and gloves. Sandy had work to do with her other patients, but she watched as Ethan walked away toward the bathroom holding his cell phone. *I hope he doesn't do it*, she thought. Sandy knew that this was enough to push Ethan into a downward spiral, knowing his history of drugs and an eating disorder. She made a mental note to talk to him again later.

Chapter 3

The Emergency Room
January 2020

At 6:50 a.m., Michael was standing next to the employee punch-in clock along with at least twelve of his colleagues. The hospital had a strict policy that no one could punch in more than seven minutes before their shift. As the clock shifted to six fifty-three, everyone began to punch in.

Most of the employees using the same time clock as Michael worked in either the ER or Facilities Management which had an office near the ER. Michael overheard a couple of the facilities guys talking; he didn't know their names, but they always argued politics. One was an older white man. His coworker was middle-aged and also white. The middle-aged man was what Michael classified as an angry white dude, and he was always harsh with the old guy. Michael couldn't understand why they ever spoke, since they never did so without it getting contentious. Today, as always, they were arguing about the president.

"He's the only one who gets anything done in this country. He's taking it back from those fucking libtards you're so attached to," said Angry Dude.

"If you only watch Fox News, that's what they'd have you believe. There are real issues here, and he is *not* taking care of business," the old guy said calmly. "I can't believe you fall for all that. Are you doing better now than you were three years ago? Didn't I hear you bellyaching about your taxes last year? And you're angry all the time, even with people who agree with you! You know there's a problem—you just won't face it."

"What the fuck do you know? You have your head up your ass," Angry Dude retorted. "I mean, take this China virus bullshit. Those fucking Chinese took all our jobs, and now they are eating God knows what and getting their own people sick as hell. Didn't that last SARS crap happen in China too? What a bunch of fuckups. And those fucking liberals just want to hand over our jobs with that free trade bullshit. Give me *this* president any day. He don't take hostages." Angry Dude was speaking forcefully, but his words had less heat than they implied.

The old guy snorted in derision. "No, he just stores kids in cages and sticks his tongue down your wife's throat and steals your money, but you're too stupid to see it. You think he's your *pal*. He hates your guts—or he would if he ever met you. Hell, *I* hate your guts, and I'm your uncle." He snorted again.

"Don't choke yourself to death, you old fuck," replied Angry Dude. They walked amicably to the office door. Michael was happy not to hear the rest of *that* conversation. Thanksgiving must be a nightmare for that family. He wandered back to his work area and to be ready for the day.

At about 0710, the morning safety huddle began. The charge nurse, Helen, had a list of the current issues that had to be addressed. The list is compiled from chart reviews, reports from supervisors on the floors, the chief medical officer.

"So there were thirteen IVs that were sent up to the floors in the last week with no labels," she started.

"There were sixteen delays in getting patients to their assigned beds." Once beds were assigned, only one hour was supposed to elapse before a patient was brought up to their assigned bed.

Michael looked quizzically at his colleague Marissa standing next to him and whispered, "They only start by giving us the bad stuff. Never a good job! Or well done." Marissa sighed and nodded.

Helen droned on, "There were two C. diff specimens not sent before the patient was transferred to the floors, resulting in a delay in treatment."

Michael whispered to Marissa, "Maybe they didn't shit down here."

"Or maybe they did, and the tech cleaned them up not knowing we needed a specimen," replied Marissa.

"Remember your customer service skills, we never say 'No problem.' We say, 'It's my pleasure,'" Helen said, never looking up from her notes.

Michael and Melissa looked at each other and rolled their eyes. "Okay, have a great day, everyone," Helen said and walked away. Michael looked at the assignment board and saw he was assigned to the main ER.

The emergency room held fifty beds as well as stretchers placed strategically for high census times. There were also two separate rows of chairs for patients that could sit up and be seen. There was a critical care room that housed four patients and a trauma bay that had three sections including one for pediatrics.

There was a separate pediatric area that held twelve beds. Then there was the rapid treatment area. This was a separate room holding ten beds for not so emergent cases, for example, a sprain, a minor surgical procedure such as drainage of a simple abscess, general complaint of pain after a minor fall, some gynecological problems. Once in the main ER, Michael selected his computer on wheels, signed in, and saw the bed numbers to which he was assigned. Six through twelve. He saw only three names, which meant that there were still three patients in beds waiting for their workup to be completed so they could be discharged, or they were waiting for a bed.

He thought, *Three empties, wonder how long that will last.*

Meanwhile, the radiology department was getting ready for their day.

At 6:45 a.m., Kyle walked into the operating room locker room to get his scrubs for the shift. He then went down to the radiology locker room to change and get his right and left lateral markers and dosimetry badge (radiation badge that is turned in every month to measure radiation exposure). He then went downstairs to say good morning to the supervisor.

"Hey, Donna, How's everything?" he said.

"Hey, Kyle! Start in the ER as usual… Have a good day."

Kyle went upstairs to the first-floor control room. John, the overnight technologist, was sitting there, waiting for relief so he could go home.

"Anything left?"

"Hey, yeah, sorry, one ER left, an abdomen. Nurse was drawing blood. But there seem to be a lot of patients waiting in triage."

"That happens. Have a good day."

"Thanks," said John. He already had his knapsack and was walking out the door.

Kyle went about his usual morning routine before his partner for the day, Jessica, came in at 8:00 a.m.

He took the container of Clorox wipes, put on gloves, and proceeded to wipe down the countertops, the portable machines, the x-ray console, as well as the x-ray table, chest board (used for patients to stand against for their x-rays A/P [front to back] and lateral [sideways]); he also had to wipe down the lead shields and thyroid collars used for patients that came over for their films.

Next, he ran the quality control checks on the x-ray console computer and portable machines. He walked over to the emergency room to check on the patient that was left over from the night shift. Kyle did not see the patient in her assigned room, so he went to the nurse. "Where is the patient in room 8?"

"Sorry," replied Sharon, the day nurse, "in the bathroom trying to get us a urine specimen."

"Okay, I'll be back later."

It was now 8:00 a.m., and Jess walked in.

"Hey, what's up?" she called out.

"Just got called for the safety huddle. Only one waiting in the ER, not ready yet."

They both went downstairs around the table in the center of the station. In walked Robert, the director of Radiology. Donna was already there, also the three radiology RNs, the supervisor of Ultrasound, Nuclear Medicine, and CT scan. They all waited.

"Does anyone have any safety issues to discuss?" asked Robert. He glanced over at each person around the table.

Emma, one of the radiology nurses, said, "We keep having delays in transport. They are never around to bring the patient back to the room after their procedure."

"Yeah," echoed Morris, the Ultrasound supervisor, "the patients are done with their study, and transport is nowhere to be found. We page them and nothing."

"I'll have to check into that," Robert replied. "Anything else?" He glanced around the table once more then turned. As he walked away, he said, "Have a good day, everyone, call me if there are any problems."

That meeting took about twenty minutes. Kyle and Jess went back upstairs to start their day.

When they got there, Kyle saw that four requisitions had already printed out.

He sighed. "Here we go, four plus the one leftover in the ER and I still have to do the critical-care run." The requisitions were all timed, and they were done in order unless there was an emergency.

The phone rang, it was Donna. "Hey, Kyle, sorry to do this to you, but we had a sick call and I need you to do the run in medical ICU as well."

"Okay, not a problem, but if we can get some help later when the ER starts ramping up, that would be great."

"I'll see what I can do." Kyle knew that would not happen.

"I'll go do the ER. You go do the run," Jess said.

"Okay—see you later." Kyle went to get the portable machine. He carefully wiped it down with the germicidal wipes that were everywhere in the hospital. He was never sure if the tech before him wiped down the machine. Kyle was meticulous about following the protocol. "Equipment is to be wiped down after every use," he remembers Robert stressing at each safety huddle. Other techs let that task go when a container of wipes were not within eyesight. Not Kyle, he went out of his way to make sure there was one available on his machine. As Kyle wiped down the bottom, he noticed a few spots of dried blood near the wheels. He wiped them off carefully.

"They're not gonna pin that on me."

*****

Michael went over to the night nurse to get report. Her name was Jenna.

"Bed 6, seventy-year-old female, here with abdominal pain waiting for CT[7] results. Probably going home. WBC slightly elevated, afebrile, lactic acid flat." What Jenna meant by this is that the patient probably had a mild infection, no fever, and no sign of a worsening infection.

"Bed 7 empty."

"Bed 8—sixty-nine-year-old male here for chest pain, EKG normal, enzymes flat, need one more at 1400 then he can go home. Oh, he has to be seen by cardiology since he has a history of an MI." This person was suspected to have had a heart attack, but the EKG was normal, as were the enzymes released by the damaged heart cells when a heart attack has really happened. In the case of someone who has had a heart attack (an MI, or myocardial infarction), there is a higher risk of another. In general, they look at more than one EKG and more than one set of enzymes to make sure the event is not evolving.

"Bed 9, twenty-one-year-old female had a little too much to drink last night, fell down a flight of stairs." She paused and looked at her notes. "Head CT normal, multiple bruises, she needs to sleep it off a bit more. Probable discharge in a few hours." She added, "Waiting for her parents to come."

"Okay, see ya later." And Jenna was off.

Michael thought, *Not bad, I will get these first two discharged, make sure the cardiologist sees bed 8. Then get ready for the onslaught.* He looked around to see whom he was working with. "Okay, the A

---

[7] CT is shorthand for computerized axial tomography, an x-ray technique that renders pictures in three dimensions. Although the pictures are still flat on the screen, you can manipulate them to get a good picture of the area being examined. They are particularly useful in emergencies, though not as good for soft tissue exams as the MRI, or magnetic resonance imagery.

team is here." He saw Angela the PA sitting at the station charting, Dr. Sulkin standing by the curtain of bed 1, and Dr. Greenstein the neurologist across from him in slot 26. *Must have been a neuro RRT*, he thought. An RRT was shorthand for rapid response team, so the patient must have had a neurological emergency, such as a stroke.

He made rounds on his three patients, checked their vital signs, looked up their labs, saw the one lab pending for the chest pain patient in bed 8, and made a mental note to get the blood draw supplies on his cart.

Michael pulled up the screen to see the total emergency room census. There were only eighteen patients in the emergency room, but it was only eight thirty in the morning.

Let's look and see what's going on around me. Michael scanned the census, saw the usual type of patient—chest pain, abdominal pain, R/O CVA (R/O means "rule out" and CVA is shorthand for cere-brovascular accident—or stroke), forehead lac (lac is shorthand for laceration or cut), R/O obstruction (obstruction in the bowel), arm pain, average run-of-the-mill ER stuff. He was a bit surprised that there was no one in trauma or critical care.

That is good, Michael thought, *since I am on for four in a row*. Each nurse was required to work thirteen shifts per month so that left them with a week of four shifts. Michael preferred to work them all in a row so he could have a stretch off with his family.

Michael, fifty-two years old, was a tall distinguished-looking African American man. He had slightly graying hair which he kept noticeably short, and a weightlifter's build. He had been a nurse for eighteen years, having graduated nursing school at the age of thir-ty-four. Prior to that, he had gone to school for finance and received his degree in business administration. He knew after working for a private financial management company for several years that it was not the career for him. It was his wife who suggested he go back to school to become a nurse. His wife, Pamela, was a nurse in labor and delivery in another hospital in the area. He never considered labor and delivery as a viable specialty for himself, but he found the chal-lenges of the emergency room interesting. He worked on a medical floor for one year and was accepted to the hospital's internship for the emergency room which consisted of a year's worth of work in the step-down unit, all the critical-care areas, and finally the emergency room. He learned a lot in that year, and he thought himself to be a seasoned nurse. He rotated through the emergency room, every day a different assignment, trauma, critical care, the rapid treatment area, all of which he found interesting.

Michael and Pamela had three boys, two still in high school and one about to finish college.

They had been able to buy a house on a good block in Jamaica, one of the nicest areas of Queens, close to his in-laws. The kids were healthy and doing well in school. He and Pamela were saving for their other two sons' college, but what parent wasn't worried about that? When he was off, Michael and his sons enjoyed sports, going to games, playing catch in the yard, taking the dog for long walks in the park, and hiking. In the summers, they loved to all go camping, hiking, and canoeing. He felt he had a good relationship with his wife and all three sons.

He was a strong family man, an attribute he got from both his parents. Both he and Pam always worried about the kids in the unconscious but never-quite-absent undercurrent of anxiety most people of color lived with daily. The attack on Trayvon Martin a few years ago crystallized his fear for his sons. One of his sons was now the age Martin had been when he was killed. But for the most part, he was optimistic and felt hard work and diligence would provide for a good outcome.

Yes, life was good, he thought.

Michael could not wait for spring. His family was planning their first camping trip of the year. This year his oldest son's spring break coincided with his high school kid's time off. He also thought about planning a large family cruise when the kids finished school for the year. He was always trying to balance saving versus living life now and giving his kids important and fun experiences.

It would be nice to have all the grandparents together on a family cruise, he thought.

"Can't wait for this stretch to be over," he said to Jenna. "I have tickets to take the boys to the Rangers-Redwings game."

The next time he took report from Jenna was a couple of weeks later.

"Did you hear about this strange virus in Seattle?" said Jenna.

"No. What about it?"

"Well, there are some nursing home residents that died from it."

"It's probably a bad flu—we all had our flu shots."

Michael was thinking, *My parents got the flu shot this year… People that live in nursing homes are debilitated and exposed to lots of things, including the flu.*

"I guess," Jenna replied. "It's easy to imagine that several old people could die from the flu in a nursing home. But for some reason, it's been on the news a lot."

"Hmmm… Well, let's finish with report, you have to go home."

"Okay. Bed 6, thirty-two-year-old female with vaginal bleeding. Awaiting sonogram to rule out miscarriage. So sad, she told me that this is her fourth attempt at having a child."

"Oh, wow, that's tough," said Michael. He made a mental note to call the ultrasound tech. He thought, *I'm glad Pam and I didn't have a problem having kids.*

"Bed 7 and 8 are empty. Bed 9—sixty-six-year-old male with abdominal pain, rule out diverticulitis." Patient reports having some blood in the stool that got worse overnight, so they brought him in. Awaiting CT results and a GI consult." She turned a page.

"Bed 10 is a seventy-nine-year-old female with fever and cough. Swab for respiratory infections sent. Rule out RSV and/or flu. Droplet precautions for now. IV fluids 100 per hour. Awaiting chest x-ray. Fifty percent aerosol mask. Probably flu. Bed 11 is empty." She paused.

"Bed 12 is a twenty-two-year-old male who got the shit kicked out of him over an iPhone. Damn, these young kids today," Jenna said. "Anyway, CT ruled out liver laceration, looks like a bunch of cracked ribs. Just got Dilaudid for pain."

"Were the police called?" Michael asked.

"Not sure," Jenna replied. "Think it started out as a friendly game and turned into some kind of fight about pictures on a phone. I didn't get into it. The parents are here, he's gonna get another H&H

and probably go home. Hopefully teach him a lesson about getting into it about stupid-assed shit." Jenna got up stiffly.

"Okay, have a good day, Mike." Jenna got her lunch bag and left.

Michael thought about the day ahead of him. "Okay, three empties—not too bad."

"Safety huddle, safety huddle..." came over the intercom. "Safety huddle, main station." Michael went over to the main desk. There was Helen again with her list. *What did we all do now?* he thought.

"Okay, folks," she started. "So the ABG machine was down last night for two hours, but it's up and running again."

Michael thought, *And I need to know that because...*

"We need better follow-up with the lactic acids for patients on the sepsis bundle. They have to be drawn every three hours for three times, but we are missing some."

Michael looked at Melissa, another nurse, and whispered, "Well, if they put in the orders, they'll get drawn." Melissa nodded.

"Again," Helen droned on, "lots of IV tubing not being labeled, guys."

Michael looked at Melissa and whispered, "Doesn't she have anything useful to say?"

"We have so much to do, and they usually change the fluids when they get up to the floors anyway," replied Melissa.

"Okay, that's all, have a good day, everyone." Helen turned and walked out.

Michael turned and walked over to his computer.

He jotted down a few notes to himself: call sono tech for bed 6, call GI for bed 9, check pain level on kid in 12, check on the RSV and flu on 10. Easy stuff to get done.

He picked up his in-hospital phone. "Hey, John, can you come over and sono this young lady in 6? GYN is waiting to see if she needs a D&C," he asked.

"Okay, I'll be over soon" was the reply.

Michael checked his computer to see who from GI service was called in on bed 9. *Oh, Dr. Palmetto, I like him, good guy*, he thought.

He picked up the phone to call Dr. Palmetto's service and left a message about the consult.

He went over to bed 12 to see the young man sleeping curled up on his side. He saw the side of his face beginning to bruise. The patient's parents were anxiously hovering over the stretcher.

"Joseph, are you okay?" said the mom. Joseph murmured something and went back to sleep.

"Are you having any pain, buddy?"

"No, I'm okay."

"And how are you two holding up?" Michael said to the parents. They both shook their heads.

Michael nodded to them. "Kids—what are you gonna do with them?"

Michael went back to his computer to begin the charting for the day. The vital signs, the assessments, review the MAR (medication administration record).

He also checked on labs for all his patients. He asked the tech, Samantha, to go in and check another temperature on bed 10. He was not ready to put on his N95 just yet. He peeked in through the window of the isolation room, looked at the monitor, saw the heart rate was 100, the O2 sat was 95 percent, respiratory rate 26. *A little fast but not bad*, he thought. *Let me check on the RSV and flu swab.* He pulled up the microsection of the labs.

Hmm, negative. She probably has some bad virus, needs some fluids, and we will probably send her home later.

Michael went to get a drink of water. Samantha came and found him by the water cooler. "Bed 10's temp is 103."

"Jeez. Let me check to see if she's due for Tylenol."

Michael looked at the medication record. He saw Tylenol was given over six hours earlier. *I'll give her some more*, he thought.

Michael went to the medication cart, entered his access code, and withdrew the Tylenol, scanned it, gowned up, took an N95 mas out of the box in the wall cupboard by the room, and went in.

"My name is Michael, I'll be your nurse for today. May I have your name and date of birth?"

He looked at the patient's name band. "Marie Rosario, March 22, 1942" came the reply in a whisper.

"I'm going to give you some Tylenol and see if we can get this fever down."

Michael scanned her patient ID band. "Here—let me sit you up and help you." He pressed the button on the side rail to move the head of the bed up. "We have to take off the oxygen mask for a second." Michael looked at the monitor as he helped Marie sit up. He took off the oxygen mask and put the two tabs of Tylenol in her mouth. As he was holding the cup of water for her to sip, the monitor started to alarm.

What the fuck? he thought. *Was that real?* He saw the sat number plummet to 79. He saw the heart rate jump to 116. It was unusual for a person's oxygen level to drop so precipitously when the oxygen mask is removed.

Marie drank the water, swallowed the Tylenol, and Michael quickly put the oxygen mask back on and took the pulse oximeter off her finger and put it on another. Perhaps it just slipped off for a moment. He looked up again at the monitor and saw the sat was 92 with a good waveform, showing it was reading her pulse accurately. The heart rate was down to 106.

Michael stood there for a few minutes, perplexed.

"How are you feeling, Marie? How is your breathing? Do you have any pain?"

"Okay," said Marie, "I feel so weak. My bones hurt."

"Well, that's normal with this high of a fever," replied Michael. He took out his stethoscope. "Mind if I have a listen to your lungs?"

"Of course not." She struggled to rise up. "But you'll have to help me sit up."

"Of course," Michael said. He put one arm underneath her armpit to lift her forward. Even with the N95 mask on and the patient wearing an oxygen mask, he could smell a strange odor coming from her mouth. It must have been extraordinarily strong to permeate the N95. Maria's mouth was dry and crusty, but there were patches of thick tan mucus at the corners. He had not seen that before. She started to cough but did not cough up anything.

The alarms started sounding again. Michael looked up at the monitor. The heart rate was 120, and the sat dropped to 85. He quickly looked at Marie and saw that the oxygen mask was still in place. *That's weird*, he thought again as he put her back down on the pillow, stood at the foot of the stretcher, and gazed at her.

Michael felt a knot in the pit of his stomach. Something was not right.

He looked at her up and down from the foot of the stretcher, trying to put the pieces together, fever, intermittent low sats, tachycardia, flu negative, conversational/exertional desaturation.[8]

Michael took her blood pressure again.

Okay, pretty normal, he thought. *Maybe up a bit high because she is anxious. Is this some kind of sepsis?* The temperature was consistent, but her BP was high rather than low. He remembered nothing jumped out at him regarding her morning labs, but she did not seem to be improving. He went out to find the ER attending physician. "Hey, Dr. P, I think you'd better come and have a look at bed 10."

Dr. P was Dr. Phibunsongkhram. He was the grandson of a Thai immigrant who had married an American woman when he was living in California. They had four sons, one of whom was Dr. P's father. Dr. P's father, also called Dr. P, was an anesthesiologist who married one of his colleagues who was nearly six feet tall and naturally blonde. They had four children, and as recombination would have it, two resembled their father and were medium height and had straight black hair. They both went into medicine as their parents had. The other two, Dr. P included, were tall and had wavy light brown hair, with very dark almond-shaped eyes and full lips. The mixture of these features made them extremely attractive. Dr. P's sister Alyssa was an accomplished pro women's basketball point guard for the Los Angeles Sparks, often compared to Nikki Teasley. She changed her name to Plum while in college because she wanted an easy name for the fans to remember. Dr. P's first name was Jack,

---

[8] Desaturation refers to a decrease in a person's oxygen saturation. Saturation should be stable when someone talks or does exercise. When desaturation happens, the assumption is there is pulmonary pathology, often pneumonia.

but it was hospital policy to call physicians by their last names. No one could say his name, thus his sobriquet Dr. P. He was raised in the West Coast also and went to UCSF medical school. He did his internship and residency in New York and decided the East Coast was where he belonged. Part of that was the occurrence of falling in love with a woman who had no intention of living anywhere but the Upper West Side of Manhattan. Luckily, she was a coder, so they could afford the astronomical amount required to buy a decent apartment and fill it with as many children as they could produce. By 2020, they already had three and were considering a fourth. Dr. P was very calm and competent, and the staff appreciated his respectful approach to the ER workplace.

"What's going on?"

"Well, she's febrile to 103, tachycardic, but the weird thing is she tanks her sats on any movement or if the oxygen is off even for a second."

"She could be septic from the flu" was the answer.

"No, RSV and flu are negative."

"Let me have a look at her chest film."

They went to the computer where Michael pulled up the film from this morning.

"Hmmm, doesn't look too bad," said Dr. P. He went to the window to peer in at the patient.

"How much fluid is she getting? That BP's a bit high," he said, looking at the monitor. Michael looked up from his computer. "A hundred cc per hour of normal saline. Want me to give her a gentle bolus for the fever?"

"No, let's hold off for now."

Just then, Kyle walked over to the room. "Sharon told me you have something brewing over here. Do you need me?"

"Thanks, Kyle, I think we're going to go with a CT now."

"Okay," Kyle said in his usually cheerful manner, "you know how to reach me."

"Actually, she does not look too bad…but maybe we should get a new set of labs, an ABG, and a chest CT. I'll put the orders in."

Michael called the respiratory therapist to draw the ABG and called radiology to set up the CT scan.

"Hey, Sam," he said to one of the aides, "could you get another temp in, say, twenty minutes? I want to have another before she goes to CT."

"Sure thing."

Michael went to check on his other patients, discharged the young man with the rib fractures, careful to explain the discharge instructions to both the patient and his parents.

"Now don't be getting into any fights over phones, please." he said jokingly to the patient and family. "Just take some Tylenol and follow up with Dr. Croce in two weeks." He added, "It's gonna hurt for a while."

Michael called the GYN attending to review the ultrasound on bed 6. He was happy to inform the patient she was not having a miscarriage. She was discharged with follow-up instructions and an appointment for the GYN clinic.

Kyle went up to the second floor to the CTICU (cardiothoracic intensive care unit).

There were ten chest x-rays to do, all follow-ups from prior open-heart surgery patients. Several were still intubated. The intensivist (the physician in charge of that ICU) followed Kyle to say, "Show me after you do the films, I want to see them before you go back down to upload."

"Okay, Dr. Harrison." Kyle went methodically to each room, going in with his usual statement, "Hi, my name is Kyle from x-ray, I am here to take a chest x-ray. May I have your name and date of birth?" It was policy to make sure the patient was identified correctly in two separate ways, either name and date of birth or name and medical record number.

He knew some patients would be unable to answer him, but as he learned in school, you never knew what the patient could hear and possibly remember, so he wanted to be as pleasant as possible. He looked carefully at each patient's ID band to confirm their name and date of birth. "I'm going to slide this hard plate under your sheets, it will only take a moment." He grabbed the pull sheet to slide the plate underneath the patient. That was a skill he had learned through the years, getting the plate underneath without pulling out any tubes or IV lines.

He walked out of the room and called, "X-ray, room 15," so anyone standing near could move the requisite six to eight feet away. Most staff jumped and moved as far away as possible.

Kyle thought, *I'm not even shooting in that direction. Whatever.* He went back into the room and told the patient gently, "Okay, all done, I am going to just slide this plate out."

"Feel better," he told each patient as he was leaving, again not knowing if they heard him or not.

Kyle patiently waited outside of each room looking for Dr. Harrison to review the films.

Often, he saw the doctor speaking to another physician or nurse and never wanted to interrupt. Unfortunately, this waiting took a lot of time. Dr. Harrison saw Kyle standing and quickly went over to him, mumbled, "Sorry about that," and began to look at the screen on the portable machine at each film.

"Can you invert this one?" Dr. Harrison said. "Sure," replied Kyle as he pressed the lung icon.

"That's better, thanks."

Dr. Harrison reviewed each film, looking for the placement of the central line, placement of the endotracheal tube, and any new lung findings on the patient.

"Thanks for waiting for me," Dr. Harrison said pleasantly.

"Sure, no worries," Kyle replied.

Next, Kyle went to the medical ICU with twelve requisitions in hand. He worried that he would never get done.

When he arrived in medical, he saw that several of the patients were on isolation. His heart sank a little, as this would add a lot of time for donning and doffing the protective gear required. He called down to Jess.

"Sorry, this is gonna take a bit longer, I've got several patients here on isolation."

"Okay, I'll call Donna and let her know."

Michael refreshed his screen and saw he had an admission into bed 11, another isolation room.

This patient was coming up from the OR holding room.

OR holding? he thought. *What's up with that?*

His phone rang. It was Catherine from the holding room.

"What's up?" Michael said

"Well, I have a sixty-eight-year-old female here for thoracic surgery with Dr. Croce." She went on, "Let me see, lobectomy for cancer, but came in and has a temp of 101.6."

"So is she admitted?" Michael asked.

"No, we were doing the admission, and she has a fever, so Croce said send her to the ER for a workup. He didn't want to admit her to his service in case something else is up."

Catherine continued with the report, including history, medications, and current vital signs.

"Okay," Michael said, "bring her down. She's going into eleven."

I wonder what's up with that? thought Michael. He went to tell the attending.

Dr. P's response was what Michael assumed. "Why do they have to send the patient to the ER? The surgeons can't do their own workups?" He sighed.

Over the loudspeaker came the announcement, "*Code blue critical care, code blue critical care.*" Michael ran in to help. "Hey, Melissa," Michael called out, "I'm running into critical care to help."

Kyle took the portable machine back downstairs to the control room to plug it in.

Jess was in the x-ray room when Kyle arrived.

"Possible hip fracture," Jess said, "and Donna called, sorry to be the one to tell you, but Hector called in for tonight and you are up for mandation."

"Okay, be right there. And seriously? I can't believe it's my turn already. On the other hand, I do need the extra money." He turned to Jess.

"Did you ID this patient already?" Kyle said.

"Yup."

"Mrs. O'Brien, we are going to roll you over onto this hard board and slide you onto the table. We have three x-rays we need to do for you, but you tell us if anything hurts."

"Okay, thank you for being so nice to me," Mrs. O'Brien said. She was frail and clearly upset. "One, two, three," they counted, and both Jess and Kyle lifted slightly and slid her effortlessly onto the x-ray table.

Kyle stayed at the door of the room, while Jess went into the control room to press the button. "X-ray," called Jess. Kyle moved just outside of the doorway. Jess shot the first two, the pelvis, and the A/P (front to back) view of the hip. These different views would help to see if there was a fracture more clearly.

Next, Kyle went into the room. "Okay, Mrs. O'Brien, are you able to bend your right knee?" he asked.

"I think so," she said tentatively.

"Okay, great, I am going to touch your leg and place your ankle on this platform to raise it."

Kyle placed the plate on the side of the left hip. "Just hold still, don't move. Just give me five seconds."

Kyle went into the doorway and nodded to Jess.

They both went back into the room. "We're going to move you back onto the stretcher now. One, two, three." They slid her over onto the stretcher.

"Would you like a warm blanket?"

"Oh yes, please, that would be so nice! You are such a nice young man."

"You have to thank my parents for that," Kyle said, laughing.

"That's so nice too! Acknowledging your parents."

"I am going to bring you back to the emergency room."

Kyle wheeled the patient back to the emergency room and placed her in the room.

"Have a nice day, I hope you feel better."

"Thank you! And thanks again for being so nice."

When Kyle returned to the control room, Jess had a disgusted look on her face.

"What?"

"Bone survey on a ninety-eight-year-old. I mean, come on, ninety-eight? What are we going to find that is even treatable?"

"Are they bringing him down?"

"Right now. Shit, this is going to back us up at least half an hour," Jess said.

Immediately a transporter appeared with an elderly gentleman on a stretcher.

"This is Mr. Goldman," she announced.

A bone survey is the first step in looking for bone disease in a patient with suspected cancer. It is a series of eighteen to twenty x-rays starting from the skull down the spine to the legs, including the right and left side of all the body parts, followed by a lateral (side) view of everything.

As Jess and Kyle were completing the bone survey, other requisitions were printing out, a few in the emergency room, plus several more portable chest x-rays in the ICUs.

"Okay," said Jess, "I'll do the ER, you take the portables."

"Sure," said Kyle.

Suddenly the loudspeaker announced, "Code *blue* emergency room. Code blue emergency room." The operator's voice was shrill and annoying.

Kyle's in-house phone rang at the same time. He knew it was time to take the portable machine over to the code area in the emergency room.

"X-ray, Kyle speaking."

"We need you in the code room," a voice said and hung up.

Kyle wheeled the portable machine into the ER, passing the many rooms and patients in stretchers and chairs in the hallway. The ER was filling up.

Kyle got to the back of the ER where he saw about a dozen people in the room. Kyle saw Michael's head bobbing up and down. He was obviously doing chest compressions.

Michael wasn't even assigned to the critical care room today, Kyle thought. *He's probably just helping out. I wish my department worked more like that.*" He and Jess worked well together, but not all the techs were good at lending a hand when one got overwhelmed.

He knew there was no way he would be getting into the room anytime soon.

He stood there, waiting.

"Where's x-ray?" someone shouted.

"Right here," said Kyle.

"Oh—okay, come in… No, wait, we're intubating."

"No worries, I'll just wait here." Kyle knew this could take a while, but he was not allowed to leave.

He watched as they called for the intubation tray, saw the emergency room physician and the respiratory therapist at the head of the bed. The patient was successfully intubated. Dr. Moore called out, "X-ray now."

"Right here," said Kyle.

"Come in."

"No, wait, BP's dropping—get the Levo," called out the nurse.

Soon there was a chain of hands passing along an IV bag and tubing into the room.

"We'd better line him." This means to insert an intravenous line into a larger vein, such as the femoral vein, the jugular vein, or the subclavian vein. These lines allow larger volumes of fluid or blood to be infused quickly.

"Tell x-ray not to leave."

"I'm not going anywhere," said Kyle.

Kyle's mobile phone rang. "Radiology, Kyle speaking."

"We need a stat chest here in 440," said the voice.

"I'm in a code in the ER, I'll be there as soon as I'm done."

"Well, can't you give me a timeline?" said the voice, irritated.

"No, sorry, I can't," said Kyle firmly. "I am in the code room. When I am done, I'll come to you."

"Well, this is stat," said the voice, growing angry.

"I am sure it is," said Kyle, "but once again, I am in a code in the emergency room, and I will be up when I am finished down here." *Click*, the voice hung up.

Kyle was used to that kind of treatment, but it never bothered him. He even was reported by staff on the floors when he did not appear in what they thought was a timely manner.

I'm only one person, I can only be in one place doing one x-ray at a time, he thought. His attention snapped back to the code room. Michael was now titrating drips; Kyle could see that the patient was not doing well by the number of IV bags now hanging.

"Where's x-ray?" someone called out. "I haven't left this spot," called Kyle.

Dr. P came back and said to Kyle, "Can you bring up the film?"

"I haven't shot it yet."

"Why not?"

"Look in the room."

"Oh—sorry." Dr. P said loudly, "Can we let x-ray come in now? We need the film."

Suddenly everyone left the room except Michael who was at the computer charting the events. Kyle was left in there with a patient with an endotracheal tube, central line, drips hanging, and, of course, no one to help him. "Hi, this is Kyle from x-ray—may I have your name and date of birth?" he asked as always. No response from the patient. He looks at the ID band, then asked, "Is this Mrs. Connolly?"

Michael looked up and said, "Hey, Kyle, and yes, this is Mrs. Connolly. Do you need help plating?" Michael and Kyle were friends, both interested in hockey, hiking, and weight training. Kyle was easygoing and agreeable, and it was easy to organize events with him.

"No, I'm good," replied Kyle. "I'm ready to shoot, why don't you step out for a second?" he said to Michael.

He expertly lifted the lines with one hand while sliding the plate underneath the sheet with the other. The patient was sedated and didn't struggle. He walked to the door and called out, "X-ray!" Everyone jumped and moved farther away.

He removed the plate as Dr. P returned to check the film for placement of the endotracheal tube and the central line.

"Okay, good. Thanks for hanging around."

"You're welcome." Kyle pushed the portable machine back to the control room where Jess was waiting, having been occupied with minor cases all along.

"Long code?"

"Yup."

"Wanna go to dinner?" Jess asked.

"Yes, please."

Kyle went down to the break room. There were three other x-ray techs all busy on their cell phones.

He thought, *Shit, I have been running my ass off, and these people have probably been sitting around waiting for their OR case to start. You would think at least one of them would have checked in with us in the ER to see if they could help. But no.*

He sat down at the table to eat his dinner and took out his own phone.

Kyle was forty-four years old. He lived in Middle Village, in the home he grew up in. He had been married briefly in his twenties, but the marriage was not successful. Luckily, there were no kids.

During that time, his parents had added a "mother-in-law" apartment to their house to accommodate Kyle's mom's parents. They continued to have the big Italian Sunday dinners, and his grandmother's tomato sauce was unmatched. Kyle remembered those dinners fondly, as well as the time he spent with his grandfather watching *Little House on the Prairie*, wrestling, and any televised sports they could find. They both loved hockey. Kyle's grandparents died a year apart slightly before Kyle separated from his wife, so it was a natural transition to move into that apartment. Slowly he replaced his grandparent's plastic-covered furniture with more comfortable and modern decor. He had some hilarious conversations with his mother about that.

"That is good furniture, Kylie, why do you want to get rid of that? You'll never find such quality," she would say. He looked over at the sofa in question, which had gold flocked upholstery on a fake Louis XV frame with gold highlights on the dark wood. The whole thing was covered with a fitted clear plastic slipcover to protect the fabric. It was fussy, ugly, and practically the hardest, bumpiest, and most horrible seating he could imagine. He had been sitting on it for years.

Years of *Little House* and wrestling. He'd had enough.

"Ma, I hate that thing. It's from the years before the dinosaurs roamed. It's like sitting on a spike, for God's sake."

"Don't swear, Kylie, you know how it upsets me. And it's still the best made furniture you'll ever find," she countered. She wasn't wrong, it was very well-made. Just hideous and uncomfortable.

"Well, why don't you take it then?" He gave her shoulders a little hug. His mother would have walked through fire for her youngest son, but she would loudly complain about it the whole time.

"Ugh! My back! You know I have a bad back!" Her furniture was all-new Lazy Boy, thanks to a gift from Kyle the previous Christmas.

"Look at this sofa!" she would say, scoffing. It was the one he was showing her to replace the gold nightmare. "It's got no style, it's so plain." Kyle just sighed and moved along with his plans. He'd been there for over fifteen years, slowly becoming the caretaker to his aging parents. He was fine with that responsibility; he loved his parents and got along with them well. He had some regrets about having no kids of his own (and he heard a lot about that from his mother too), but overall, he was satisfied with his life. He was happy in his own space but close enough if his folks needed anything. His mother still made tomato sauce every Sunday, but truth be told, Kyle thought Grandma's was better. Not that he ever said *that* out loud.

It was getting close to the end of Michael's shift. Jenna was due in again. Maria's temp came down a little with the Tylenol and the fluids. Her CT scan was pending. Michael was jotting down notes to tell Jenna.

The new patient, Mrs. Irene Hoffman, was brought up into bed 11. She indeed was having a bit of breathing difficulty, but Michael thought, *She has lung cancer. Maybe the temp is just inflammatory.*

Since she was placed in the isolation room, Michael did get another N95 mask out to go into the room.

"Hi, my name is Michael. I'll be your nurse for the next hour or so, and then your nurse will be Jenna." The woman nodded. "How are you feeling? Do you have any pain?"

Mrs. Hoffman answered, "Yes, but ever since they diagnosed this damn cancer, I have always had a bit of trouble. I have a little pain in my chest, but it's not too bad."

"Have you had a fever recently?"

"No, not that I recall…" was the answer.

Michael used the scanner to retake the temp. Sure enough, 101.8. "Well, you're hot. Let me go out and check your orders. Can I get you anything?"

"I'm okay," said Mrs. Hoffman. "If I'm not going to have surgery, can I have some water, please?"

"Sure thing," said Michael.

He pulled up her orders on the computer. RSV, flu swab, CBC, BMP lactic acid, ABG, chest x-ray, blood cultures. These lab tests would help to figure out what might be causing her fever.

Michael started getting his supplies ready. Then he drew the blood and sent it to the lab.

Jenna came in and got report. Michael went home.

That night he was watching the news with his wife, Pamela.

"BREAKING NEWS!" went across the bottom of the screen. "First cases of CORONAVIRUS HITS U.S."

Michael felt his heart race. He looked over at Pam, then his two boys playing video games. He started to think, *What if I have brought this home to Pam? Or the kids?*

Chapter 4

The Orthopedic Floor
January 2020

Fran had finally made it. She was a nurse. Six months of orientation and she was finally getting the hang of it. Knee and hip replacements, back surgeries, some complicated shoulder surgeries. Her preceptor Janine had told her all about the nuances of the orthopedic surgeons. "You have to baby them."

"They all have different techniques, different ways to rehab the patient, different equipment, different dressings."

Fran thought, *How am I going to remember who likes what?*

"Once you get to know them, they don't yell at you as much," Janine said, smiling. Fran was not sure she believed her; she would just have to find out.

"I can handle this," she'd say to herself. "I worked so hard to get here. I should be able to take a surgeon yelling at me once in a while."

Fran worked the 7:00 p.m. to 7:00 a.m. shift. She came on nervously by 6:30 p.m. to see her assignment. She had only six patients and one empty bed. The nurse's aide assigned to her was Shauna, a veteran evening-shift employee, and she knew that Paula was coming on for the 11:00 p.m. to 7:00 a.m. shift. Fran worked the night shift so she could care for her children during the day.

She started by looking over the earlier vital signs, blood pressures, pulses, temperatures. It was important to note if any postsurgical patient has spiked a temperature as it could imply the onset of an infection.

Thank God, no one has a temp, she said to herself. She breathed a sigh of relief. Having to call the surgeon late at night to tell them their patient had a temperature was painful, as they always got so hot-tempered, asked a million questions, many of which she did not have the answer for.

"What was the preoperative chest x-ray?"

"Was he coughing?"

"Did you look at the wound?"

Answering those questions with "I do not know" or "I will have to get back to you on that" was cause for quite the lecture on the other end of the phone.

Next, Fran walked into each room to introduce herself, careful to wash her hands before and after each encounter. She had her speech worked out for each patient.

"Hi, my name is Fran, and I'll be your nurse for the next twelve hours."

"How are you feeling?"

"On a scale of zero to ten, zero being no pain and ten being the worst pain in the world, where is yours?"

"I'd like to look at your dressing now."

She knew to do this early in the shift so the patient could get a good night's rest as most would have physical therapy the next day beginning at six o clock in the morning.

For those patients, she had to remember to call for their breakfast trays early so they could eat before they began their therapy.

Initial rounds took about two hours. So at nine o'clock, she had her first drink of water for the shift and went to the bathroom. *I see why nurses have to have large bladders*, she thought. From about 9:00 p.m. to 10:00 p.m., she had to read up on the latest policies on her computer and sign off that she read them. She went and read the minutes from the last staff meeting and signed off on that. She looked at all the notices on the bulletin boards to see if there was any news she missed. Most things happened during the day shift, so it was up to the night staff to read up on all the happenings of the hospital.

It was time to start the next set of rounds.

She walked down the hallway to start her assessments and vital signs. It was after midnight. The unit, called 2 South, was in the shape of a long rectangle with thirty-two beds. Most were two-person rooms, but there was a private room at each corner. Those were the VIP rooms. They were decorated, with thoughtful paint and wallpaper and matching draperies. There was a refrigerator, large flat-screen TV, and extra space for a guest to stay over. Fran wondered how much extra these private rooms cost. In the center of the unit there were several small nursing stations and one large one at the entrance to the unit. The supply and medication room were also in the center with a badge entry.

Fran felt important to have badge entry now.

There was a sizeable break room with a microwave and a television for the staff. There was also a coffeepot provided by the hospital, but all the staff had chipped in to buy a Keurig coffeepot. The patients that stayed in the private rooms were not always nice. They tended to be demanding. *Gee, do they think I'm the maid?* Fran wondered as she went to get a pitcher of ice for Mr. Harris and his wife.

"Oh, dear," said Mrs. Harris with a bit of arrogance. "I did say six cups, you only brought me four. And Arthur needs straws with that too. So please run along and get that for us now, dear. Thank you," she said dismissively.

Fran did as she was told and brought the cups and the straws into the room. "Where would you like me to put them?

"Over on the table, dear. Oh! And Arthur needs to go to the bathroom now."

Fran put on her cheeriest face and said, "I'm going to go and get Paula. Mr. Harris needs two people to get him up."

"Okay, dear, but hurry up, please. And he's not using the commode, I want him to go into the bathroom now."

Fran knew Arthur was not going to be able to walk that far on his first day after knee surgery.

She went to check his activity orders although she knew he didn't have bathroom privileges yet.

Fran and Paula came back in the room. "Mrs. Harris, your husband has to use the commode for another day—it's doctor's orders. It's also extremely late—after midnight—and you should go and get some rest too."

"I'm not leaving Arthur. That's why we have this nice big room. So I can stay here."

"Okay, Mrs. Harris, we will put Mr. Harris on the commode, and then you both need to get some rest. He has a big day of physical therapy tomorrow."

Fran and Paula finally got out of the room forty-five minutes later. They had put Arthur on the commode, got him back to bed, put his CPM machine on, and got Mrs. Harris a blanket.

Fran asked Paula, "Does it always take this long with everyone?"

"No," said Paula," you gotta set limits with some of these people, or they will walk all over you." Fran went over to her computer to document the encounter with Mr. Harris. She had five more patients to check in on, medications to give, IV sites to check.

A call light went off.

Paula called out, "Pain med in room 246."

That was Fran's room. She went into the MAR (medication administration record) to see what the patient could take for pain, got the keys, took out one tablet of Percocet, and gave it to the patient.

She was happy with her progress so far.

She checked in on her other patients who were, thankfully, sleeping.

It was 3:00 a.m. Time for her break. Fran was too nervous to sit and eat anything, so she sat at her computer station to catch up on the charting. All the check-off sheets—pain scale, Morse fall scale, Cincinnati sleep scale, Braden scale (all compulsory charting for each patient)—Fran had to do all her regular charting consisting of an assessment of body systems, intake and output, status of activity, teaching done, as well as a nursing diagnosis and care plan for each patient.

I wish they would stop with these scales! she thought. *It's so much charting.*

At 4:30 a.m., another patient called for pain medication. It was time to take some people off and put others back on CPM machines. CPM—continuous passive motion—helped people who had their knees replaced achieve full range of motion.

Paula called and asked her to help assist another patient to the bathroom.

The orthopedic patients were physically heavy to take care of. *On the other hand, they get better*, Fran thought. *They get to go home all fixed up.*

At 6:00 a.m., she was making another set of rounds. *Good, everyone's quiet for the moment.* Fran had three finger sticks to do for blood glucose level. She called for the early trays and gave the patients their insulin.

This was a good night. *I hope it stays like this*, she thought.

At 7:00 a.m., she gave report to the day nurse. She went through each patient's history, surgery, pain level, and plan for the day. By seven thirty, she was ready to go home to start another shift with her kids.

Now my day really starts, she thought.

She made herself a cup of tea and sat on the couch. She was tired but knew sleep was hours away if at all. The kids would be waking up soon full of energy, and they would need breakfast and would be ready to play.

Thank God, they are still asleep, Fran thought. *I have a few minutes to breathe and maybe get in a shower.* Fran sipped her tea and turned on the news. She was fascinated about the news coming out of China about this new coronavirus. *What does this mean for here?* she wondered. Fran was always a news buff, actively following politics, health, and social issues. She also listened to the Greek news channel Cosmos. But she had no time for that now. *I'd better hurry up and shower before the kids get up*, she thought as she turned off the television.

Here I am, thirty-five years old, on my own with two young children. How did that happen? she wondered.

Fran was a petite, attractive young Greek woman. Her real name was Filia, but she preferred Fran to be more American. With her long flowing brown hair, she was considered pretty by most standards. Her deep-set big brown eyes and full lips made her an eye-opener to those who saw her walking on the street.

Her life didn't go the way she had expected when she was a little girl. Fran was raised by a single mom, Patty. Patty, whose real name was Patia, had been married before and had two children, so Fran had two half-sibs that were much older. She had met them only once. Fran spent some of her childhood years living in Greece. She had lived on a farm, an hour away from civilization. She remembered her grandma teaching her how to milk the cows and boil the milk. She remembered the village pharmacist treating her with herbs for any illness. She only met her father once, right before he died of alcoholism and kidney failure. He spent the last year of his life on dialysis.

Patty had hidden Fran from him most of her life as he was a nasty drunk. They lived for a while in the house built by her grandfather. Fran remembered the addition of a bathroom her grandfather built outside the home. Everyone was excited, but you had to walk a path through the garden to get to it. When it was too cold, everyone urinated in a bucket inside their bedrooms. After her grandfather died, her mom's sister had the house demolished and built a new modern one. Part of her still craved the outdoors, the mountains, the fresh air. *Maybe one day I will buy a house in upstate New York*, she thought. Her mind wandered, then she snapped back to reality. *Get in the shower.*

Fran had been in college for event planning. She happened upon a great internship that led her to her first career.

She worked throughout college as a production assistant to party planners for celebrities. Among other tasks, she stuffed swag bags for parties. As a perk, she got to attend a few and saw more than her share of celebrities. This internship turned into a position where she was running a part of the company and planning the parties.

She was making good money, but spending it as fast as it came in. Fran loved clothes, jewelry, buying gifts for her mom. She was even able to buy herself a one-bedroom condominium. But she never established a savings account.

The party planning business wasn't all glamorous. She was on call twenty-four seven. She found herself sleeping in a closet, more than once, at the event venue. She had to carry a bag with her toothbrush, makeup, and a change of underwear. This was not the life she wanted. When she was home in her freshly painted and decorated condo, she was sleeping most of the time.

There was no time for socialization, going out with friends, or seeing her mom.

She did manage to strike up a friendship with her downstairs neighbor Rob. They spent some time talking here and there on their shared deck space. Fran thought Rob was attractive but never thought of him as a potential partner.

Their friendship evolved into a few dates, out to dinner, bowling, a hike. They were great friends. Fran didn't remember at what point their friendship turned romantic, but when she turned twenty-five, Rob asked her to marry him. Fran said yes, even though she knew she had some reservations.

Rob did seem to enjoy drinking a little too much for her comfort. She didn't think much of it at the beginning. He only drank when they went out to a restaurant, maybe a glass of wine on the deck as they looked out at the sunset. Still, he seemed romantic and crazy about her. Fran got pregnant immediately after they were married. Rob seemed happy, but Fran knew he wasn't. He began staying out late, excuse after excuse.

He had all sorts of excuses—met a friend for a drink, had to work late, went to a game with people from work.

Fran went through the pregnancy pretty much alone. Rob didn't go to doctor's appointments with her, and it didn't seem to please him when they found out they were having a son. Rob Jr.—or Robby as they called him—was born the summer of 2011. He was a beautiful baby with dark hair, a full chubby face, and smiling brown eyes. Fran was so in love.

Rob began to drink even more.

He soon began coming home falling down drunk. He first became nasty, then he became scary. He took no interest in little Robby.

Fran did not take a long maternity leave; her party planning company needed her back right away. She was afraid to leave their son home with Rob, so her cousin would come over to babysit.

Fran thought he would change as Robby grew more into a person, interacting, playing, but Rob grew even more distant.

Fran knew where this was going, but she didn't want to believe it. They had a beautiful son. Between them, they had two condominiums. Fran would realize later that she was smart to have kept her own place.

Sometimes after a night of managing her parties, she took little Robby and stayed upstairs. When Robby was one year old, he had a grand mal seizure. A seizure is erratic electrical activity in the brain, and it is very scary to witness. People having a seizure can jerk uncontrollably, lose consciousness, can bite their own tongue, be incontinent of urine. Sometimes they can stop breathing. Fran rushed him to the hospital where the doctors couldn't find anything really wrong. They did a multitude of tests, CT scan, EEG, blood tests, everything was negative. They sent him home.

Rob was nowhere to be found during this ordeal. Fran was devastated. Little Robby seemed okay, but somehow things were different. He was no longer playful or gurgling, and he slept a lot. Fran attributed it to the medication. After a few weeks when Robby was lethargic, she took him back to the emergency room. He had no fever or overt symptoms. An EEG revealed he had been having silent seizures all along.

Fran racked her brain trying to think if it was anything she had done during the pregnancy to deserve a sick child.

Riddled with guilt, she quit her job to spend all her time with Robby. Fortunately, she had saved a fair amount of money to be okay for a while, and Rob was still working and paying the condo fees on both places. But he wasn't ever there.

He was unprepared to deal with being a father, let alone one of a sick child.

One night, when Rob came home in a particularly nasty mood, he began to yell at Fran.

"I didn't want to do this. I didn't want a baby. Now all we have is this sick kid!" he screamed. He began to knock things off the tables and even threw their wedding picture on the floor and smashed it.

"I hate you, you bitch, what have you done to my life? Get the fuck out."

Fran grabbed her clothes and the baby's clothes and ran upstairs to her own condo.

She did not know whether to call the police. She was scared out of her mind.

Fran figured Rob would sleep it off and apologize at some point. But at this time, she had Robby to care for. She had to figure out a way to care for him.

As time went on, she stayed up in her own condominium and she rarely saw Rob, but she did not care. She had research to do for Robby.

Fran contacted the early intervention program from the state. Robby was too young yet to be evaluated for applied behavioral analysis. Fran would have to wait for that type of assistance. Meanwhile, Fran continued her research on how to take care of her child. She read everything she could about his eating rituals, and she tried to make sense of his little communication. Robby showed no emotional attachment to Fran. He never laughed, he never responded to toys, music, or cartoons. After a while, Fran became his personal assistant; she did not feel like his mother.

She found out over time that Robby only would eat foods with a runny consistency. He had texture issues. If Fran gave him a piece of bread or a cookie and he ended up holding crumbs in his hand, this would cause him to wail uncontrollably.

At eighteen months, she began the ABA (applied behavioral analysis) program. This is a system of rewards, usually snacks for certain behaviors. She worked with the therapist and Robby on all these techniques. Robby would be expected to pick up a toy, walk toward an object, or focus on a picture, and for this, he would get a sweet snack like an M&M. It did not work. ABA, as Fran found out later, was geared toward children with autism, and her child had brain damage. She allowed the therapy to continue. Occupational therapy came in, and they worked with Robby on picking up a spoon, taking off his socks, trying to say words. Robby just screamed until he got his snack.

63

Fran wondered what she was going to do if he did not improve. Who would take care of him?

She also did not have a job, and money was going to start running out.

During this time, her husband told her he met a woman online and thought he was in love. Fran was secretly thrilled—this was the way out.

"Honey, this is the best thing," Fran said. "I am happy for you." Fran was letting her husband be the one to walk out on her.

This could work, she thought.

After two months, Rob came back. "I want us to be a family again. I love you and our family—I want us all to be together. I swear I will be better."

Fran had given this a lot of thought. She wanted a sibling for Robby. "I need someone else in his life that will love him."

She let Rob back for two months during which time she became pregnant.

Rob behaved himself for a while. One day, when Fran came back from food shopping, she noticed that Robby was asleep. That was not usual for him.

"What did you do?" she screamed at Rob.

"Nothing, he was tired." Fran knew this was not the case. When she was washing Robby's sippy cup, she found a white substance.

"What the fuck did you give him?" she screamed.

"I only gave him a quarter of a Xanax to calm him down—see how nice he's sleeping?"

"Get out!" she screamed. "I'm not going to have another baby with you here."

"Wait, you're pregnant? How could you do this? What if this baby is retarded just like Robby? What are you gonna do then?"

Rob left. But he didn't leave Fran alone. He began stalking her. He keyed her car, he tried to run her over. Fran went to the court to obtain an order of protection. She was afraid every day. Fran called her mom who had moved to Greece five years earlier. She had been living with her older children.

"Mom, I need you."

Patty flew back and moved in.

Neighborhood friends would call her to tell her that Rob was in the area. Fran would carefully choose when she would leave the apartment. Now that her mom was back, she could figure out what to do next.

Rob was not out of her life yet. He called her, harassed her, begged her forgiveness. Fran knew he was using multiple substances, and she could not afford to have him near her. She was three months pregnant and had a disabled child.

What the fuck am I doing? she thought. Her life was in total turmoil. This had been going on for almost two years.

One incident happened that changed the course of Fran's life.

One day Robby started screaming and crying. He would not stop despite Frans's best efforts.

Candy, toys, music, nothing stopped Robby's incessant screaming.

Fran got down on the floor, took Robby by the shoulders, and shook him.

"What the fuck do you want from me? Stop being a fuckin' idiot! Just fuckin' talk. It's not hard, just tell me what you want! What the fuck did I do to deserve this?" She grabbed Robby by the arms and tried to rock him. Still, he screamed. Fran screamed along with him. This lasted for what seemed like hours.

Robby looked scared.

I wish I could call someone, Fran thought. *I need a friend that understands—I need someone to help me.*

They both fell asleep on the floor by the front door.

When Fran woke up the next morning on the floor, she looked at her sleeping son. He looked so beautiful and peaceful lying there, his breathing regular, his face relaxed.

Fran knew at that moment she had to become a nurse. It was the only option. There was nothing else that mattered anymore. She wanted to learn how to take care of Robby. Lilly was born six months later, a healthy, beautiful baby. Fran watched her sleep every night until she surpassed the age that Robby had a seizure at. A full year of no sleep.

*****

Fran came in at her usual time of 6:30 p.m. She looked at the assignment sheet and saw that she was assigned to her usual district. *All seven beds filled*, she thought, *then no admissions for me.* Fran liked it when her assignment was full with no pending discharges because that meant no admissions. Fran was getting the hang of the night shift, she started to develop her own routine.

She signed in to her computer, scanned over her patients' vital signs, outstanding orders, and checked all the medications.

She saw that there were two patients scheduled for discharge in the morning. Fran would start the discharge teaching and paperwork for the day nurse. *That's how you make friends, be part of the team*, she thought. *Just get the work done.*

She started making her rounds with her computer to chart her assessments, pain level, do the required scales, "everyone scores high on the fall scale here—what do they think? they are orthopedic patients." She remembered the nursing process from school, potential for injury related to… Her mind wandered.

A call bell went off. Fran was working with a float aide tonight. She was anticipating problems working with the float aide, because they didn't have any kind of relationship, and so she couldn't know how much self-motivation she could hope for.

Unfortunately, her worst fears were confirmed. When she went to look, she found the aide was sitting at the nursing station talking intently on her phone. Fran was not one to cause trouble, so she went to answer the call bell herself.

"Mrs. Troiano, how can I help you."

"I don't feel well" was the reply.

"Do you have pain?" She went to the patient and pulled back the sheets, putting her hand reassuringly on Mrs. Troiano's arm. "Can you rate it?" Fran went to look at her incisions. Mrs. Troiano had bilateral knee replacement surgery a little over twenty-four hours earlier.

"It's not that. I feel warm, and my shoulders hurt."

"Can you describe the shoulder pain?" Fran said.

"Well, it's not like a real pain, it's like an ache, like maybe I slept wrong, but I haven't really moved. Maybe I'm just stiff, don't worry about it. I had a lot of visitors here today—it was my daughter's birthday. Maybe I just overdid it."

"Could be," murmured Fran. *Probably not*, she thought.

"Let me take your vital signs." Fran hooked up the NIBP (automatic blood pressure cuff), put the pulse ox on, and took her temperature.

"You have a bit of a fever, but just 100.3." The patient's pulse was 98. She compared these readings with the ones earlier, when the patient's temperature had been normal at 98.8 and pulse had been 72. *Hmm*, Fran thought back to nursing school *Potential for infection related to incisions. Think, think, think*, Fran thought. She remembered one of her nursing instructors saying, "Don't ask a question unless you already know the answer."

"Let me take a look at your surgical sites." Fran looked carefully with her Maglite at the knee incisions. They looked normal, no real redness, no swelling, no drainage.

She looked at the computer to see when Mrs. Troiano had Tylenol. She saw it was last given ten hours ago.

"Would you like some Tylenol?"

"Sure, why not?"

"I am going to call the physician's assistant on call and let her know about your temperature and pulse," Fran said to Mrs. Troiano.

Wow, this could end up being a busier night than I bargained for, she thought.

She put in a call to Annie, the surgical PA on call.

"Hey, Annie, it's Fran on 2 South, I am here with Mrs. Troiano—"

"Who's the attending?" Annie interrupted abruptly.

"It's Henderson's patient," Fran reported. "Oh shit" was the reply.

Dr. Henderson was one of those physicians that got angry if things did not go perfectly.

"Did you call him?" Annie said angrily.

"No, I called you," Fran replied.

"Well, what do her knees look like?" Annie asked impatiently.

"They look fine to me. Do you want to come have a look? Also, she says her shoulders hurt."

"Well, that's just from the temp," replied Annie, sounding annoyed. "Hmm, no, just give her some Tylenol and I'll be up later."

Before Fran could reply, Annie had hung up.

Wow, talk about obnoxious, I wonder what bug is up her ass, Fran thought.

Fran went to the medication cart, scanned in, took out the Tylenol, and brought it to her patient. "Here you go," she said gently as she helped Mrs. Troiano sit up and take the medication with some water.

Fran noticed an odor coming from the patient's mouth. *She probably hasn't brushed her teeth in a while,* she thought. Aloud, she said, "Would you like to rinse your mouth?" "Oh god, yes! I've had this awful taste in my mouth all damn day. I think it's strange, I brushed my teeth after dinner."

Fran got the patient some mouthwash, helped her with the rinse basin, put her CPM machines on, and went on to see her other patients.

"Mary," she said to the float aide, "could you please check the temp for Mrs. Troiano in 234 in an hour? I am concerned about her."

"When I get to my 11:00 p.m. temps" was the reply.

"No," said Fran firmly, "she febrile now, so I want her temperature taken again by ten." Mary walked by, mumbling something to herself. Fran shook her head and went on to the next room.

Fran went to see her other patients, gave out nighttime pain medications. Fran made it a point to offer her patients their pain medication before bedtime so that they could sleep through the night. She knew that most of them had a grueling day of physical therapy coming up. She had several 10:00 p.m. finger sticks for her diabetic patients, and often they required insulin. As each night wore on, she became more confident in her organization skills. She even began to get some charting done as she spent time in every room getting to know her patients. For the most part, Fran only had minor problems with the patient in the private VIP rooms, but she was comfortable setting limits when necessary.

At 10:00 p.m., Mary shuffled over to her and said, "You know, that patient's temp in 37 is still high."

"Well, what is it?" said Fran shortly.

"It's 100.8" came the reply as Mary had already turned her back and walked down the hallway.

Fran went after her. "Did you take her other vital signs by chance?"

"No" was the reply as she never stopped walking.

What am I missing? Fran thought. *Her incisions looked good. Her shoulders were hurting probably due to the fever…* She mentally went down a checklist as she walked toward the room with the NIPB.

"Mrs. Troiano, let's see what's going on, I see your temperature is still up."

"I don't know. I know I'm not feeling well." Fran hooked up the NIBP. *Blood pressure normal. Pulse 104, a little higher. Oxygen saturation 92, a little lower*, she thought.

Think, Fran, think! Postoperative pneumonia? Let me get her the incentive spirometer.

"Mrs. Troiano, maybe you have not been exercising your lungs enough. I would like you to do some more of your breathing exercises." She handed her the incentive spirometer and watched as she performed it. "Remember, the focus is on the inhale. Breathe in deep like this…" Fran demonstrated. "The idea is to get the blue ball all the way up to here." She pointed to the 1,000 mark.

Mrs. Troiano was able to hit the 1000 mark with no problem, but she began to cough after each deep breath.

"Good, that's good!" encouraged Fran. "You probably have some secretions left in the lower part of the lungs, that happens after anesthesia." Fran was somewhat relieved, although she knew she would have to call Annie at this hour.

Fran picked up her phone and called Annie.

"Ortho, Annie."

"Hey, Annie, Fran. Mrs. Troiano's temp is 100.8. Her sat is 92 on room air, pulse 104. I got her to do her incentive, she got up to 1,000, a bit of a cough."

"Probably postop atelectasis" was the reply. "Let's get a chest film. I'll put in the order. Take her temps every three hours and let me know if she goes higher."

"That makes sense. Okay, right," replied Fran. "Portable, right? She won't be able to stand."

"Okay, portable." The phone went dead.

By 11:00 p.m., the x-ray was done. Fran again called Annie. "Film's up."

"Okay, I'll look and call you." Fran knew she would not.

Okay, Fran thought, *I've got this. I'll just keep an eye on her and make her do the incentive a few times. She will be okay—I hope.*

Fran went over to talk to her closest colleague on the unit, Debra. Debra had been a nurse on that unit for over five years.

"Hey, Debra, I have a patient, Mrs. Troiano in 37. She is Henderson's patient. She spiked to 100.8, sats on room air 92, pulse a bit up from earlier. I called Annie twice. We did the incentive, she ordered a chest x-ray. Any other suggestions?"

"Did you call Henderson?"

"No. I thought Annie would do that."

"Not always. Annie is probably watching Netflix by now."

"Do you think I should call him? It's almost one AM."

"Not if you don't want to get screamed at."

"So I should wait until the morning and hand it off to the day shift?"

"Just write a good note, include everything you did."

"Okay, I will. Thanks."

"No problem."

Fran went to make another set of quick rounds before she went on break. She was comfortable enough now to take a short break, have a cup of tea, maybe turn on the news for a few minutes.

She went in to see Mrs. Troiano first. *Good, she is sleeping.* Fran counted her respiratory rate, 22, regular. *Okay, she seems good.*

Fran stepped into the break room, made a cup of tea, and turned on the news.

FIRST CASES OF CORONAVIRUS TURN UP IN A NURSING HOME IN SEATTLE... She stopped listening as the news anchor droned on with the details.

Fran's eyes widened. *It's here in the US,* she thought. *What does that mean? Is there going to be some sort of apocalypse?* Her mind wandered. *Maybe I should warn my friends and family. Get a grip, Fran. The government is prepared for this sort of thing. They have scientists and doctors and the CDC and the WHO. Am I the only one thinking about this? I should stop, I'm going to go nuts.* She decided to end her break and go back out to the floor.

It was 4:00 a.m. Time for vital signs and assessments. Fran took her computer / med cart and made her last set of rounds. She offered patients pain medications, reviewed vital signs, removed the CPM machines as ordered. She looked at her watch, 4:45 a.m. *Not too much longer. I think I'm going to stop on the way home and pick up a few things.*

Mary came up to her. "That patient you are worried about—temp still high."

"How high?"

"It's 101.2."

Shit, Fran thought. Out loud, she said, "Thanks, Mary."

She went in the room. Mrs. Troiano was definitely short of breath. Fran took out her stethoscope and listened to her lungs. *Rhonchi anteriorly,* she thought. *What does that mean? It must be mucus... I have to get her to cough.* She said out loud, "Mrs. Troiano, let's do your coughing exercises."

"I'll try" came the weak reply.

Fran put the sat monitor on. It showed 85 percent. That was alarming.

"Mrs. Troiano, are you okay?" She shook her shoulder lightly. There was no response.

"Hey, guys!" she screamed out of the room. "Call an RRT. Get me an oxygen mask, someone!"

"RRT, 2 South, RRT, 2 South" was heard over the loudspeaker.

71

Annie was the first to arrive.

"What happened?"

"She was sleeping an hour ago, now she dropped her sats, spiked a higher temp."

"And you didn't call me?"

"No, I called an RRT—she not responding!"

Suddenly the room was filled with people. Respiratory, a nurse from the ICU, the intensivist on call.

"What's going on?" said Dr. Wright, the intensivist. Fran started to speak only to be interrupted by Annie.

"I've been monitoring her all night, she started with a low-grade fever, responded to Tylenol, told the nurse to do some more incentive with her, ordered a chest film."

"Did you look at the film?" said Dr. Wright

"Uh, I got called to 2 North for a bleeder, then the RRT."

"Let me look at the film." Suddenly by magic, Annie was all over it. She swiped Fran's computer away and signed her out, signed on, and pulled up the x-ray.

They looked at it together. "Nothing really here," said Dr. Wright.

Fran had gone into the room to take vital signs again. She called out to Dr. Wright, BP normal, pulse 110, sat 89 on 50 percent aerosol mask. Mrs. Troiano was awake. "Am I okay?"

"Yes," said Fran reassuringly, "you are just fine." Fran knew she was not.

Annie tried to step in to give orders.

Dr. Wright, now understanding what had happened, spoke to Fran, "I'm going to put in an order for a chest CT."

"Got it," Fran said. She glared at Annie.

"Who is her attending?"

"Henderson," said Fran. Dr. Wright looked at Annie. "Call him. Then write transfer orders for the ICU." Annie started to take Fran's computer again. "No, you can't use this now, I need to pick up orders and chart."

Annie turned around and walked off to the nurses' station.

Dr. Wright said to Fran, "Good job, young lady—it's possible this is a PE." A PE is shorthand for pulmonary embolism, a large blood clot in the lungs that can be extremely dangerous. Anyone who has had orthopedic surgery is more at risk for a blood clot. "Has she been on Lovenox?" Lovenox is a drug that interrupts the clotting mechanism and is used to prevent the very thing they were worried about, the formation of a dangerous clot or embolus.

"Yes."

"Call me when they come to take her to CT."

"Of course, Dr. Wright." Fran looked up to see Annie glaring at her from the nurses' station.

As soon as Fran met her gaze, she looked down.

Fran thought, *Well, if she had bothered to come up the first time I called, this might have gone down differently.*

Debra came over to offer support. "Well, you were right about something going on with this patient."

"I wish I wasn't." Fran felt slightly queasy.

It was now 6:00 a.m. She had orders to pick up, notes and vital signs to chart. She had to call transport to take Mrs. Troiano down to radiology. She had to call report to the ICU, also update her other patients' notes and give report to the next shift.

It was 8:00 a.m. before she was able to leave. She drove to the nearest Costco and started filling up her cart with rice, canned goods, coffee, frozen foods, snacks for the kids. She thought about Mrs. Troiano. *I hope she's okay*, she thought. *She was on Lovenox, it shouldn't be a PE.* Fran kept thinking about the new reports of the coronavirus.

Couldn't be that. It's not here in this state, or is it?

She looked at the cart in front of her at the checkout line. It was filled with bottles of rubbing alcohol, cases of water, batteries, toilet paper, and flashlights. Fran was amused. *Are we having a hurricane?* Fran turned around and looked at the carts behind her. Cleaning products, Lysol spray, Tylenol, paper goods were in everyone's basket. *Why is no one buying any food?* She looked in her cart. *Maybe I am the ignorant one.* With a sigh, Fran got off the line and went to the paper goods and cleaning aisles. *Wow, they haven't stocked this place yet*, she thought, looking at the partially empty shelves. Grabbing a few rolls of toilet paper, paper towels, Lysol spray, detergent, and Clorox, Fran thought, *I don't know why I am getting caught up in this. I'm panic buying like everyone around me.* Fran got back on the checkout line. She got home, unpacked her things. "What's with all the cleaning supplies?" her mom said. "I don't know, everyone around me was buying them, so I got caught up and got us some stuff too. Mom. I just need to shower, then I want to spend some time with the kids and you."

Fran was sitting on the floor playing with Lilly and her dollhouse, watching Robby run around with his iPad and blanket, and thought, *I wonder how long I have to stay in surgery before they will let me go to pediatrics?* That was, after all, her reason for becoming a nurse. *Maybe I will look online for pediatric jobs or jobs with brain-injured patients. Or maybe I'm not ready, I'm just getting the hang of this.* She let her mind focus on the kids during her days off. *There will be plenty of time to worry about health care when I get back to work.*

Chapter 5

Critical Care
February 2020

Sandy already knew Maureen was in a bad mood, and it was only eight thirty in the morning. Sandy had been off for three days. She came back on a Friday. Her first patient, a seventy-year-old man, Mr. Berger, had been kept intubated overnight as he was too agitated to extubate immediately after his mitral valve replacement. Sandy was determined to get him extubated on her shift.

Her second patient was a sixty-two-year-old woman with lung cancer who underwent a lobectomy (removal of part of the lung to cure the cancer) the day before.

Maureen was talking out loud. "This fuckin' thing, I don't know why no one here know how to slave the ALINE to the monitor." This means getting the arterial line readings to show up on the monitor. "I always get left finding another ALINE cable and doing it. Great way to start the day," she said, annoyed.

"Can I help you with anything?"

"Yeah, actually, you can. I have to go to that fucking section council meeting today and you will have to cover me. So I'm setting up the slave so you can see it from your room."

"Oh, okay," Sandy said nervously. "Can you show me what I need to do for the IABP?"

"You won't need to do anything for the *pump*, but you might have to do something for the *patient*," Maureen said sarcastically.

"What's section council?" Sandy asked earnestly.

"Why? If you want to be on the committee instead of me, you can have it."

"Well, uh, no, but I was just wondering what the purpose is," Sandy inquired.

"We just talk about shit that's never going to happen."

"Okay," said Sandy. She knew she wasn't going to get anything more out of Maureen today. "Just tell me when you have to go and let me know what you want me to do." Maureen did not answer.

Sandy went up to Ethan to vent. "I don't know what bug is up Mo's ass today, she is meaner than usual."

Ethan chuckled. "That's Mo, you'll love her when you get to know her better."

"I hope that will be sooner than later." She paused. "She has this meeting today. I asked her what it was for, and she wouldn't tell me, just said something about a whole lot of shit that never happens."

"Well, she is partly right, I'm on that committee too."

"Well, thank God, someone can tell me about it. Doesn't it involve all of the staff here?"

"Sort of. It's me, the evening unit secretary Jan, five other nurses, I forget who they all are, some are on nights, our head nurse, someone from administration. We talk about staff satisfaction, scheduling, how we alternate getting certain holidays off. Then we talk about skin problems, infection control stuff, you know, just stuff like that. Nothing ever really comes of it, it's partly a gripe session. That's really about it. No biggie."

"Oh, okay," said Sandy. She walked back to her patients' rooms. *I guess it is no big deal*, she thought.

At nine thirty, Maureen walked over to Sandy. "I'm gonna go now to the meeting. You should be okay. I set the insulin pump to ring in an hour, just do a finger stick and use the protocol. By then I should be back. If anything, get me."

"No problem."

Maureen walked into the break room. She saw that she was the only one there. She checked her watch. "They did say nine thirty, didn't they?" she mumbled to herself. "Where the fuck is everyone? I don't have time for this shit." Just as she was pouring herself some coffee, in walked Jan, the evening secretary, and Gina, the assistant director of nursing. Gina put down a box of Dunkin' Donuts on the table. *Oh yeah*, Maureen thought, *doughnuts, now that will just fix everything. Why does everyone think that feeding nurses will solve everything? It's just fuckin' insulting.*

Maureen was fuming inside.

Next, Nero came in. "I hope this doesn't go too long. I'm tripled today." Gina said nothing.

Maureen checked her watch again. "Can we just get started, some of us have patients to take care of."

"Let's wait another minute or two, and sorry, but Dayna is in another meeting, so she won't be able to make it today," Gina said with her sincerest voice. Dayna was the director of nursing. "Where's Ethan? Isn't he a member of this committee?"

I think that might be just a tad more important than him coming in here for a meeting. *And* we're gonna need him as a nurse when we all die from being overworked like this." Maureen leaned over to Nero. "I thought this *was* Dayna's scheduled meeting, this is bullshit." Maureen leaned back in her chair, took a sip of her coffee, and sighed. Maureen made an obvious gesture of checking her watch again. Nine forty-five. She stared at Gina.

"Okay," Gina said, "I guess we'll get started. Let me first say that our incidence of pressure injury this quarter was below the national benchmark, so good job, people." The room was silent.

Maureen thought, *If she's looking for applause, she's not getting it here.*

"So anyone have anything they would like to share?" Gina said as she looked down at her legal pad. She held her pen as if she was going to begin taking notes. Maureen looked at Nero and rolled her eyes. "Mo, do you have anything you'd like to say?" Gina said.

"No, I'll pass."

Ethan rushed in the door, "sorry I'm late," was in class." He took a seat.

Nero said, "Why do we have to float to step-down?" Gina jotted something on her pad.

"Remember, you work for the hospital and not just the unit. The nurses from step-down have to float here to help you out sometimes."

Maureen said, "But they can't take a full assignment here, yet we have to take a full assignment there. And quite frankly, we've discussed this subject ad nauseum, nothing ever gets resolved, so can we just move on?"

"It's just that some of us are unprepared for the different workload on step-down, we were never trained for it," Nero said defeatedly.

Gina looked down at her notes and sighed. "I don't have anything else, unless there is something else you all want to talk about." This was received in silence. Nero looked up and responded: "what about this virus in the nursing home in Seattle that's been on the news?" "We haven't been told anything yet," Gina replied, eyes never leaving her notes "Okay, everyone, thank you for your hard work. Have a nice day."

Maureen got up, walked out, shaking her head. "What a waste of time."

Sandy went to work on Mr. Berger first. She lowered the sedation to see how he would wake up. "Mr. Berger, it's Sandy, can you open your eyes?" she said, shaking him gently. "Mr. Berger, wake up, let's get this tube out." The patient opened his eyes and looked startled. He started to move his hands up toward the endotracheal tube. Sandy put her hand gently on his.

"It's okay, you just need to wake up, and we'll do a few tests and get that tube out of you." Mr. Berger nodded. "Do you have pain in your chest now?" The patient nodded no. "That's good because I want you to stay awake now. Can you lift your head off the pillow?" Mr. Berger did. "Can you stick your tongue out?" He did. "That's really good. I think if you stay that way, nice and calm, I'm gonna call Denise to see if we can move on getting you talking." Mr. Berger nodded again. Sandy took her phone out and called Denise, the respiratory therapist. "Denise, I think Mr. Berger is ready."

"Okay, be right there" was the answer. Sandy noticed that Dr. Camarie was standing outside of Mr. Berger's room. She immediately became nervous. Dr. Camarie, the medical director, had a habit of showing up at all times to check up on patients. He also had the responsibility of overseeing proper usage of the ICU beds.

"How's that young gentleman doing? Are you going to extubate him soon, Sandy?" he asked.

Sandy was surprised he even knew her name.

"Why, yes, I think he will be extubated. He is meeting all parameters so far."

"Good," said Dr. Camarie, "we might need his bed later. Who has that patient?" Dr. Camarie gestured to the patient on the IABP.

"That's Maureen's patient."

Dr. Camarie smiled knowingly. "Oh, Mo, is she out having a cigarette again?" Sandy nodded. "I keep telling that young woman to quit that nasty habit, but Mo listens to nobody." Sandy was getting the sense that Dr. Camarie was more involved on the unit than she had originally thought. He seemed to know all the nurses by name.

Sandy glanced over at Maureen's patient on the IABP. *I really want to go and have a good look at the IABP for next time*, she thought. Her attention turned toward Mr. Berger who was patiently waiting to be extubated. That was her priority.

Denise came down, and fortunately, it was an easy extubation. Mr. Berger met all his weaning parameters and was successfully extubated. Sandy called down for the post-extubation chest x-ray. Sandy helped him sit up and taught him his deep breathing exercises and how to splint his chest to diminish the pain. "Mr. Berger, this is particularly important. Hold the pillow and press it into your chest while you take a deep breath in." Sandy demonstrated. "Now cough."

"Ow! That hurts."

"I know, it does. Let's have you take a sip of water, then I can get an order for you to take some pain pills instead of the injection, which will make you too sleepy."

I have to admit, thought Sandy, *this patient is one of the more cooperative and easy patients to take care of. I'm so glad he is doing well."* Out loud, she said, "Mr. Berger, I am going to call your wife and tell her you did great." Mr. Berger nodded and drifted to sleep.

Sandy saw all the staff returning from the meeting, so she quickly went over to Maureen's patient. She was looking at the monitor, the arterial line, and the insulin drip when Maureen came up behind her.

"Almost time for the finger stick."

"It still had a few minutes to go."

"Okay, I'll take it from here, thanks."

"How was the meeting?"

"Usual crap."

Sandy went on to see her second patient, Mrs. Moss. She reviewed the orders again. She thought, *I must get an IV in, take out the central line, get her up and moving. Shouldn't be too bad of a shift. But I do have that empty bed… Always a risk for a problem.*

Sandy saw Ethan walking toward her, shaking his head. "What's up?"

"Oh, the meeting."

"Why what happened?"

"Well, someone brought up this coronavirus thing in Seattle and asked if we are doing anything here."

"Oh really," Sandy said nonchalantly, "I heard something about a bunch of people dying in a nursing home. It's flu season after all, it's probably the flu. So what did they say?"

"Nothing," said Ethan, "they said nothing. One of the administrators said it's not in this state. How do they know?"

"Why? Are you worried?" Sandy said, concerned.

"I don't know if we should be worried or not. It seems to affect people that are older and with medical conditions or immune system problems."

"Like everyone in this unit," Sandy replied.

"Yes, like everyone here."

"Well, we can't worry about it now. We have patients' lives to save. Come with me, we have to help this patient get cleaned up. He just got extubated."

"Okay, coming."

They could never know how correct they were to be concerned.

Sandy went over to Maureen to see if she could ask a few questions about the IABP. Maureen waved her off.

Wow, after our last interaction, I thought we were getting friendly. I guess not.

"*RRT, 2 South, RRT, 2 South*" came over the loudspeaker. Sandy knew what that meant. She had an empty bed. This next patient could be hers.

The phone rang just as she finished the thought. "Sandy, take report on this RRT patient," Her charge nurse said, holding up the phone.

"Sure," she said. *I wonder what this is?* Sandy thought. She picked up the phone.

"Hey, it's Britney from 2 South, I want to give report on Mrs. Cantor."

"Okay, shoot."

Britney continued. "Mrs. Cantor is an eighty-one-year-old female with a history of congestive heart failure, aortic stenosis, diabetes, anxiety. She was admitted with CHF exacerbation to tweak her meds. They were talking about an echo, pulmonary function tests, and maybe a stress test to see if she would qualify for a TAVR."

Sandy was jotting down notes. "Anyway, today she complained of severe shortness of breath. So we first diuresed her"—which means they administered a strong diuretic, a water pill type of drug, to rev up her kidneys and get rid of excess fluid—"got her up, gave her a respiratory treatment, but she dropped her sat to the eighties, so we called the RRT. She is on 100 percent NRB"—NRB stands for non-rebreather mask, which delivers the highest concentration of oxygen that can be given without a breathing tube—"we have a chest x-ray pending, and labs are pending too. Any questions?"

"No, thanks," said Sandy.

"What bed?"

"Fifty-seven."

"Okay, I'll call transport."

Sandy thought, *Let me be on top of this. This makes my third patient, but I can handle this. Okay, CHF exacerbation, diuretics, beta-blockers perhaps. Let me check her blood sugar.* Sandy was already adding her to her assignment on the computer so she could see her labs.

Within ten minutes, the patient was brought up by Britney and a transporter.

They helped Sandy and Ethan settle her into the room.

"Hi, Mrs. Cantor, I'm Sandy, your nurse, and this is Ethan, our star nurse's aide. We are here to figure out what's going on and help you feel better."

"Hi, Mrs. Cantor, I'm Ethan, I'll be helping Sandy get you all settled here."

Ethan was already thinking back to his classes on cardiology. *Hmm, CHF, heart is overloaded, fluid in the lungs…*

Ethan attached her to the monitor. "I'll get her vital signs."

"Thanks, Ethan."

Sandy looked up at the monitor. "Hmm, sinus tach 105, a little fast for my liking." Ethan called out, "Blood pressure's normal." Sandy could see it on the monitor.

When the saturation curve came up, Sandy saw it read 86. "Can you get a better waveform, Ethan? Try a different finger."

"Nope, still 86." Ethan splayed out Mrs. Cantor's fingers on his own hand. "Come here, look at her fingers," he said to Sandy. She went into the room. They were a purplish color and cool.

"Now that's strange." Sandy went to check that the non-rebreather bag was inflated to the fullest.

"Can you get a temp, please?" she asked Ethan.

"Mrs. Cantor, how are you feeling?"

"Oh, not well, this old ticker is worn out, I think." Sandy noticed that she was taking very deep breaths but rapidly, at least twenty-four times per minute. A regular respiratory rate was fourteen to twenty times per minute. She was really working to breathe.

Ethan held up the thermometer so Sandy could see—101.8. That was a significant fever.

Sandy took a deep breath before she said anything.

"Mrs. Cantor, you're running a bit of a temperature."

"Really? Why do you think that is?"

"Well, I'm not sure at the moment, but that's why you're here so we can find out."

"Thank you."

Sandy took out her phone to call the PA.

"Keith," said the voice at the end.

"Hey, Keith, Sandy, this new admit from 2 South, Mrs. Cantor, she's running a temp of 101.8, and her sat is 86 on 100 percent NRB."

"I'm putting in orders. Do you know if she had an x-ray downstairs?"

"She did, will you have a look?" *Click.* The phone went dead.

Sandy pulled up the radiologist report of the earlier chest x-ray. It had not been dictated yet. She pulled up the film, but she really did not know how to read x-rays. Ethan stood over her and looked as well. "I wish we knew how to read these things."

"Me too."

Keith was on the unit moments later. He said, "Something's up with the chest film. Pulmonary said to send her for a chest CT."

Sandy went to look at the new orders. "CBC diff, BMP, LACTIC ACID, Blood cultures X 2, UAC with culture, chest x-ray, chest CT with contrast. IV fluid NS@50cc/hr" were the new orders. Most of those were routine labs, but there were blood cultures to check for germs in the blood and urine.

Sandy gathered the supplies needed and sent off the blood work and urine.

Sandy also put up the IV fluids. Ethan was standing around, trying to absorb all that was happening. "So, Sandy, should she have IV fluids if we think this is fluid overload?"

"Well, she is febrile, so yes, and they only ordered 50 cc per hour as compared to the sepsis protocol, which would require a large bolus based on her weight."

"Okay." Ethan was processing this.

Dr. Camarie was suddenly standing in front of the room. "Good explanation, young lady. Yes, Ethan, she is correct, we have to treat the sepsis with fluids but not enough to overload her."

"Thanks, Doc."

"Wow, Dr. Camarie knows you?"

"Hell yaz, that doc knows everyone and everything. He's really a great guy."

Sandy called for a transporter to help her take Mrs. Cantor down to CT. She hooked up the portable monitor, got a portable oxygen tank, and waited. Soon a transporter came up from the office to help her push the bed.

In the elevator, they went to the basement where CT was located.

Sandy's eyes were on the monitor the whole way down. *Hmm, still tachycardic, sats hovering around 88 percent.* This was concerning to her. *I just want to get her to CT and back upstairs*, she thought.

Once in CT, the tech helped her pull Mrs. Cantor over to the table, and the CT was completed in a matter of minutes. Once back in her room upstairs, Sandy hooked her up to the central monitor and adjusted her face mask and cables.

"Are you comfortable?" she asked. She noticed that Mrs. Cantor had a respiratory rate of twenty-six, a bit fast, but the sat was holding at 89 percent. This was still concerning as she was still on the 100 percent non-rebreather mask.

Maureen sauntered over to Sandy's room.

"What ya get?"

"Not sure yet. CHF, respiratory failure, low sats, febrile, just got back from CT scan."

"Did we flu swab her?" Maureen said sarcastically. "You know it *is* the flu season."

"I didn't get an order for that."

"Well, maybe ya should." Maureen walked away.

Sandy thought, *Now why didn't I think of that?*

She called Keith and got an order for the rapid flu swab.

Sandy called the lab to send up the swab, as it had to be in a certain container with culture medium and sent right back.

"Ethan, I'm gonna get the swab, can you bring it down?"

"Sure, just tell me when. I'm gonna be in 59 doing a bath."

Sandy walked into the room. "Mrs. Cantor, I am going to take a flu swab. This will be a bit uncomfortable. I have to put this all the way into the back of your throat through your nose."

"But I had my flu shot!"

"I am sure you did, but with your fever and low oxygen in your blood, we have to make sure."

"Okay, whatever you say."

"I'm just going to pull down the mask for a moment to get the swab."

Sandy lifted the mask gently and began to put the swab in the patient's nose. She looked at her face, which suddenly turned a gray/blue color. Sandy quickly looked up at the monitor only to see the sat was reading 68 percent.

"Mrs. Cantor, can you hear me?" No response. "Mrs. Cantor!" she yelled as she shook her shoulder.

Sandy yelled out, "I need help!" as she pushed the red button on the back wall.

Keith came running in as did Maureen, Ethan, the respiratory therapist, and most of the nurses on the unit.

"Get the cart—get the intubation tray," Maureen directed.

Maureen grabbed a surgical mask and one for Sandy. "Hurry, put this on, you need it to assist with the intubation. Get gloves on too."

Sandy put on the mask. Denise was already at the head of the bed, having removed the headboard. Keith was there too.

Maureen gave Sandy a little push. "Get up there, it's your patient."

Keith yelled, "Someone open the tray." Sandy looked up at Maureen, who nodded at her. "Get me two milligrams of Versed and twenty milligrams of etomidate!"

Etomidate is a nonbarbiturate hypnotic drug that totally relaxes but does not paralyze the muscles. It was essential to avoid the natural struggling to prevent hurting the patient. She looked at Maureen.

"I'll get it." Maureen walked briskly to the med room and came back with two syringes.

Sandy opened the tray. She thought, *Please don't let me fuck this up.*

"Okay, push the Versed and the etomidate." Sandy got to the IV and pushed the drugs. The patient relaxed, as though all her body had just deflated.

Denise expertly got the laryngoscope and endotracheal tube. "Give me some pressure," she said to Keith." Keith put his finger on the patient's throat and pushed down gently. That pressure straightened the airway and helped smooth the intubation.

"Got it," said Denise and expertly slid the tube into the airway.

Maureen came in and helped her secure the endotracheal tube.

"Someone bag her while I get the vent," Denise said. Sandy took the Ambu bag and started rhythmically squeezing the bag to inflate the patient's lungs. Keith listened to both her lungs to make sure the tube was in the right place. Emergency intubations were fraught with potential problems, including putting the tube down too far. Anatomically, the right lung was slightly higher than the left, and so when the tube went too far, it would go into the right main bronchus and only ventilate the right lung. Keith heard equal sounds on the left and right.

"Let's get a gas and an x-ray," he said.

"As soon as I get the vent," Denise replied.

Sandy looked at the door and saw Ethan standing there. He nodded to her as if to say good job.

Sandy's heart was pounding as she looked down at Mrs. Cantor. *Please don't die*, she thought. She looked up to see if Maureen was still there, but Maureen was already back in her own room.

"Keith, can you order some sedation? She's gonna wake up soon and start fighting the vent."

"I'll put the orders in. Let's also start her on antibiotics."

Keith put in all the ICU orders including the ventilator settings, placement of an NGT (a tube from the nose into the stomach that can be used to take excess stomach contents away or used to put liquid food into the stomach), medication orders including IV antibiotics, pulmonary and infectious disease consultations, additional blood work, RSV, and flu swab. And one thing that was like stab in Sandy's gut, *COVID-19 PCR, droplet precautions.*

WTF? Sandy stared at the order. The color drained from her face. She called Ethan over and pointed to the order. He looked and then looked directly at Sandy.

"And so it starts," he said and walked away. He came back with a box of surgical masks and placed them outside of Mrs. Cantor's room.

"Did you talk about this at the section meeting the other day?"

"No, not really, we just talked about it being some virus in Seattle."

Sandy was not sure if she should tell the other nurses working that day. She went over to Keith.

"COVID swab? Droplet precautions? Is it here in the building? Are there other patients with it? Did we know about this already? Is there a plan?"

Her mind was racing, trying to think about all the patients she had cared for over the last few weeks and their symptoms.

"Slow down," Keith said, "it's just a precaution. We don't think it's here. But there are new CDC recommendations for patients presenting with certain symptoms." He thought. "Besides, the hospital is not doing its own testing, it's a send-out to the CDC." He was arguing with himself. "She just came in for CHF exacerbation. So she might be dead before we get it back. So what's the point. But it was Camarie's recommendation."

"But why isn't anyone here saying anything?" Sandy went on.

"Because there is nothing to say yet." He shrugged. He wasn't sure what to think himself, but he knew he had a boatload of work and no time to argue the point of every nurse who wanted to freak out.

Sandy looked around at all the nurses working on the unit that day. Maureen, Stacy, Jan, Pete, Nero, Rasheeda, Ahmed, Bill, the unit clerk Lucille, and Ethan. She looked at the nursing students on the unit happily exploring the supply room, the emergency equipment, making rounds with their professor. It was if the world was swirling around her. She felt like she was now in a vacuum, but out of control. *Snap out of it, Sandy*, she said to herself. *If there was something to worry about, we would have got it in our employee emails or a notice or a memo in the break room. They wouldn't have said* nothing! *Right?*

Sandy put on her blue plastic gown and her surgical mask and went in to Mrs. Cantor. She listened to her lungs, abdomen, heart, felt her peripheral pulses, and checked her central line dressing site. When she suctioned the endotracheal tube, she was startled. Thick brown malodorous sludge came out of the tube. *Ugh*, she thought, *those are some nasty secretions. Let me tell Keith, maybe he wants to order a sputum C&S.*

She called Keith and got the order. Sandy now had three patients to care for. *I'd better start prioritizing. Okay*, she thought, *I have Mrs. Moss and Mr. Berger.*

Mr. Berger had been newly extubated and was having pain. She did the swallow test with a sip of water. "Good, no coughing. Okay, Mr. Berger, I want to give you some oxycodone [a painkiller] and then get you out of bed."

Sandy went to the medication room and signed out 10 milligrams of oxycodone and gave it to Mr. Berger. "We're gonna let that kick in, then we will assist you out of bed to a chair."

"Okay. Do you think I'm ready to get up? I just had open-heart surgery."

"That's the best thing we can do for you. We have to get you up and moving, and if there are no complications, your tubes will all come out tomorrow and you will go to a regular room. Now I want to show you your incentive spirometer." Sandy got out the device and a pillow and demonstrated the pulmonary toilet exercises. These involved deep breathing and purposely coughing to open up all the parts of the lungs.

"Hey, Ethan, can we get Mr. Berger up in about fifteen minutes?"

"Sure, meet ya there."

She went on to Mrs. Moss, careful to keep an eye on the central monitor to check on Mrs. Cantor as she walked by. *Okay*, she thought, *holding steady, BP normal, sat 90 percent, could be a little better. Maybe we'd better put in a Foley with a temperature probe. I'll ask Keith.* Sandy made a mental note.

She washed her hands and went in to see Mrs. Moss. "Okay, lots of things to do for you today. First, I am going to put an IV in your arm, then I'm gonna take that thing out of your neck."

"Okay, great, it's so itchy."

Sandy had her supplies ready and expertly put an IV into Mrs. Moss's arm. She flushed it and placed a dressing over the site. "That should do it. Now I am going to lie you flat for a moment and take that IV out of your neck. You're going to feel me pulling on the tape. That's the worst part."

Sandy removed the tape, got a large gauze pad, and placed it over the entry site of the central line.

"Okay, now take a deep breath and hold it." Mrs. Moss did as she was told.

As she held her breath, Sandy slid out the catheter in her neck and pressed down on the site. "Good job. I'm just going to hold this in place until I am sure the bleeding has stopped, then I'll sit you up. I'll call Keith after that and see if he wants to pull your chest tube, then we'll get you into the chair. You might even get to transfer to a regular room later today."

"Wow, that was pretty easy so far," commented Mrs. Moss.

When Sandy went back to Mr. Berger's room, Ethan was there already setting up the chair. He had the stand-and-lift device already there.

She made sure to pass by the central monitor again to check on Mrs. Cantor. "Okay, Mr. Berger, this handy-dandy machine is going to help you get out of bed." She and Ethan stood on either side of Mr. Berger.

They placed the stand device in front of him. "Now, put your feet on this platform and hold on here." Ethan pointed. "Now on the count of three, pull yourself up, and we will put the seat down behind you. One, two, three, *up!*" Mr. Berger stood. They quickly put the seat together behind him. "Now just lean back."

"What'll they think of next?" said Mr. Berger.

They moved the lift device in the front of his chair. "Okay, one last time, on three, you stand then sit all the way back in this big comfy chair we have for you."

Soon, Mr. Berger was seated in his recliner chair.

"I'm gonna go," said Sandy. "Can you finish setting him up? I have to go and check on Mrs. Cantor."

"Sure thing, hon," said Ethan.

Soon, Sandy was gowned and masked up and back in Mrs. Cantor's room. Maureen stood outside the doorway. Sandy looked up.

89

Maureen motioned with her hand she was going out for a smoke. "Nothing to do, back in a sec." Sandy just nodded. When Maureen was gone, she rolled her eyes.

Disgusting habit, she thought. *Whatever.*

Sandy hung the antibiotic. She set the pump for thirty minutes. She looked at the monitor again. Heart rate 110. *Hmm,* she thought, *maybe I'd better check her temp again.* It was 101.2, still significantly febrile.

Well, we've already sent blood cultures, sputum culture, urine culture. Nothing to do but wait and see if the antibiotics work, Sandy thought. *Are we missing something? She's stable for now. Let me see if I can get transfer orders on Mrs. Moss.*

Sandy reviewed the transfer orders, called the floor, and gave report. She kept an eye on Mrs. Cantor's monitor as she was on the phone.

"This is Mrs. Paula Moss, date of birth, September 24, 1957, who had a right upper lobectomy two days ago. Vitals stable, afebrile, chest tube removed this morning, x-ray shows no pneumothorax"—meaning her lungs had not collapsed after the chest tube was removed. "Central line is out, peripheral IV is in the right lower arm, no fluids. She is out of bed, advancing diet today to regular. Nasal O2 2 liters per minute"—oxygen flowing into the nose at two liters per minute, a minimal amount of support as needed. "Pain level at highest 6 over 10, refused pain medication but took 650 milligrams of Tylenol this morning at 0945. She ambulated about half the hallway this morning due to increased activity."

"Okay, send her up" was the reply.

Sandy called transport and got Mrs. Moss into the wheelchair.

"Good luck, Mrs. Moss, be well," Sandy said cheerfully.

"Thank you! And thanks for all your wonderful care." She smiled at Sandy.

Now Sandy had another empty bed.

Mrs. Cantor's son Joel walked into the unit. He went up to the nurses' station to inquire about his mother. Sandy saw the unit secretary point in her direction. Sandy gulped hard. *Uh-oh, what am I going to tell him?*

"Hi, I'm Joel Cantor, and that is my mom. What happened to her? I thought she was here for a workup for open-heart surgery."

"Hi, Joel, I'm Sandy, your mom's nurse. What happened today is that your mom couldn't breathe and was brought up here for closer monitoring. The saturation of oxygen in her blood dropped so much that we had to put her on her breathing machine to assist her."

"What about her heart? Was that the problem?" Joel asked excitedly.

"Well, we don't exactly know right now. We're doing some tests to see what is going on. Your mom has a fever, which is unusual. We have to see what is causing the fever before we even think about doing any surgery," Sandy explained.

Joel had to be satisfied with that, although he was even more anxious about his mother than when he arrived. He had expected the time after the surgery to be difficult, but for her to have deteriorated so much before the surgery was inexplicable. He pulled out his cell phone and called his sister and uncle to let the rest of the family know what was going on. It was not a call he was happy to make.

Sandy went back to check on Mr. Berger, who was doing well. He was up in the chair and had tolerated his liquid diet, so she obtained an order to advance him to regular food. His wife, Carol, was there, so they spoke for a while. "So how's my husband doing?"

"He did really great."

"What's next?"

"Well, we begin to walk him further. We will take out his central line today or tomorrow, his chest tube will come out in another day, and he will be ready to transfer to the regular floor. His doctor will resume all his medications before he leaves, but he will begin a beta-blocker to keep his heart rate slow and steady."

"What about pain," Carol said

"Well, most of the pain comes from having the chest tube in. He will get pain medication when he asks, and after the tube comes out, he probably will only need Tylenol. Excuse me, I have to go see my other patient, I'll be back in a bit. Your husband has his call light if he needs anything. I'll tell Ethan to take him for another walk after lunch."

Sandy saw Joel nervously pacing back and forth in front of his mother's room. He was talking excitedly on his cell phone.

Sandy washed her hands, put on a mask and gloves, and went into the room to check on Mrs. Cantor. She looked up at the monitor and paused. She knew Joel was watching her every move. Sandy made an exaggerated show of each part of her assessment so Joel could see she was performing well. Sandy remembered fondly one of Mo's old sayings: "If you can't kill 'em with kindness, baffle 'em with bullshit." Sandy tried to hide a chuckle. How true this was right now. She spoke softly to her patient although she was sedated. "Mrs. Cantor, I am going to listen to your lungs, check your pulses again and all your medications. Then I have to suction you to get out some of those secretions."

"Can I come in?" said Joel from outside the door. "Yes, you can, but I have to ask you to wear a mask."

"Why?"

"Because your mother is running a fever and we have a flu swab and other tests pending, so we want to protect the other patients."

Joel seemed satisfied for the moment, but Sandy sensed he might end up being trouble.

Joel stepped into the room and looked at all the equipment and monitor.

Here it comes, thought Sandy. *All the questions.* She was right.

"What's that?" Joel asked, pointing to the waveform of the respirations.

"That is a respiratory waveform so we can see how fast she is breathing, and that blue number is the oxygen saturation." Sandy thought if she flooded him with information, he might be calmer.

"That red wave is her blood pressure, and you can see the number displayed next to it, so her blood pressure is stable for now."

Next Joel went over to the IV infusion pumps and appeared to study them.

Sandy saw him and spoke up.

"Okay, so that is just IV fluids so we can hang her antibiotics. That other medication is a drug called Levophed to help keep her blood pressure up, and I will lower it as necessary to maintain a normal blood pressure."

She saw Joel looking at his mother from the end of the bed. He seemed frightened to approach her. "You can go up to her and talk to her.

"Can she hear me?"

"She's sedated, but some patients report that they have heard conversation after the sedation is turned down or off."

"What's that tube in her nose for?"

"Well, right now, that is a tube that will prevent her from vomiting, and later we will use it to give her some feeding and medications, as necessary."

"Hi, Mom," Joel said meekly.

"You can hold her hand," Sandy said. "Here, I'll get you a chair, and you can sit next to her for a while."

Sandy busied herself tidying the room, checking on the supply of linens in the cupboard, emptying the Foley catheter.

"I'm going to suction her now, so if that will upset you, you may leave the room."

"No, I want to stay."

"Okay, but your mom will cough and look a bit uncomfortable for a few moments, and I don't want you to be upset."

Sandy went to the bedside, hooked up the in-line catheter to the tubing, and threaded it down the endotracheal tube. The patient began to gag and cough, her head jumping off the pillow for a moment. "It's okay, okay," Sandy said reassuringly, "it's okay, I'm almost done."

Joel jumped up. "Are you hurting her?"

"No, it doesn't hurt, but it does cause discomfort, but it's only for a moment or two." She knew that Joel saw the dark thick secretions that were suctioned up.

"What's that from?"

"Well, there might be some germs down there, and sometimes they don't look very pleasant, that's why we have to get them out." Sandy tried to change the subject. "Did you update your family?"

"Yes, I called my uncle, mom's brother in California. Most of the family is there." He turned away from his mother to face Sandy. "Did you know there is a cruise ship that is quarantined there with passengers on it with some kind of virus?"

"No, I didn't know that," Sandy replied casually.

"Well, they are saying that it is very contagious, and they are not letting anyone off the ship." Sandy felt her heart quicken, but her poker face never let on.

"Were you just in California?"

"Yes, I live there. I knew Mom was not feeling well and they were evaluating her for surgery, so I was on my way here anyway, and now all this happened."

"I am going to have Ethan come in here, and we are going to turn your mother. Why don't you go out and get a cup of coffee. There is a cafeteria downstairs. There are a few things we need to do for your mom to make her more comfortable."

"Okay. When can I come back up?"

"Maybe give us thirty minutes, please."

Joel took off his mask and stepped out.

"There's a sink right over there." Sandy pointed. "You can wash your hands."

Sandy took off her gloves, washed her hands, took off her mask, and stepped out of the room. She looked around the unit for Ethan, but saw he was in another room doing vital signs and preparing a chair for a patient to get out of bed.

She walked by the door and motioned for him to come.

"Waz up?" he said, poking his head out of the doorway.

"Waz up is shit's getting real, and you have to come in 57 with me and turn, and we have to talk."

"Okay, I'll be there as soon as I finish up."

Sandy went to her computer to chart and took out her cell phone. She googled "cruise ship California coronavirus."

There it was, plain as day. "Diamond Princess Cruise ships held at the Port of Oakland dock amid concern of outbreak of coronavirus."

Sandy did a bit of her charting as she was waiting for Ethan to help her with a turn.

Ethan walked over to her, and she held out her cell phone to him. He read the headline. His eyes widened. "So that's California."

"Guess where Mrs. Cantor's son just came from?"

"California?"

"You got it. It has to be in New York by now. I just don't get why no one is saying anything. Everyone seems to be acting strange, agitated, like something's up but no one wants to say." Sandy and Ethan washed their hands, put on blue plastic gowns and surgical masks, and went into Mrs. Cantor's room. They began giving her a bath. She was diaphoretic, pale, and dropped her blood pressure and sats (oxygen saturation) whenever they turned her.

"Careful, let's get the sheets under fast so we don't drop her sat too much."

"Wait, let me go up on her Levo a bit first."

"Understood," replied Ethan. "This is freaky."

"She is starting to look a bit dusky." Mrs. Cantor's sat had dropped to seventy-nine. Sandy was staring at her, looked at the vent settings again.

"Hm, we have some wiggle room to go up—let me call Keith."

They finished positioning her and removed their PPE, washed, and went out of the room.

Sandy picked up her phone.

"Yes?"

"Keith, it's Sandy, Mrs. Cantor de-sats with any little movement. Would you like to change any vent settings?"

"What's her FIO2?" Keith asked.

"It's 70 percent."

"Let's go up to 80 percent, can you put the order in for me?"

"Sure," Sandy said. Nurses were only allowed to put in emergent orders, but she always saw Maureen and other veteran nurses doing it, so she entered the order.

Sandy called Denise and told her.

"Be right over."

Sandy went in to check on Mr. Berger, then sat down to chart.

Over the loudspeaker came the booming voice, "*Code blue* cardio critical care, code blue cardio critical care."

Sandy, Maureen, Ahmed, and Nero all stopped what they were doing and looked at the other side of the unit. "I'll go," Sandy said. If one side of the unit had a code, a nurse from the other side was supposed to respond.

Sandy walked over to find Keith writing orders. Pete was in the room with Denise, the respiratory therapist, the anesthesiologist, the pulmonary fellow, along with Jan, the charge nurse.

"What happened here?" Sandy said to Keith

"Respiratory failure, probable pneumonia."

Sandy called into the room, "Whatcha need in there?"

"Can you get some more Versed, maybe five milligrams, and twenty milligrams etomidate?" called out Dr. Holmes, the pulmonary critical care fellow. Sandy noticed that Dr. Camarie, the medical director of the ICU, was standing by the room as well, looking quite concerned. He was a tall man, with dark-gray-streaked hair. He was always impeccably dressed, favoring brilliantly white shirts and French cuffs with gold cuff links. Sandy could never understand how he could keep those cuffs clean. Whether he was rounding or teaching on the unit, he maintained a quiet professionalism that was unusual. He was always optimistic and was never rude or condescending to the staff. "Sure, let me get keys." Sandy grabbed the keys from Jan's pocket and ran into the med room to sign out the meds.

She drew them each up in a separate syringe and handed them into Jan. "Five milligrams Versed, twenty milligrams etomidate," she said as she passed each syringe into the room.

"Can't seem to sedate this one properly," Jan said as she took the syringes. "Thanks."

Sandy looked into the room and saw a young African American man, no more than twenty-five years old. She went over to Keith who was still putting in orders. *Wait, he is so young, he has pneumonia? He's getting intubated? What's going on?* she said to herself.

She peered over Keith's shoulder and saw the orders, the sepsis bundle protocol. This is a standard set of orders to collect specimens that would determine what was causing the infection, and empiric antibiotics to start until the culture and sensitivities were resulted.

She saw RSV, flu swab and COVID PCR. Keith looked up at her. Sandy stared back at him. Sandy once again investigated the room. The anesthesiologist and the pulmonary fellow were wearing gowns and N95 masks, plus the anesthesiologist was wearing a face shield.

Denise, the respiratory therapist, Pete, and Jan were wearing regular surgical masks.

Sandy looked at Keith who had an N95 mask around his neck. "What's wrong with this picture?" She stared at him, eyes burning, tearing up. What was worrying her was that half the team in the room with a patient with a presumed life-threatening infection were wearing insufficient PPE.

"I don't know, I am just doing the scut work around here."

Sandy knew this was not the right time to start in with Keith. He looked stressed out enough.

She turned to walk away toward the other side of the unit.

"Hey, Sandy, come back for a minute." She walked back. From underneath the desk, Keith pulled out another N95 mask and handed it to her. "Don't say where you got this." She nodded, put the mask in her scrub jacket pocket, and walked back.

Sandy's mind was reeling from what she just witnessed. *I think I need to take a break today*, she thought.

When she got back to the other side of the unit, Maureen was the first to approach her.

"What happened over there, you look like you're about to crash!"

"Twenty-five-year-old, just a baby, being intubated for respiratory failure. Maybe pneumonia."

"Twenty-five-year-old with pneumonia? On a vent?" Nero repeated. "WTF? I want to go have a look."

"Have at it," said Maureen. "When you've seen one intubation, you've seen them all."

"But this guy was different!" Sandy said. "He's only twenty-five. It took twice the dose of etomidate and Versed to sedate him."

Maureen shrugged. "It is what it is. I have to get back to my patients. But I'll tell you all something, don't ever let anyone do that shit to me. I've been a DNR ever since I became a nurse."

Sandy thought, *She doesn't really mean that. Or does she?* She shrugged.

Sandy waited until Nero got back. "Wow," he said, "they still can't get that kid to calm down. They had to put him on fentanyl."

"Nero, can you watch for me, I need to take a break."

"Sure."

Sandy told him a bit about each of her two patients and that she had an empty.

"I won't be long, just need to clear my head."

Sandy walked down to the first floor. There was a lounge with a few comfortable chairs and vending machines. It was a visitor lounge, but many of the staff came in there because it was usually quiet and calm, and there was a place to put your feet up for a few minutes.

As she was walking down the corridor to the lounge, she saw Dan, the PA from the first floor.

They had known each other from when Sandy worked on the med surg unit.

"Hey, Dan, I haven't seen you in forever!" She noticed Dan was wearing a blue plastic isolation gown, a mask, and gloves. Sandy thought that was strange.

"What are you doing down here?" Dan said. "I thought you are upstairs on 2 now."

"I am upstairs, I just needed a moment, and I was going into the lounge over there." Sandy pointed ahead.

"Well, you shouldn't be down here. You have a break room on 2, don't you?"

"What are you—the hall police now? And why are you in PPE in the hallway?"

She walked past Dan and into the lounge where she sat and stared at the vending machine for a moment, wondering if she should get a snack. *What the fuck was that all about? Dan and I were friends. Why is he acting so weird now? and why on earth was he in isolation garb in the hallway?*

Sandy's mind wandered again. *First, Mrs. Cantor, then that new young man, intubated, desaturating, ordering COVID PCRs, Keith giving me an N95, is this all related? Does Dan know something?*

Sandy's mind was going a mile a minute. *What if? Why is no one saying anything? They just had the section meeting a few days ago. Wouldn't they discuss any infection control issues if there were any?* Sandy's heart was pounding. She knew in her heart that COVID was here in this hospital. *But Keith had said the test was a send-out, no results for five to six days. What do we do in the meantime while we wait? What do we treat them with? What would come next?*

Sandy thought about the things she'd seen in the news about how hard it was to treat the infected patients in Wuhan, China. She heard that doctors and nurses were catching the disease. She thought maybe one of them had actually died. She started to feel afraid, and then chided herself. *No matter what, you became a nurse to help, and that's what you were meant to do. Get over yourself.* She went back and forth between fear and acceptance a few times. Finally, she got up and went back to work. She didn't recognize that act as courage, only one of many she would display in the coming days.

Chapter 6

The Emergency Room
February 2020

Michael arrived at work at his usual time of 0650. He punched in at the usual time of 0653. He had wondered about his patient from last week, Maria Rosado. Jenna had not been on the night before. He was taking report from one of the newer nurses in the emergency room, Greg. "There was a patient over in number 10, Maria Rosado, do you happen to know what happened to her?"

"Uh, sorry, no."

"Oh, that's okay, I'm guessing she went to step-down or maybe even went home. I'll look at the census later. Thanks anyway."

Over the loudspeaker came the usual "Safety huddle, main desk, safety huddle, main desk." Everyone congregated around the main desk to hear Helen and her list.

"So, guys, try not to call the help desk for the next few days. I was told they are working on a project. If you have IT trouble, see the charge nurse."

"What the fuck?" Mike whispered to Greg. "What's that all about?"

"I don't know, they are always updating that IT shit. Probably nothing."

"Yeah, you're right."

Helen droned on, "So remember, it's flu season now. If you are showing symptoms of the flu, please stay home. We have been getting a number of patients testing positive for the flu. Please remember our transmission-based precautions." She looked around at the staff. "If you are in triage and a patient comes in with flu-like symptoms, please make sure you give them a mask." She paused to look at her list.

"Okay, guys, those tubings, I can't keep telling you they need to be labeled. I'm gonna have to start writing people up for that if it keeps up. Thirty-four in the last week." She sighed.

"Okay, one final thing, the masks, gowns, and gloves will now be stored in the locked supply room. Please take only what you need and use them sparingly. They are expensive, and we have been over budget in the supply area lately." She folded her list.

"Okay, thanks, have a nice day." Helen walked off before anyone could say anything.

Michael remembered watching the news last week with Pamela; he went after Helen to ask her a question, but she was in her office already.

I'll ask her later. I'd better get Greg out of here.

He was not comfortable with the safety huddle this morning. He sensed there was more going on than was being told.

Michael was assigned to triage. Greg went over the patients that were waiting for various things, lab tests, x-rays, consults. The emergency room was crowded today, and the waiting room was full.

Michael hated triage. He preferred the action of the main or critical care or trauma. He hated all the little nonsense that people came into the ER for, especially things that could have waited for a physician's office to handle.

Why, if you have been having pain in your side for three weeks, do you decide to come to the ER now? he thought as he smiled at the first patient.

"So did you have a fall or bang into something?" he asked the twenty-five-year-old woman that came in complaining of pain in her right side.

"Uh, no, not that I remember."

"So any drug or alcohol use?"

"Well, maybe on the weekends. I go out with my friends, and we party."

Okay, priority IV, he thought.

"Have a seat, and someone will be with you shortly."

On February 14, James Denninger was just finishing his sales pitch about the new pharmaceutical cream chorobenthol. Of course, in his business, they did not call it a sales pitch. They called it detailing and made it seem as though they were only offering academic evidence that the drug was better than its closest competitor, metholintol. He was in the office of a dermatologist located in the Faculty Practice suites of one of the biggest hospitals in New York City.

He knew all about the practice. How many doctors, how many PAs, how many technicians, how much support staff, what the doctors mostly prescribed. He knew all the staff by name and what kind of treats they liked. He never arrived empty-handed and was therefore always welcome in the office. It didn't hurt that he was in his late twenties and above average in looks, with deep blue eyes and dark hair. He was charming and well-mannered, and he was at the top of his game.

What he didn't know was that while waiting for Dr. Singh in the reception room, he'd been exposed to the illness that he would carry to all his sales calls that day, carry home to his boyfriend in the condo they shared, and carry to his mother who was undergoing chemotherapy for breast cancer.

James went home for the evening after a long day. His boyfriend, Will, was home cooking dinner.

"Long day?" Will asked, seeing James's face.

"Always."

"Well, have I got a treat for you! I picked up steaks today and am going to broil them along with fresh corn, baked potato, and your favorite dessert—blueberries and fresh cream."

James smiled. "What did I do to deserve this treatment?"

"Nothing, you are just you, that's all." Will gave James a kiss on the cheek. "Go wash up. I'll pour us a glass of wine, and dinner will be ready in about ten minutes."

James went into the bathroom and looked in the mirror. He turned sideways. *Have more work to do on those triceps*, he thought. He looked down at his fingers and realized they were white with a bluish tinge. He rubbed his hands together vigorously. *Must be the cold*, he thought. He went into dinner. The table was beautifully set, as usual. Will was as fastidious about how things looked as he was about how food tasted.

"Okay, let's dig in." James took a sip of wine and immediately felt nauseated.

He took a sip of water. He did not want to let Will know since he had taken the time to prepare this wonderful dinner.

James cut his steak and found his appetite had vanished, and he still felt slightly queasy.

"What's wrong, love?" Will noticed everything.

"I don't know, must have picked something up in one of the doctor's offices I visited today. You know, flu going around and all."

"You don't have to eat. I can just put this all away and heat it up later." He bustled around and took the dishes away. "Maybe you should go lie down."

"I think I'd better—I'm really sorry."

James went into the bedroom, washed his face, brushed his teeth, put on a fresh pair of boxers and a T-shirt, and got into bed.

When Will came to bed later that night, he found James shivering underneath the covers. He felt his head. It was ridiculously hot.

"James, what's going on? Are you okay?"

"I think I need to go to the hospital—I feel awful."

They arrived at the triage desk where Michael was working. Michael had stayed an extra four hours since the ER was unusually busy.

"Hi, my name is Michael. What brings you to the ER tonight?"

Will said, "This is my boyfriend, James. He was nauseous earlier tonight, and then he was shivering and felt like he had a fever."

"Any cough or sore throat?" Michael asked.

"Maybe a little," James said.

Michael put on a pair of gloves to take vital signs. He noted the blood pressure was normal, temperature 101, pulse a little elevated, but that would be normal with the fever. The big outlier was the oxygen saturation at 81 percent. His respiratory rate was high too, 24 times per minute.

Michael swallowed hard. He switched fingers and told James to take two deep slow breaths; the saturation still read 82 percent.

Michael tried to hide the worry on his face. Out loud, he said, "I think we will get you back to a bed in the main unit."

"What's wrong with him?" said Will, sounding worried.

"That's what you're here to find out," Michael replied, again trying to hide his increasing concern. He stepped away and called the charge nurse.

He brought Will and James back to room 10, an isolation room.

Michael handed off report to the nurse in the main ER, Natalie, and went back to triage for his last few minutes.

On the drive home, Michael switched on the news station.

The radio news anchor said, "The number of deaths from the novel coronavirus has risen to more than 2,600 across the world. Europe's biggest outbreak is in Italy, where seven people have died, and restrictions have been imposed on some municipalities. South Korea announced 231 new cases today with the nationwide total surging past 830. More than half of those are associated with a branch of a religious group. US stock markets plunged this morning on mounting worries about the spread of the coronavirus outside China to major economies including South Korea and Italy."

It's not that bad, Michael thought. *It's not really all over the US.* But still, Michael could not get that feeling out of his gut.

When Michael got home, he decided to undress in the garage. He got out a large black garbage bag and put his scrubs, socks, shoes, even underwear and undershirt in it.

His family was all asleep, so he jumped into the downstairs shower and then put the towel he used into the garbage bag as well. He threw the whole thing in the washer and set it for hot, and poured in laundry detergent and, for good measure, some ammonia. Only then did he feel safe enough to relax. He went into the den and turned on the CNN late-night business news.

He poured himself a small amount of scotch and sat on the sofa.

The news was kind of benign. "With the summer wedding season around the corner, the coronavirus outbreak could leave brides-to-be in panic. Some may be unable to get the wedding gown they want for their big day. China is a leading supplier of wedding gowns. As much as 80 percent of the world's gowns are produced there, according to the American Bridal Prom Industry Association. Many factories in China have remained closed this year as the country attempts to curb the spread of the coronavirus."

Wow, Michael thought, *commerce being affected? But bridal gowns? Who is thinking about that now?*

"Never interested in government details, the president now wants to purge officials of dubious loyalty. Wall Street is reminding Americans a weakened executive branch carries risks. The two-day plunge in financial markets reflects growing alarm over the threat coronavirus poses to the economy. Containing that threat depends in large part on the skillfulness of the administration's response in concert with governments abroad. That response has not inspired much confidence this week, even as the number of known coronavirus cases in the US remains small."[9]

Michael turned off the TV. He sat there for a few moments, finishing his drink.

What's going on? he thought. *Bridal gown shortage, markets down? How is this all fitting in?* He looked up at all the family pictures on the wall over the fireplace. His wedding picture, him and the boys hiking, his youngest son's Little League picture. He straightened all the frames on the wall.

At least I don't have to think about it for the next two days. Michael went upstairs to bed.

He tried to drift off, but the only thoughts that would pop into his head were all the really horrible cases he had witnessed. The two young women who had been rear-ended in their small car, causing the car to flip and catch on fire. They both arrived in the ER with 90 percent second- and third-degree burns. One of them was a nurse. Before they could get her tubed, she cried out, "DNR! No intubation! Let me die!" The surgical staff wanted to press on, but she was adamant. Her hair was burned off, and raw red skin was all over her face and neck. Both her feet were charred. If she had survived, she would have been seriously deformed. The irony was she worked in the burn unit and knew exactly what was in store for her. She started

---

[9] CNN, February 2020.

begging for morphine. Michael could not get the keys to narcotics fast enough. But it was the other one who gave him nightmares. She was slightly older and had a one-year-old child. She said, "You have to save me, no matter what!" and the first thing they did after intubating her was take her to the OR to amputate both her legs in order to decrease the burned surface.

He remembered triaging an old man who came in by ambulance. Even the EMTs looked green while they gave report, and it was no time at all before the smell emerged. He had been found at home by a young neighbor who was helping him by fixing his meals. He would just ask her to leave the plate, but by the third day, it was clear he could not walk or move from the chair in which she first found him. He kept wrapped up in a blanket. She asked him to show her what was wrong with his leg, and when he removed the blanket, she could see his whole leg was necrotic and crawling with maggots. He had advanced arterial insufficiency, and his leg had died from lack of blood flow. The smell nearly overpowered her, but she stayed with him in the ambulance. Michael gave her full credit for empathy; he could barely stay in the room, and the man's leg was fully covered.

He drifted back and forth worrying about what would happen if the virus from Europe or China or wherever it started came to New York. He started thinking about the possibility he could bring it home and infect his beloved wife and children. The thought got him up and out of bed briefly; he went back to the den and looked at the scrapbook of their last camping trip. That calmed him down enough to get him to sleep.

Michael woke up the next day thinking about the last patient he had triaged. *I hope it was just the flu*, he thought. He struggled to push the thought of a young man with a sat in the 80s from his mind.

Pamela was off, too, so they busied themselves with the never-ending projects around the house. The boys were in school, so after their chores, they looked online at cabinets for the kitchen. They had been wanting to redo the kitchen for quite some time. Pam had always wanted a blue and white kitchen.

"Honey, with all the overtime I've been putting in, maybe in the next six months we can actually do it." He looked at his wife, no longer the young beauty he fell in love with, but more lovely to him than ever. He pulled her close and said the things into her ear that are for only between two people. Pam smiled and said, "The kids won't be back for hours—let's go back to bed for a bit."

Days off always fly by, Michael thought as he was getting his things ready for work in the morning. He had already packed his lunch, set out his scrubs, and put a special hamper with a garbage bag in the garage. *Just in case*, he thought. *In case of what, I don't know. But just in case.*

Michael felt uneasy driving to work the next day. Instead of turning on the news radio station, he listened to the jazz station.

Michael got in earlier than usual. It was too early to punch in, so he went to the desktop computer and pulled up the ICU census.

There they all were: Maria Rosado, Irene Hoffman, and James Denninger. He went up to the ICU to see what was going on. He went up to the night charge nurse who was getting ready to sign off for the day.

"Excuse me," he said, "but I took care of these three down in the ER when they first came in. I wanted to check up on them. I see they are all on airborne precautions. Do we know anything new?"

Jasmine, the night assistant head nurse, shook her head. "We really don't know, but they all have pneumonia, respiratory failure, and sepsis syndrome. Some weird ARDS." ARDS is an acronym for adult respiratory distress syndrome and described a group of signs and symptoms that are usually caused by a lung infection.

"Sorry—I didn't want to interrupt your report, was just wondering. Have a good day," he said to Jasmine and Roseanne. They continued with report and did not look up.

Michael walked by each of the rooms. He looked at Maria, on a vent, sedated, drips to maintain her blood pressure, a dialysis catheter on CRRT (continuous renal replacement therapy). This acts as an artificial kidney to clean the blood as the kidneys do.

Two doors down was Irene Hoffman, also on a ventilator, sedated, with multiple drips. He looked up at her monitor. *Low BP, low sats, high temp, looks like sepsis*, Michael thought.

He passed by James's room. There sat Will, looking so distraught. Michael knocked on the glass pane of the window. Will looked up and came out.

He threw his arms around Michael and sobbed. "I don't know what happened! He was just a little nauseous, then the temperature, and they tell us it's not the flu." He paused to wipe his eyes. "He has pneumonia! He couldn't breathe. They had to put him on the breathing machine." His words were rushed. He was exasperated. "What happened to him? Do you know? It isn't HIV—he had all the tests, and they were negative."

Michael looked in the room and saw James, again, on a ventilator, sedated, multiple drips. *The same as Maria and Irene, except James is about half their age*, he thought.

He patted Will. "I am sure they will get to the bottom of this. I see he is on all the right medicines," he said, trying to offer some hope. "I have to go back to the ER now, but I'll stop up again to check on you and James."

"Thank you for coming up, I appreciate it so much," said Will.

Michael walked away.

As he went down the hallway to leave the unit, he bumped into Kyle, who was up there doing the morning x-ray run. Michael was surprised as Kyle was the usual tech in the emergency room.

"Hey, Kyle, I see you have the unit today."

"Hey, how you doing?" returned Kyle with his usual smile on. "Yeah, sick call, we have to double up today."

"Doing well, you know, another day, another dollar. And yourself?"

"Same old, same old. Sure are a lot of stat portables up here today."

Michael paused a moment. "So who are you shooting now?" Kyle looked at his set of requisitions.

"Well, I have twelve to shoot here out of twenty patients."

"Do you mind if I see if the three I took care of in the ER are on your list?"

"Knock yourself out." There they were, Rosado, Hoffman, and Denninger.

Michael wondered if their chest films would be similar. He made a mental note to check on them later. "Thanks, Kyle. Looking forward to that Rangers game on Sunday?"

"You bet! Can't wait to see the boys too," he said, referring to Michael's two who were still at home.

As he continued down the hall, he saw Kyle placing a gown, N95, and gloves on to walk into Maria's room first.

Please be safe, Kyle, he thought.

Kyle walked in with his usual smile. He knew none of these sedated patients could hear him, but he lived by his self-imposed rules of decency, respect, and professionalism. "Hi, my name is Kyle from x-ray. I am going to put you on a plate and do a chest x-ray. May I have your name and date of birth," he asked, knowing there would be no answer. "Okay, Maria Rosado," he said out loud as he compared her ID band with the requisition.

Kyle gently slipped the plate under the sheet over the mattress, a trick he had learned early on so the patient would not have to be lifted up by the shoulders and possibly dislodge any tubes or IVs. "You might feel something hard under your back for a moment."

The x-ray took seconds. "Maria, I am going to just pull the plate out from under you." It was done before he could finish the sentence.

Kyle removed his PPE and went to the doorway of the next room. He opened the PPE cabinet on the wall to put on the next set. "Hmm, not much here." He grabbed an N95, gown, and gloves and was putting them on when one of the nurses, Jasmine, approached him. "You can't take all that PPE from here."

"What?" Kyle asked. No one had ever said that to him.

"Our stock is low."

"If I have to go into *your* isolation rooms and shoot films, I have to wear *your* PPE."

Jasmine sighed and walked away. "Whatever," she muttered under her breath. Kyle went into Irene's room, repeating the entire process. Next, he went into James's room where Will was sitting. "Excuse me, I'm Kyle from x-ray, and I have to do a chest film, so I will have to ask you to step out for a moment."

"Of course! Will you know the result right away?"

Kyle could tell he was nervous. "The result will be uploaded to the computer, and the doctor will be able to look at it and tell you the results."

"Okay, thank you. Please be gentle, I'm so worried."

"Of course," Kyle replied. He went into the room to see a man, younger than himself, on a ventilator, sedated, tubes and lines and drips. He took a deep breath through his N95. *I wonder what's wrong with this guy? He looks like he is in great shape.* As he slid the plate out from beneath the sheet, he said gently, "Be well, guy, I'll be thinking about you."

He removed his PPE and pushed the portable machine out. "You can go back in now." He saw the anguish in Will's eyes. "I'll be praying for James."

Kyle walked away with tears in his eyes. *This is new—this is such a young man. This could be me.* Kyle finished the rest of the run and went down to the break room after wiping down the portable machine with germicidal wipes.

He sat down for a moment and had a glass of water.

What is happening that people are coming in and getting so sick so quickly? And why are they yelling at me about taking PPE from the units? That's what we've always done.

Kyle sat there staring at his water, and his thoughts roamed back to 2014 when he was preparing for his third Ironman Triathlon. His mind carried him to the place where he felt solace and calm. Putting on his wet suit, jumping off his friend's dock into the canal, and swimming to the buoy that marked the mile distance. How good it felt to take those long bike rides while looking at the beach and smelling the salt water, how mesmerizing the road had become, looking forward to coming up on a hill and the challenge of charging the hill, then the run where mile after mile his thoughts could go just about anywhere, focusing on even, steady breathing while thinking of his grandpa watching TV, his grandma's tomato sauce, the pleasure his dad had while watching him finish the race. It had been six years now since his last race, and although he still trained hard on his days off, he had not registered for another race. *Maybe I should do another one, while there's still time.* Kyle snapped back to the present. It was time to go back to work.

Michael clocked in at 0653. He saw he was assigned to the critical care room for this shift. He walked into the room to find only one patient and three empty beds. He knew he would have to likely transfer that one patient up to critical care or downgrade them to step-down level. Greg, the night nurse, was waiting to give report.

"What's up?"

"How are you? How was your night?"

"Uh, good enough—I mean busy. Sorry, didn't have time to finish stocking all the cubicles. Got pretty crazy in here between 3:00 a.m. and 5:00 a.m."

"Well, you want to tell me about this woman here in bed 2 first?" Michael said.

He looked over at bed 2 and saw the youngish woman on a ventilator, hand mittens on for safety, propofol drip (to keep her sedated), Levophed drip (to keep her blood pressure up), IV fluids, central line, Foley catheter, the usual critical care items all in place. Michael looked up at her monitor and saw sinus tachycardia (a fast but essentially normal rhythm), oxygen sat 92 percent, blood pressure normal, and temp 100.8. Michael was already thinking, *Okay, sepsis—but she looks so young.*

Greg started report, "Sonia Mendoza, forty-one, came in about 4:30 a.m. complaining of three days of fever and a dry cough. Her sats were in the 80s, but the weird thing is she was talking on her cell phone like nothing was wrong. No real surgical history except a C-section ten years ago. Medical history, nothing to tell." He paused to look at his notes. "She comes in, and they send her in here, and I'm like, she looks great, what does she need critical care for? Then I hook her up to the monitor and see her sats—83, 84, 85. We put her on 50 percent venti, she improves, then tanks again, get her up to 80 percent, she's good for a while, then tanks again, then 100 percent NRB, so she's good but she keeps taking off the mask to call people. So I tell her, like, you have to keep this mask on, and she's okay for a while, still talking a mile a minute, then her husband comes in, and she takes off the mask to talk to him. I was charting, then I hear the alarm ringing, and I turn around to see the sat at 74." He paused for the effect to sink in. Michael looked properly expectant.

"I'm thinking what the fuck? 'Cause she's still talking. I run over there, switch the finger, still reading like 78, I put the NRB back on, but this time she doesn't come up. So I call out to main, and Dr. P comes in, looks at her x-ray, and decides to intubate."

"So she was awake the entire time?" Michael asked.

"Yeah. Dr. P talked to her and her husband and said it was probably a bad pneumonia, and we couldn't take the chance with her sats so low, so they agreed to intubation. But she was a wild one, took six milligrams Versed"—a strong tranquilizer—"and twenty milligrams etomidate to chill her. Then she tanked her BP, so Levophed, then of course, she needed the propofol since she kept waking up and fighting, so we had to put the mittens on. She has been quiet ever since, but I had to go up a few times on the Levo. We put a temperature probe Foley in, and you can see she is still febrile. They started on Zosyn and Vanco after she was pancultured"—this means blood, urine, and respiratory secretions were all sent to the lab to look for the germ causing the sepsis—"no results yet, other labs, normal. They ordered a chest CT this morning and ICU consult, but they have no beds right now." Greg took a breath.

"Did you do RSV and flu?"

"Yup, all negative. So just waiting on a bed in ICU."

"What are her vent settings?" Michael asked.

"AC 18, FIO2 80 percent, TV 400, PEEP 10." These settings were remarkably high and indicated an almost heroic amount of respiratory support.

"What? So she's on 80 percent FIO2 and PEEP of 10, and she's only satting low nineties?" Greg nodded confirmation.

"By the way, even though she didn't complain of a cough, when you suction her, it's gross. Thick brown, bad odor. That's why they are going to do the chest CT."

Michael looked over at the mess by cubicle number 4. "Wow, what happened over there?"

Greg shook his head slowly. "That was the 3:00 a.m. party. Eighty-four-year-old male comes in from a nursing home, probably aspirated." Often when older people get pneumonia, it is at least in part because they burped up a little and inhaled the stomach contents. The syndrome is called aspiration pneumonia, and it is difficult because there is a chemical component (the stomach acid) and the infectious component (the germs in the vomitus).

Greg continued. "Family rescinds his DNR"—stands for *do not resuscitate*—"so he gets intubated. X-ray looks like an atypical pneumonia. So we do a CT chest. Dr. P comes in to have a look at him after seeing the CT results. He says this is not aspiration, this is something else. So we do the whole workup, RSV, flu, paraflu, all negative, pan culture, start him on the usual antibiotic combo. At 3:45 a.m., he drops his heart rate to the thirties, we call a medical, do three rounds of drugs and CPR, pronounced by 4:05 a.m. Family in here wailing they are going to sue us, sue the nursing home. We actually had to call security to escort them out. They wouldn't leave the body."

"Are they gonna get a post?" Michael was referring to a postmortem, also called an autopsy. "Probably not. Old person comes in from a nursing home and dies, nothing suspicious about that."

"But you said that Dr. P thought this was an atypical pneumonia."

"Yeah, but he wasn't an ME case, so I guess we won't know."

"Have you been hearing the news about this coronavirus that's staring to crop up all over the place?" Michael asked.

"Yeah, but it's says it's been in China and South Korea and Italy," Greg replied.

"Well, it's in some states here too."

"Yeah, but I heard some nursing home in Seattle and maybe like Texas." He put his things together, clearly ready to get out. "Okay, gotta run, I'm back tonight."

"Have a good one," Michael replied reflexively. He started to think. *Seattle and Texas, if it's spreading there, we know it's in the US. Why can't it be here in New York?*

Michael went over to Sonia and began his assessment. He went to get a surgical mask to suction her, but there were none in her cubicle. He went to bed 1. *No masks? What the fuck?* he thought. Out loud, he called to main, "I need some masks in here." Samantha, the ER tech, walked in with a box.

"Use them sparingly, they are locked up."

"Locked up? Why?"

"Don't know, you'll have to ask Helen."

I think I'll do that when we have the safety huddle, Michael thought. He got up to straighten and stock the space in bed 4.

Michael got suction tubing and a new cannister for behind the bed. He looked in the cart and replaced the supplies for drawing blood and doing arterial sticks. He added the biohazard bags for sending specimens to the lab. Michael got out a temp probe Foley catheter, an irrigation set, emesis basins, and stocked the bedside cart. When Michael was done, he went back over to Sonia, who was quite sedated, and started a head-to-toe assessment. He had his computer on wheels with him so he could document as he went along. Michael was thankful that the technology in the emergency room allowed all the vital signs to populate right on the flow sheet in the computer. All he had to do was click, and he could trend everything.

He reviewed her sats over the last few hours. Only when her FIO2 (oxygen delivered by the ventilator) was raised did her sats come up to normal.

Why should a young woman with no prior medical history get this sick? he thought.

Michael thought about all the new reports he had watched on TV and listened to on the radio.

Am I the only one who thinks that coronavirus is here in New York? I can't be.

He trended a few other of the patients' labs.

This is fucked up. Administration is not saying anything. We are not prepared. He thought about asking Helen about the decision to lock up the PPE (personal protective equipment) without explanation.

He continued his assessment of Sonia, listened to her lungs, checked all her pulses, looked at her Foley catheter, measured the output, looked at her central line dressing, and checked placement of the NGT. He started her morning dose of vancomycin and lowered the dose of the Levophed. He sat down with his computer and began the rest of his charting, the sedation scale, Braden scale for skin injury, all the required documentation.

He knew there was a reason for this, all the "evidenced-based practice," a term that everyone threw around for the last few years. A lot of people think that the way medicine is practiced is the way they show it on TV. They think a patient comes in with a mysterious, inexplicable set of symptoms, and it takes a doctor like House to pull some arcane crap out of his head, and suddenly the patient can be cured. What really happens is that most illnesses are well studied; they have a fairly well-described set of signs (something that is observable, such as a lab test, an x-ray finding, or a rash) and symptoms (pain, fever, loss of appetite—something the patient is experiencing). The patient goes to his/her provider and gets examined. It is up to the clinician to connect the dots. If the dots do not add up, maybe the clinician does a little reading or discusses with a colleague. In any case, the clinician then makes a diagnosis. Most clinicians with good training and even halfway good experience can figure out what is wrong, and that's when evidence comes in. All around the world, there is medical research being done. The research tries to answer the question "How do I treat this person?" or "What's the best antibiotic to use for this diagnosis?" and other questions all clinicians need the answers for. Nurses also do research—about the best way to evaluate pain, how to help with nausea, how to prevent bed sores, to name just a few. This body of knowledge is the basis of evidence-based medicine, and it informs all the care done in the hospital.

He called over to radiology to set up the CT scan of Sonia's chest. The tech told him he was a bit behind, so they agreed on 9:30 a.m.

Michael heard the intercom, "Safety huddle main desk, safety huddle main desk."

He knew he could not attend as he was in the critical care room and there would be no one to relieve him to attend the meeting. He would just have to rely on his colleagues to update him later. Michael also wanted to talk to Helen. He called the bed coordinator to see if there would be a bed for Sonia anytime soon. "Maybe later" was the answer.

Michael got the call that another patient was being brought into critical care. *And so the day starts*, Michael thought.

In came two police officers, the paramedics, and EMTs with an elderly woman on the stretcher, CPR in progress. That means one medic was pumping the woman's chest to help her heart move the blood around, and the other was breathing for her through an endo-tracheal tube that had been inserted in the field, using a device called an Ambu bag. All the medics were wearing N95 masks. Michael had never seen medics in N95s before, and he had worked in the ER for over fifteen years. He started thinking about what they knew that he didn't know. The knot, ever present in his gut, tightened. Michael wondered, *How is it that the police are wearing* gloves and masks *now?* He tried to suppress his feeling of dread, and concentrate on the patient.

Michael kept an eye on the two officers just walking around the code room, hands on their belts, and one officer had a clipboard with paperwork he was filling out.

"Bed 1," Michael said. Two more nurses and an ER tech came into the room. They gathered around the stretcher. Respiratory therapy went to get the ventilator. Michael got on one side of the stretcher to get ready to transfer the patient onto the critical care stretcher. "Everything clear?" Michael said. He wanted to make sure there were no tubes or lines hanging down to get caught as they moved her from the stretcher to the ER bed. "Clear" was the response from all involved. "On my count, one, two, three," Michael said. The team moved the patient expertly over to the critical care stretcher, not missing a beat of CPR.

One of Michael's colleagues would have to stay in the room with him since there were now two critical patients and one in cardiac arrest with an active code in progress.

That nurse was a newer nurse to the ER, Kim. The room was now full of residents.

Dr. P was now in the room. "Stop compressions, feel for a pulse." He was leading the code. Kim got the twelve lead EKG electrodes on. The rhythm was flat line, but wavy enough to try to shock.

Michael was at the head of the bed feeling for a carotid with the other hand on the femoral pulse. Dr. P looked up at the monitor. "No pulse," called out Michael. "Charge to 300," ordered Dr. P. He picked up the paddles. "Get ready to clear. Clear!" He looked to make sure everyone was off the bed and no one was touching the patient or the bed. "All clear," he said and defibrillated the patient. Her body arched slightly. He looked over at the EKG machine and saw the line was flat.

"Continue compressions. Do we have access?"

"Yes, IO in left tibia," called out a resident. An IO is a line that goes directly into a bone. Even though most people think of bones as solid, they have a hollow core, and it has a direct link to the blood vessels.

"Amp of EPI and continue compressions," called out Dr. P. "Do we know what happened here?"

"Family called EMS. She was down when we got there."

"Prior medical problems?"

"Don't know the history," called out a medic.

"Is family here? Can we ask someone?" Dr. P was becoming frustrated. "Do we have any idea of her DNR status?" He was agitated, slapping his pen against the bed rail. "Do we have anything on this patient?" The pen slapping got faster.

"No."

"Okay, hold compressions—check for a pulse please. How long so far?" Dr. P asked the scribe nurse. He looked at the EKG, still flat line.

"Kim, can you please go check on the other patient in bed 2?" Michael called out at the same time.

"Here eighteen minutes, don't know about the field," read off the scribe.

"Gentlemen?" he asked, referring to the paramedics.

"Maybe twenty minutes."

"One more round—epi, then 1 amp of calcium. Continue compressions." Dr. P waited one minute after the drugs were pushed through the IO.

"Hold compressions, feel for a pulse." Michael looked up at Dr. P and shook his head. The EKG showed flat line.

"Anyone have any ideas?" said Dr. P. The room was silent.

"Okay, time of death—10:56 a.m. Please, can someone try to reach the family for me?"

Michael went over to check on Sonia. During the code, extraordinarily little attention was paid to her status.

Two ER techs began the arduous process of cleaning up the deceased and wrapping the body for the morgue. They weren't sure if this case would be reviewed by the medical examiner, and so they left the lines and tubes in. They left part of the shroud open and covered her with a clean blanket. She was ready for the family to say goodbye.

Michael performed another assessment on Sonia, and Kim was still in the room. "Kim, can you help me turn her, I want to look at her skin."

"Sure," she replied.

Kim went over to one side of the stretcher, placed her arms over the patient, grabbed the loose sheet, and pulled Sonia onto her side. Michael took that opportunity to listen to her lungs posteriorly and check her skin for any bruising, rashes, or breakdown. He noticed a little redness on her buttocks and sacral area. "Hold her while I get some barrier cream," he told Kim. "The last thing she needs is a pressure injury even before she gets up to the ICU." He gently rubbed her back and buttock area with barrier cream and placed a pillow underneath her back to support her on her side. He hoped ICU would take her to put her into a proper bed soon. The ER stretchers were awfully hard and thin. Just the act of turning her made her O2 saturation drop briefly. Michael was alarmed that her status was so fragile.

The rest of the shift was less eventful. Michael and Kim got some more critical patients. A neuro RRT stroke, a STEMI (a person having a heart attack that was visible on the EKG) where he had to activate the cath lab team, a drug overdose. All these types of patients had their own protocols, which Michael was entirely familiar with. He knew whom to call, when to call, what supplies he needed at hand. He moved effortlessly throughout the rest of the shift, but always keeping an eye on Sonia.

Sonia continued to require a high concentration of oxygen via the ventilator. Whenever the respiratory therapist thought she was in a stable place and turned down the FIO2 on the ventilator, it resulted in a profound decrease in her oxygen saturation. She also required a fair amount of sedation to keep her calm, keep her from fighting with the ventilator. In addition to the propofol, which was running at the maximum rate allowable, Michael had to ask Dr. P for an order for a Versed drip, as Sonia kept overbreathing the ventilator.

That's strange, Michael thought. *She's not a large woman, she shouldn't require that much sedation.*

Dr. P came back into the critical care room. "How's she doing?"

"Keeps needing more sedation to keep her synchronous. I find that strange. She's not a big girl."

"Her CT looks awful, like atypical bilateral viral pneumonia," Dr. P said with concern. "Looks like she has some pleural effusions as well." This means that fluid was collecting in a pool between the two membranes that encase the lungs. Michael pulled up the CT on his computer where Dr. P pointed out the abnormalities.

"You see here"—Dr. P pointed—"all this patchy white stuff, those are ground glass opacities, and over here"—he pointed again— "there is vascular dilatation. This is surprisingly advanced disease in such a young woman."

Michael just nodded. "Should she be on some kind of isolation? If we are thinking viral, then this could be like the flu, and we do isolate people with the flu."

"She probably should," said Dr. P, "but she is vented, so there are no secretions being vented into the air. But there were when we intubated her…" His voice trailed off as he exited the room.

Michael called the bed coordinator, "We have to get this patient upstairs into the ICU, and she is going to need isolation."

"Okay—working on it" was the reply.

It was Friday. Kyle was in the control room for the safety huddle. Robert looked down at his notes. "First, we have had some mix-ups with images being sent with the wrong patient ID." Everyone looked at one another. "This can't happen." He emphasized. "Everyone must identify the patient properly with name and date of birth."

"Well, the ER tries to send people over before they get past triage, so some of them don't even have their name band on," someone contributed.

"Don't do the study" was the answer. "Please make sure the code carts are checked on each shift upstairs and downstairs. We have had a few missing signatures. Anything else?" Everyone was quiet. "Have a nice day." Robert walked away.

Kyle walked over to the computer where several requisitions had already printed out.

"A lot of chest pain" was in the "reason for x-ray" space on the requisition. Kyle shook his head. He took the portable machine and wheeled it over to the emergency room.

The emergency room was in its usual chaotic state. People calling out for help from the cubicles, health-care workers all around trying to talk to patients, the central station crowded with all the consultants, nurses, clerks. Alarms could be heard from the central monitoring station as well as from the cubicles themselves. Desk phones were constantly ringing, cell phones were buzzing or beeping, and IV drip controllers were adding their alarms to the mix.

Stretchers and wheelchairs impeded Kyle's path. Then Kyle saw something unusual. *What the hell?* he thought.

Dr. Young came out of a patient's cubicle and was in a full hazmat suit, complete with goggles, OR hat, and N95 mask.

That's strange, Kyle thought, *no one else is wearing anything like that.* "What's that about?" Kyle whispered to Michael.

"She's just nuts. She was talking about this virus in China, and suddenly she appeared today in full hazmat gear."

"The ER director told her to take it off. She is scaring the patients, but she refused."

"What a weirdo."

"I wonder if she knows something we don't," Kyle answered.

"I would hope we'd all know something if this was really an issue? Hoping it's just flu season." Kyle brought the portable machine into the patient's room. "Hi, my name is Kyle from x-ray, may I have your name and date of birth?"

"Jason Fields, September 22, 1955." Kyle checked the name band.

"I'm here to do your chest x-ray. I see it says on the requisition you are having pain in your chest?"

"I guess, but I have this cough, and I had a fever last night."

Shit, Kyle thought, *they always do this. They put in chest pain because it's the first selection on the menu.*

"Excuse me a minute, Mr. Fields." Kyle stepped out and went to the nurse in the next room.

"Hey, Michael, do you have this guy in 8, Mr. Fields?"

"No, sorry," said Michael, "that's Julie's patient."

Kyle went and found Julie at the nursing station charting.

"Hey, Julie, the req says chest pain, but he told me he has a cough and fever. Is he on isolation for the flu?"

"Well, there is no order for isolation. I'm kinda busy here, Kyle, look in his chart if you want."

"I don't have time to read everyone's chart," Kyle mumbled to himself. But he put on a surgical mask he obtained from the PPE cabinet outside the room and went back into the room.

"Sorry for the delay. I'm just going to put this plate behind you."

"Why are you wearing a mask?"

"Well, when you said you had a cough, we have to wear a mask to protect the other patients."

"You're the first one to do that."

"I'm sorry if I startled you. Can you take a deep breath and hold it? X-ray, bed 8," shouted Kyle. Kyle took the plate out. "Feel better, Mr. Fields."

Kyle washed his hands, took off his mask, and went back to the control room to upload the film.

His thoughts started to wander. *How is it that the emergency room staff are not aware that a patient has a cough, yet when I go in, I seem to be the first one to notice it? That means that people have been in and out of this room with no mask and then walking around the ER, taking care of other patients. No orders for isolation until* after *the chest film has been taken, then all of a sudden, the patient is now on isolation. That means if the patient has something contagious, the x-ray staff has been already exposed—that's totally fucked up.* Kyle thought about having this discussion with the other techs but was afraid he would be singled out for being hysterical.

Still, something was wrong with this process. Meanwhile, requisitions kept printing out from the emergency room, chest x-ray, reason, chest pain. Kyle went to the cabinet to get more masks.

The box was empty.

Chapter 7

The Orthopedic Floor
February 2020

Thursday arrived, and Fran was back at work. She looked at the assignment. *Only five patients. That means two empties*, she thought. Everyone hated the empties because admissions were such a lot of work. Fran went through her usual routine. She took report from the day nurse, signed into her computer, reviewed labs, vital signs, orders, and medications. Fran saw that there was a patient in room 239 that she had not noticed before. She was in a new district since she had been off for two days.

Danielle Rosen was a fifty-two-year-old woman that had a right knee replacement six days prior. *That's strange*, thought Fran, *usually patients are discharged by now. There must be more to the story.* The day nurse had not said anything unusual during report except that Danielle was nasty and rude to most of the staff.

Fran went in to talk to her. "Hi, Ms. Rosen. I'm Fran, and I will be here with you until seven tomorrow morning." Danielle said nothing. "Can I get you anything?"

"Yeah, ice, and a lot of it."

"Okay, my pleasure," Fran said, but was worried about how this would play out for the shift if they started off on the wrong foot.

Fran brought back the ice and asked, "May I take your vital signs?"

"What are you asking me for? Everyone just does it."

"Well, I always ask before I touch someone."

"Okay," said Danielle, "but can I have some ice first?"

"Sure." Fran gave her a cup filled with ice and a spoon.

"Oh, that feels good, you don't know. My mouth is so dry all the time."

"Really? Why do you think that is?" Fran inquired.

"I really don't know."

"If you don't mind me asking," Fran said slowly, "usually a young woman like yourself with a simple knee replacement surgery is home by now."

"I know, I was supposed to go to a short-term rehab, but there was a problem with my insurance, so they made me stay here. I live alone, so I don't have any help." She paused. "Also, I had pain in my chest yesterday, so the doctor wanted to do a few tests. Can you go see if there are any results?"

"Okay," Fran said, "I'll go check on that for you."

Fran went up to the nursing station. A few of the nurses were sitting around on the computers and phones.

"Does anyone know anything about Ms. Rosen in 39?"

"Oh, she's a pain in the ass," said one voice, not even looking up. Fran rolled her eyes.

"Well, she said she had chest pain yesterday and there is some kind of workup going on."

"No, that's what they said to make her stop having every doctor in the directory called." Fran pulled up her records. She found nothing about a workup.

Then she saw the progress note from the psychiatrist: "52-year-old female living alone admitted for right knee replacement. Reports history of anxiety, on no medications. Pt now 6 days post op and reports having chest pain. Vital signs WNL, EKG WNL, labs normal. Diagnosis: Situational anxiety, start Xanax .25 mg po every 6 hours as needed."

Fran felt relieved. She went about her assessments, medications, and charting on her four other patients.

At midnight, it was time to do another set of rounds. Four of her patients were sleeping.

Danielle was awake.

"Are you okay?" Fran asked.

"No, I am having that pain again. Isn't there anything you can do?"

"Let me take your vital signs."

Danielle stuck out her arm. Fran had the NIBP machine. Danielle's blood pressure was normal, her pulse was 100, and her sat was only 90 percent on room air. *Gee, that's odd,* Fran thought. A young woman with a sat of 90 percent was unusual.

"How's your breathing?" Fran inquired

"Well, I'm breathing," Danielle said shortly. "Not that great, but I'm breathing."

"What do you mean not that great?"

"It's nothing, so they tell me, but it just feels like I have a tight bra on."

Fran looked up on her computer to see when Danielle had her last Xanax.

"Do you think you are feeling anxious?"

"I don't know. That's what everyone keeps saying, that I'm anxious. So it must be true."

"Do you have any pain now?"

"Yes, I keep telling everyone, I have pain in my chest. Goddamn it, everyone should just stop bothering me and send me the hell out of here already. I'm sick of this shit. I tell them I can't breathe right, I tell them I feel pain in my chest. They tell me I'm anxious—whatever. Just get out now, please. And shut the door."

Fran felt defeated. She thought she had struck up a relationship with Danielle, but she was just as nasty to her as everyone else said she was to them.

But what if? *What if she really is having trouble breathing? What if she is having chest pain? Her sat was only 90, but that's not something I want to call someone about. They'll think I'm crazy.* Fran went out to the desk again.

"Seriously, guys, did anyone think that maybe this patient Danielle was telling the truth about her breathing and chest pain?"

One of the nurses laughed without even looking up from her phone.

"Yeah, right, she can't breathe, she has pain. Give her some Tylenol and Xanax, get her outta here."

"I am going on break," Fran announced. "Can someone just look in on her for me?"

"Sure, we all will" came a chorus from the nurses' station.

Fran sat in the break room having her tea. *We were always taught to believe patients when they tell us they are having pain. Pain is subjective.* She remembered her nursing professors stating emphatically, "Pain is what the patient says it is."

Maybe I'm making too much out of it. Fran sighed. *I hope I am.*

Fran came back from break a little earlier than normal. There was something in her gut. Again, she remembered one of her nursing professors saying, "Trust your gut, it always serves you right. Better to be wrong and do the right thing." Fran went into Danielle's room with the NIBP.

Danielle was moaning. "Hurts, hurts, hurts."

"What hurts?" Fran said frantically.

"Chest." Danielle could barely get the words out. She put the sat monitor on. Eighty-five.

Fran looked closely at Danielle. Her eyes were wide open and not focused. She started biting her tongue.

Fran screamed, "Call a code, someone call a code! Get the cart."

She heard the loudspeaker, "*Code blue* 2 South. Code *blue* 2 South." She felt for a pulse, nothing.

People were swarming the room, and Fran had begun compressions.

Someone called, "Get the intubation tray." Fran was pushed out of the way. She stood in the doorway watching the critical care team take over.

Much later, she heard, "Time of death, 4:42 a.m.," from the intensivist.

Fran looked at the same nurses that had been laughing at her in the nurses' station. They were not laughing now.

Fran managed to get through the rest of the night without incident.

She went home, called her mom on the way.

"Meet me in the hallway with a towel and a garbage bag. I'm not bringing my uniform and shoes in the apartment."

Fran was off for only one day. She was having her tea in the morning and was listening to her favorite Greek news station. She did not like what she heard.

> "How Greece Can Reopen Without Ruining Its Coronavirus Containment Success"
> Early February 2020
> Prime minister Kyriakos Mitsotakis announced restrictive measures with an entire lockdown of the country. 3500 medical professionals have been recruited and ICU beds have been doubled in capacity. Coordination with philanthropic organizations such as Stavros Niarchos Foundation and the Onassis Foundation have donated to ensure that local 3 D printing vendors are producing health care equipment. Easter church services will be canceled. (W. Antholis and F. Letsas, May 26, 2020)

Wait, what? Fran thought. *It's only February, and the prime minister is canceling Easter services?* She felt a sense of dread wash over her.

She grabbed her mom and the kids and went shopping at Costco. They bought paper products, all sizes of plastic bags, frozen items, meat, a few new toys for the kids, canned goods. She wandered into the auto supply and gardening areas. "What do we need here?" Patty asked. Fran's eyes were darting around. Suddenly she saw a few things and threw them in the cart. Gardening gloves, painting masks, two auto technician jumpsuits.

"What do we need with all these things?" Patty asked again.

"Mom, just don't ask, please."

Fran even managed to get a few scrub tops and pants.

"Doesn't the hospital supply you with scrubs?" her mom asked.

"Yes, but I want to have extra just in case."

"In case of what?"

"I don't know, Mom, just in case."

They got home and unpacked all their items.

Fran took all the gloves, masks, and the auto technician jumpsuits and placed them in the hall closet in a plastic box. She felt better.

They spent the rest of the day playing with the new toys the kids got. Both Robby and Lilly were happy. Fran could tell Robby's expressions now.

He had a certain grunt when he liked something, and blowing bubbles was just the thing. Fran watched as each bubble floated in the room with Robby reaching for it and Lilly running around after each one.

She watched as each bubble picked up the light from the room and as each one burst. Her mind wandered back to Danielle Rosen. *Is life that fragile?* she mused.

Fran had to work the next three shifts in a row. It was her weekend on, and she scheduled herself on Monday as well so she could have a stretch off during the week.

After the kids went to bed, she took the plastic bin with the gloves, masks, jumpsuits, and garbage bags and put them in her trunk.

Fran slept a little later than usual. The kids were still sleeping. She knew they were going to want pancakes for breakfast. Robby was attracted when Fran made different-shaped pancakes, so he ate better. She lay in bed and thought about her last shift on.

Is COVID-19 here? Why is no one saying anything? Does the hospital have a plan? Am I being paranoid? I know I am on the orthopedic unit, and it is a clean surgical floor, but...

Remembering her infection control from school, she was aware of how things spread. *What if some of these patients had traveled?*

Fran remembered all the news reports. There were only a few cases on the United States, and they were nowhere near here. California, Texas, Seattle, all extremely far away from New York. Fran spent another morning entertaining the kids, giving her mother a much-needed break. She had Robby and Lilly in the kitchen as they fashioned shapes out of the pancake mix. Robby liked to help, so Fran gave him a little of the dough to play with. Robby ate well this morning, but Fran knew what that meant, a large diaper to change later. Fran sighed. *Look at my life*, she thought. I have a brain-damaged child, another one that does not get much attention although God knows she needs it, and I live with my mom. What will happen to me? Fran turned her focus back to the kids.

What can we play that will keep them occupied for a while, that Robby will understand? she asked herself. *Nothing.* So she strapped Robby in the stroller and started a game of "you're it" with Lilly. Fran felt exhausted, but she managed to play for a full thirty minutes. Robby loved being pushed in the stroller even if it was just around the apartment. Lilly was delighted. She could go all day, Fran thought. Lilly loved her brother, and they developed a special type of communication with him. It was as if she could read his mind. *Thank God Lilly loves him*, Fran thought. *Maybe someday when I save money, I can buy a big house upstate where there will be enough space for everyone. I want a large property where they can play outside"* She secretly hoped that Lilly would always want to care for her brother, but knew that when the time came, it would be up to her daughter. Fran snapped back to the day ahead. *Why am I thinking about things that are light-years ahead of me?*

She would try to take a nap around 2:00 p.m. to be rested for the night. Fran had become used to little sleep. Patty kept the kids entertained with a few Disney movies so Fran could nap. Fran got up from her nap about four thirty. She knew she had to prepare dinner for the kids and her mom. She often felt guilty on how much she relied on her mom to take care of everything, especially Robby, who, although was growing physically, mentally was staying at the age of a ten-month-old. *Will he ever progress past this?* Fran thought. *How am I going to take care of him when he is a teen or an adult?* She thought about that often, but now it was time to focus on the three shifts ahead of her.

Fran arrived at her unit at 6:30 p.m. She had found a good parking spot this evening, right by the entrance to the hospital. *Luck must be on my side tonight*, she thought. *Maybe it means I'll have a good night.*

Once on 2 South, she looked at the assignment sheet. Six patients, one empty. *Okay, that's not so bad.* She began to take report on her patients from Laura, the day nurse.

Laura had a reputation of a quick-paced report. She wanted to leave as soon as Fran arrived and always looked to change her assignment to the nurse that arrived the earliest, and that was always Fran. Laura was impatiently tapping her fingers on her computer station as Fran arrived.

What the hell. It was only 6:40 p.m. Laura looked up at her. "Are you ready?" she said impatiently. Fran knew how to stand up for herself albeit politely.

"Uh, actually, no. It's only six forty, and I have to put my things away in my locker and get my stuff."

Laura muttered something under her breath as Fran walked into the locker room.

Fran came back ten minutes later, and even though she could have dragged it out another ten minutes to make Laura wait, she did not.

Fran sat down next to Laura. "How are you? How was the day?"

"Can we get on with it? I have to get out of here and pick up dinner on the way home." Fran decided not to say anything.

"Okay, 232, John Samuels, forty-five, status post-posterior cervical discectomy, medicated for pain at 1800, ambulating without assistance," Laura droned on. Fran was jotting notes on her report sheet.

Most of the report was routine, hip replacements, hip fracture, knee replacements, until they got to 237. "Edna Cobb, eighty-one, came from Brooklyn South Nursing home after a fall with hip fracture. ORIF"—which stands for open reduction and internal fixation, a routine way to fix a broken hip so the patient can get out of bed much sooner—"done by Dr. Gregorio. This is day number 6 post-op."

"How come she is not in rehab?" Fran asked.

"Well, she started spiking a temp yesterday, and they called in ID to do a workup."

"Do we think it's pneumonia or site infection?" Fran asked.

"I don't know what we think," replied Laura sarcastically, "but I think I want to get the hell out of here, so let me finish." Fran held her tongue.

"So her last temp was only 100.4," Laura droned on. "I gave her Tylenol earlier when she was 101.6, so it came down a bit. She has some pain but does not want anything stronger. The Tylenol seems to be holding the fever and the pain. Vitals are stable. She has been out of bed working with PT every day except for yesterday when she started spiking. She refused PT yesterday, saying she was just too tired. Maybe you can get her to get up tonight." Laura started to put her things together to leave. Almost as an afterthought, she said, "Oh, and she's on isolation."

"For what?"

"I really don't know. We just put her on isolation since the fever and cough."

"Oh, you didn't mention she had a cough."

"Uh, sorry, she does."

"So droplet precautions or airborne precautions?" Fran said, remembering her transmission-based precautions. Laura looked at her quizzically. "Are we wearing surgical masks or N95s?" Fran asked.

"Oh, surgical, there is half a box outside her door," Laura said as she got up. "Have a nice night," she said as she walked off.

Fran sat for a moment, absorbing the rushed report she just received. *We don't put many people on isolation here*, she thought.

Fran pulled up her assignment on the computer to start going through her labs. She went right away to Mrs. Cobb. Edna Cobb was a slight African American woman, probably no more than a hundred pounds. She looked cachectic, which means she had extraordinarily little facial fat, giving her a skeletal look. She was surprisingly well-kept for having come in from a nursing home, with her nails painted pink, her hair neatly braided, and wearing her own pink nightgown that was several sizes too big. She also looked fatigued as though she'd been working hard. When Fran started to assess her, she noted that Mrs. Cobb was breathing at twenty-eight times per minute. Fran knew that was a lot of work, especially for a frail, elderly woman who had just had surgery.

The room had multiple pictures of smiling faces of children and probably grandchildren. There was a large vase of flowers on the windowsill. It was clear her family was incredibly involved, and this person was loved and cared for.

Edna Cobb was a lifelong Brooklyn resident. She was born at King's County Hospital and grew up in Brownsville, living through the deterioration of that neighborhood. Because her mother was strict, Edna finished high school with good grades. As a Black woman, her opportunities were limited. Through her church connections, she was able to get work in hospital housekeeping when she was nineteen years old; 1199 was a strong union at her hospital, so she was able to be employed her whole life with benefits many of her neighbors didn't have. She was focused and hardworking and was promoted up through the ranks. She was a housekeeping supervisor by the time she retired. That work enabled her to move out of Brownsville and into a house she and her husband bought in Williamsburg in the early 1960s. She and her husband raised their three children there; they took care of her mother at that house and then her husband's father. It was the center of her family's life. Edna did not forget her neighbors in Brownsville, returning often to visit friends and attending the same church on Liberty Avenue that her mother had. She volunteered at the church outreach kitchen and was well-known for bringing a hot meal to her friends who were in worse circumstances, taking one or more of her children with her. She modeled the behavior she wanted to see in her own children, and she was successful. She credited God with her good luck, as she called it.

Edna was sleeping. Mrs. Cobb was wearing a 40 percent aerosol mask, a detail Laura had omitted.

Fran shook her head. She saw Lisa down the hall coming toward her. Lisa had been there since 3:00 p.m. "Hey, Lisa, how has this patient been doing since you got on?" Fran asked as she put on a surgical mask and went into the room.

Lisa came over to the door of 237. "I really don't know. I have been on with her most days this week, and she seems to be sicker."

"What do you mean?"

"Well, she's not eating. Also, she started off excited about her PT sessions, and now she just seems to be not interested in getting better anymore. Her family was here earlier and even brought her grandchildren to perk her up, but she told them all to go home, that she wasn't feeling well."

Fran digested all this information from Lisa. *I get more information from the nurse's aides than the nurses*, she thought. "Hey, Lisa, when you get a chance, can you get another box of masks for here, I'm sure we will run out soon."

"Sorry, no can do. Masks are now locked up."

"What? Seriously? Why?"

"I don't know, above my pay grade. But so are gowns and the N95 masks."

"And nobody knows why?"

"Well, not me," Lisa said. "I gotta go finish vitals, so call me if you need me."

"Okay, I will, thanks."

Fran looked at her computer as she stood in Edna's room. Her other five patients did not need any routine medications except for the 10:00 p.m. finger sticks. Lisa came back to tell Fran one of her patients needed pain medication.

"Mr. Ferguson in 234 says his knee is really hurting."

"Okay, I'll take care of it." Fran washed her hands and removed her mask. She walked with her computer to the room. "Hi, Mr. Ferguson, can you rate your pain on a scale of one to ten?"

"Oh, honey, it's an eleven tonight."

"I am so sorry to hear that."

"Let me look at that knee, and I'll get your medicine right away." The suture line looked benign, no redness or swelling. Fran looked at the MAR and saw oxycodone 5 milligrams for mild pain and 10 milligrams for severe pain. Since Mr. Ferguson was a large man, Fran opted for the 10 milligrams. She scanned into the medication drawer, took out two pills, and gave them to the patient. "Thanks, honey, now maybe I'll get some rest."

"Of course," said Fran. "Here is your call bell. You call me if you need anything. Remember to ring if you need to use the bathroom—no walking by yourself!"

"Okay, thanks, honey."

Fran did not mind being called honey by some of her patients. Some of her colleagues did. *If it makes them happy and they are not cursing at me, I'll take honey any day*, she thought.

Fran continued to push her computer / medication cart to each room. She went inside to check on each patient. She had the clipboard with each patient's vital signs on it, but she made sure to count their respirations, look at their color, check the IV site, and put the call bell close to each one.

Fran went back to Edna's room. She put on a surgical mask and went inside.

She stood at the foot of the bed for a few moments, watching Edna breathe. *Hmm, slightly labored, a bit fast, but not distressed.* Fran did not want to wake her but tried to evaluate her color. It's a bit difficult, but she managed to look at Edna's nail beds with her Maglite. She noted a slight bluish tinge. She thought, *Am I imagining this?* She felt Edna's hands, cool to touch. Fran again went back to her nursing school days. *Cool extremities, slight bluish tinge equals hypoxia*, she thought. *Let me get the sat monitor.*

Fran walked the length of the hallway, and the NIBP machine was nowhere to be found.

She found Lisa. "Lisa, could you please find the NIBP machine and bring it to 237?"

"Okay, I'll see if I can find it. That thing is always disappearing."

"Thanks."

Fran brought her computer over to Mrs. Cobb's door and started to chart while she was waiting for the NIPB machine. She had become expert at all the scales and required documentation and flew through that part of the charting. She decided to review Mrs. Cobb's history. "81-year-old female s/p fall in nursing home. Hx CVA left side with right sided weakness. Cachectic appearing, alert and oriented. VSS, will get routine labs and type and screen. Prep for OR with DR. Gregorio. Pt. understands and agrees with need for surgery at this time. Consent signed."

Well, that wasn't particularly helpful, Fran sighed. *If you want to find out information about the patient, you have to ask them or talk to the nurses' aides.*

Lisa came back with the NIBP machine. "Whew, you have no idea where this thing was," said Lisa, out of breath.

"Where?"

"Two North had it hidden in their utility room."

"Why would they have it?"

"Because one of their aides thinks she deserves her own, so she sneaks over here to steal ours and hides it there."

"Why would she think she deserves her own NIPB machine?"

"Well, between you and me and the wall, it's Yang, and she keep babbling about some virus in China and she thinks it's here, so she wants her own NIPB so she doesn't have to share. Isn't that ridiculous?" Lisa said, grinning.

"Yes, we don't have enough to go around. There are only two per floor," Fran replied, but she knew whoever Yang was, she was probably right.

Fran put on a surgical mask after washing her hands and went into the room. Edna seemed to be sleeping soundly. "Edna, it's Fran the nurse. I just want to take your vital signs."

Edna opened her eyes briefly and said, "Okay..."

Fran could tell she was weak with her barely audible voice. She took her vital signs. *Hmm, BP normal, HR 100, not bad, sat 89 on 40 percent aerosol mask, not good.* Out loud, she said, "Edna, I want to take your temperature." Edna did not respond. She scanned her forehead, 101.0.

"Edna, I need you to wake up and talk to me."

"Okay...but I'm so tired."

"I know and I'm sorry, but I just want to ask you a few questions. How is your breathing?"

"It's fine, I think." Fran could see that her respirations were twenty-six, a little elevated but not too bad.

"How's your pain?"

"What pain?"

"In your hip."

"Oh, I don't have any pain there now."

"Well, do you have pain anywhere else?"

"My chest feels tight."

"Can you describe it?"

"Like when my granddaughter hugs me too tight. But I like it when little Edna hugs me that tight, so I just am imagining it's her."

Fran knew she had to call the PA on call. She went up to the board and saw it was Annie.

Oh, great, get ready for another fight, she thought.

Fran picked up her phone. "Annie," she heard on the other end.

"Hey, Annie, it's Fran. Mrs. Cobb in 237, heart rate is 100, sat is 89 percent on 40 percent aerosol mask, normal BP, has a temp, 101. She is also complaining of chest tightness."

"What's a normal BP for you?" Annie asked in a snarky voice. She always sounded annoyed.

"It's 124/74." Fran was tempted to say, "Is that normal enough for you?" but she held her tongue.

"What about the hip. That's why she was here, you know," she asked with a sound of annoyance.

"I know why she is here, but obviously something else is going on. Her hip is fine, non-painful, site looks good, no dressing. She is almost seven days post-op." That was a strangely long hospitalization for a hip replacement.

"Whose case is she?"

"Dr. Gregorio."

"Did you call him?"

"No, I called you." Fran had about enough of Annie's obnoxious tone. "Look, I'm calling you because you're on call for this service. I don't want a repeat of the last time, so why don't you just come up and evaluate the patient." Fran hung up.

Jeez, she muttered to herself, *the PAs are worse than the attendings. If I called Dr. Gregorio, he would ask me if I called the PA. I guess you can't win either way.*

Fran went over to the nurses' station to see if there was anyone she could vent to. Three out of the six nurses on shift were there on their phones.

"Anyone have any problems with Annie? She is so obnoxious, doesn't want to come up to see the patients. Doesn't want to call the attendings. What's up with that?"

Laura looked up. "She's always that way, wants to get out of doing her job, always in the on-call room probably ordering out and watching Netflix again."

"So what do we do about it?"

"Keep bugging her."

Fran thought, *I have to tell the mid-levels to do their jobs? And take their lip? They don't pay me enough for that.*

Fran went back to 237 to check again on Mrs. Cobb. She took all her vitals again. No change.

Her sat was up to 90 percent on her 40 percent aerosol mask. That was still quite low.

Fran looked at Edna's medication record and saw that she was due for Tylenol. She scanned the medication, put on a gown, mask, and gloves, and brought it into the room.

"Mrs. Cobb, I want you to take some Tylenol for the fever. It will help with the pain in your chest too."

"Okay." Her voice was weak and tenuous.

"Here, let me help you sit up."

Fran slid down the mask just enough for Edna to take the Tylenol and have a sip of water.

"Thank you."

Fran removed her PPE and stayed outside the room to chart as she waited for Annie.

She did her nursing note and began to chart on some of her other patients while she waited. Lisa came down the hall and asked Fran to help her get another patient to the commode. "I am usually good by myself, but this guy is just too big for me alone."

"Of course," Fran said.

They went into 235 where Mr. Martone was waiting. "Jeez, what took you gals so long, I really have to go."

137

"We are right here," Lisa said gently. "Let's get you up." She had the stand-and-lift device all ready.

Fran and Lisa stood on either side of Mr. Martone and assisted him to the commode.

"I might be a while—can you close the curtain?"

"Okay," Lisa said, "here's your call bell. Please do not get up by yourself."

As Fran exited the room, she saw Annie by 237, Mrs. Cobb's room. "I was looking for you."

"Well, here I am, I do have other patients to take care of."

"Oh yeah, right."

"So what's happening again here?" Annie looked like she had just woken up. Her hair was in a messy ponytail, her scrubs were wrinkled, and she had a stain on her scrub top. Fran held her tongue.

"Well, as I informed you over the phone, Mrs. Cobb is on 40 percent aerosol mask, but her sat hovers around 88 to 90 percent." She is a bit tachy, her temp is 101, I just gave her Tylenol. Her hip looks fine, but she is complaining of chest tightness."

Annie stared off into space. Fran was not sure she was even thinking about anything. Her look was vacant.

"Would you like to start with a chest x-ray and an EKG perhaps? Why don't you go put those orders in?" She was a little resentful that she had to tell the experienced PA what to do, especially because she was a new nurse.

Annie went to the desk to use a computer. Fran went to get Lisa to do the EKG. She saw the orders pop up on her screen and called down to x-ray and told them. Within ten minutes, a tech came up, investigated the room, saw the isolation sign.

"What is she on isolation for?"

"Well, we're trying to figure that out," Fran replied. "She has a fever and low oxygen saturation."

"Okay," replied John as he began to gown up. Fran stayed outside as John called, "X-ray."

"Can you wait here and pull it up so I can get the PA to come have a look?"

"Sure."

Fran walked over to the desk where Annie was now chatting with the other nurses. "Excuse me for interrupting, but John has the x-ray on the portable machine. Do you want to have a look?"

Annie got up and came over to the room. She stared at the film. Fran was not sure she even knew what she was looking at.

They stood side by side staring at the film. "I can tell you, that is not a normal chest," said John. "You see that." He pointed to some white haziness in the lung fields.

John's pager went off. "I gotta get going. I will have the film up in the system in about ten."

Annie stared into Mrs. Cobb's room. "Do you want to go in and listen to her lungs?"

Lisa was in there doing the EKG. She came out and handed the paper to Annie. Annie stared at the paper, again appearing to not know what to do. "I'm an ortho PA. I don't know all this medical stuff."

"Well, how about we call a medical consult?" Fran offered. "Maybe she has developed a post-op pneumonia. I'm sure about one thing, these sats are going to go down if we try to titrate her off of oxygen, so her hip is no longer the problem."

"I'm going to call for an ICU consult and see if we can upgrade her to at least step-down," Annie offered.

"Good idea." Annie went off to the station to make the calls.

Ugh, that's like pulling teeth, Fran thought as she went off to check on her other patients. It was 3:00 a.m., and she was supposed to be on break, but she knew this was not going to be a night for that.

Fran walked around the unit. She saw Lisa and the other aide, Trevor putting on isolation garb.

The patient was not hers, but she decided to investigate.

"Lisa, why is this guy on isolation, did he have ortho surgery?"

"Yeah, looks like a knee something surgery, he's got a dressing," replied Lisa. "I don't know why he is on isolation. We just do what the sign says."

Fran decided to investigate. She went up to the tracking board at the station. There were symbols for things like isolation, NPO (which was a Latin abbreviation for "nil per os," meaning nothing by mouth), pending discharge, awaiting labs, DNR status. All were symbols that only the staff knew.

Fran saw the isolation symbol on eight of the rooms. *That's unusual*, Fran thought. *We hardly ever get isolation on a clean orthopedic unit.*

She walked down the length of the unit and around to the other side and stopped briefly to peer into the rooms labeled isolation. She could tell from the door by the equipment in the room whether there had been a knee surgery, a hip or back surgery.

What she was not prepared to see was eight patients on oxygen. That was highly unusual for an orthopedic unit. *What is going on here?*

Fran's eyes widened as she remembered listening to her favorite Greek news station Cosmos. *Shit. I hope Annie isn't on call for all of these patients.*

Chapter 8

The next day, Sandy arrived at work expecting to have her same assignment. She looked up at the assignment board and saw Mr. Berger was up for transfer. Room 237 was empty. Sandy saw that her assignment was at the other end of the unit with the young man she had seen get intubated yesterday. She went over to the night nurse she had given report to before leaving. She stared in the empty room, which had been cleaned out completely. This was called a terminal clean, done for an isolation room. It included a change of bedside curtains, window curtains, walls washed, bedside tables, drawers opened and washed inside, and an airing out of the room.

"What happened?" she asked Amira.

"About 3:00 a.m., her sats dropped into the 60s. We put the FIO2 up to 100 percent, added more PEEP, then she developed a pneumothorax. They put a chest tube in, but by then, she brady'ed down. We did CPR, maybe a few rounds, then her son was called. He told us to stop, that she would not want this, so we did."

Sandy felt the tears coming, not only because she felt bad for Mrs. Cantor and Joel, but also, this was a scary time right now and she did not know what to think. In general, her patients always improved and went home, and she was not used to one of her patients dying. It made the anxiety of everything she was seeing in the news very personal. She didn't recognize how much she depended on a good outcome for her patients to feel satisfaction in her work.

Amira handed a folded piece of paper to her. "What's this?"

"A note Joel left you."

Sandy walked to the side and opened the note. It read:

Thank you for being so kind to mom.
Please take care of yourself.
They are not telling you everything.
Joel

Sandy felt her heart stop. Who was Joel? What did he know? She started thinking about all she had seen on TV. COVID-19 was here, right in New York. *We just can't prove it yet*, she thought. *By the time the PCRs come back, the patients will all be dead. And no one will care.*

She walked over to take report on Raymond Jackson, the twenty-five-year-old young man that was in serious trouble. She did not see Maureen today; she knew that she had pretty much the same schedule, but Maureen had called in sick.

She went over to Jason, one of the newer night nurses to take report.

She looked in the room to see Raymond, and her eyes surveyed the infusion pumps, the monitor, the ventilator, the central line, the dialysis catheter. Raymond was just a jumble of tubes and wires now. Sandy looked around the unit to see whom she was working with. She saw Jan, the charge nurse, and Jerry, a veteran nurse, there. *Good*, she thought, *someone more senior than me.*

It seems the turnover in the critical care unit had sped up lately and she was now more senior than many. There was Jackie. *Okay, good. I like Jackie, I can talk to her.* Across from her were Patricia and Rena. *Okay, good crew today.*

Raymond Jackson, twenty-five, was her only patient today since he was so ill. Jan knew that Sandy had wanted all the critical care experience that could be thrown at her, so she assigned the sickest patient to her. Although grateful, Sandy was nervous. *I'll try not to let on that I might shit myself today.* She sat down, pulled up Raymond on the computer, and started to take report. Raymond Jackson had been born and raised in Queens. His father, Lloyd, worked for the New York City Transit Authority in track maintenance. His mother,

Darlene, was an administrative assistant for the owner of a large construction company. Neither of his parents had been to college, and their fondest dream was for Raymond to go to college. He was the older of their two children. His younger sister April was still in high school. Raymond had more than fulfilled their dreams by graduating from City College with a degree in electrical engineering and landing a job (at the MTA, where his dad worked in a different department) before he even graduated. He was very athletic despite having asthma, and his favorite game was basketball. At six feet, four inches tall, he was built for it. Raymond was the point guard for his team. He had substantial handling skills of the ball and knew how to facilitate the ball getting to the other four members. He had plays in his head all the time. He always kept the opposition guessing.

He played on his high school team, and it nearly derailed his plans because he was so popular. He had many girls who were interested in him, and if not for his mother, he might have become a father incredibly early in life. One of his mother's best friends was a nurse who worked with people who had HIV, and his mother would talk about how important condoms were from the time Raymond was young.

At first, his mother had argued with her friend. Darlene Jackson was staffing the coffee table after church one day when Ray was about twelve, and her friend JoAnne (the nurse) was helping. JoAnne was going on again about how young people are never taught real life skills. "What do you mean? Ray can cook, he knows how to do laundry, he's the one who made this coffee!"

Darlene was determined to make her kids self-reliant. "He also knows how to fix things—his dad is on top of that."

"Yes, but I'll bet you haven't talked to him about sex yet," JoAnne countered.

"Oh, you! You are too obsessed with sex!" Darlene said, but she laughed, and they talked about the date night she and Lloyd had on Valentine's Day. Darlene said, "I put a bow in all the important places!" She and Lloyd liked to keep the spark going, and she was proud of her swimmer's body. JoAnne was her best friend, and not hypocritical about how much she liked sex. But Darlene wasn't sure when or how she should bring it up with Raymond. It wasn't that long ago he still believed in Santa. Still, she needed to figure it out. "I don't know how to start!" she said to JoAnne. She and JoAnne talked about it endlessly. She and Lloyd also discussed it, and they decided that Lloyd should start the conversation. Ray was always glued to his father whenever he was home, and at twelve, he still thought his father was the smartest guy around. Ray did not become a father in high school, despite his great popularity, nor did he get any STIs, a nice side effect of consistent condom use. As Raymond got older, taller, and even better looking, he always remembered to use condoms. He was gentle and kind as well as athletic. He had an enviable sex life.

In addition to working, basketball, and his active social life, Raymond was deeply involved with his church. He had a wonderful voice and was tapped early by the pastor to be in the choir. He loved to sing and never missed practice or a service.

On Sunday, February 23, he woke with an asthma attack. He hadn't had any wheezing in years, but since January he had had two minor exacerbations. He used his inhaler, had some coffee which really helped, and got ready for church. By the time he got there, he knew this was going to be a bad attack, and he left the back room where he was putting on his choir robes and went looking for his mother's friend JoAnne.

"Oh, baby, you need to go to the ER. You're really wheezing bad," she said. "I don't even need a stethoscope to hear how tight you are. Come on, I'm gonna get your mom and April, and we'll go. I'll tell the reverend." Lloyd was working and wasn't at church.

Sunday was a whole wasted day in the ER. He was discharged at 6:00 p.m., and his mother took him back to the family house. "You're staying with me for a few days." Ray didn't argue, he still felt horrible.

By the following Sunday, he was back in the hospital, unable to get enough air, intubated, and chemically paralyzed.

Sandy took a deep breath, signed on to the computer, and pulled up the chart on Raymond. She read the notes written by the various disciplines on his case.

Jason sat down next to her with his computer. "You ready?"

"I hope so."

"Okay, so this is Raymond Jackson, his parents call him Ray. He was brought in yesterday in respiratory failure, required intubation, lots of sedation, pressors, dialysis, and now you see him. The only medical history he has is asthma which had been well controlled until earlier this year. He had two minor exacerbations in January, and on February 23, he woke with an attack, went to church anyway, ended up in the ER where he was treated and discharged, presumably feeling well. He presented a week later, and this is his condition."

"His parents are Lloyd and Darlene, and they are in the waiting room. They have not left since he came in, and are naturally quite distraught. Social history, no drugs, no smoking ever, works as an electrical engineer, big popular basketball player both in high school and college. Point guard. That means he has skills," he said nervously. Jason was trying to impress Sandy with his basketball knowledge. He always felt nervous around her, and one day he tried to analyze why. That was when he realized he liked her, and that made it harder to talk to her. "Family involved in the church. Ray here sings there every Sunday, volunteers with church programs. Seems like an all-around great guy."

"Tell me the events leading up to this admission, please," Sandy said, oblivious of Jason's attempts to be charming.

"He came in through the emergency room night before last, um, so that would be March 4. His mom says he had a bad asthma attack in church." Jason looked down at the EMR notes. "Anyway, they put him on HIGH-FLOW at thirty liters, after his sats were in the eighties. His sats improved slightly. The ER nurse says he was talking on his cell phone almost the whole time." He paused to take a breath. "They did a chest film, with patchy infiltrates according to the radiology report. They started IV vanco and Merrem,[10] like broad-spectrum coverage." Jason was nodding and trying to look confident to let Sandy know he knew his antibiotics. She was unimpressed.

---

[10] Merrem is the trade name for meropenem, a strong broad-spectrum antibiotic.

"Did they think he had any abdominal signs? That would be the reason for the Merrem," replied Sandy, realizing she was beginning to sound a bit like Maureen.

"Uh, no, I don't think so," said Jason, sounding a bit sheepish.

Sandy was already on Ray's lab page. She was thinking, *His hemoglobin and hematocrit, so low for a young athlete. White count not elevated, strange.* Then she realized Jason was still talking.

"He got up here on HIGH-FLOW, and we increased the liter flow to forty liters. He was still talking away according to Pete. He was tachycardic, so we put in another peripheral IV, just in case." Sandy looked up, noted the two peripheral lines now saline locked and two central lines infusing. "We gave him some fluids after seeing his temp of 102. But vitals stayed stable except for the tachycardia. At about 2:00 p.m., he complained of chest pain, and Pete told me his sats suddenly went into the sixties. They called a code and intubated him." Sandy remembered.

"He was ridiculously hard to sedate," Jason continued.

"Yeah, I was here for that," Sandy said. "I got them extra etomidate and Versed. What's he on now?"

"Propofol at fifty micrograms, Versed at four milligrams, Nimbex at two micrograms with room to titrate up on the Versed and Nimbex. Train of four[11] is to be kept at two out of four."

"I see Levo," Sandy said.

"Well, after intubation and all that sedation, he tanked." Meaning his blood pressure dropped.

"Levo is at two micrograms per kilogram."

"What? Are you sure?" Sandy leaned in for a closer look. That would have been a huge dose. "You mean .02 micrograms per kilogram per minute." Sandy realized she was emulating Maureen more and more. *I don't want to end up like her,* she thought.

---

[11] Train of four is a technique to check muscle responsiveness. The deep sedation required for intubation and mechanical ventilation often causes nerve and muscle problems even after the drugs are stopped. Monitoring how functional the muscle is during deep sedation helps to prevent residual paralysis. It allows the drug given to be adjusted up or down based on the neuromuscular response.

"Oh, yeah, sorry, I guess I am getting tired," Jason answered, mortified.

"I am sure you are," Sandy said sympathetically. She was not going to become a bitch like Maureen.

"Anyway, he bumped up his BUN and creatinine, so he now has a RIJ dialysis catheter." What Jason was explaining was a decrease in kidney function and the need to perform temporary dialysis to perform the usual work of the kidneys. "He has a left internal jugular triple lumen catheter, a right radial arterial line, a temperature probe Foley catheter, but he is oliguric." Meaning that he is not producing as much urine as expected. This was all consistent with the picture of someone with an overwhelming infection and kidney failure.

"Uh, vent settings, please," Sandy said.

"Oh yeah, right. AC 18, TV 400, FIO2 80 percent, PEEP 10." Those were aggressive settings for near maximal ventilatory support.

"Wow, he's up there," Sandy commented. "He's a big guy, why only 400 c tidal volume?" That was a small volume for a man who was 6 feet, 4 inches tall and 180 pounds.

"I thought that too," said Jason.

"Probably because of the high PEEP," Sandy said, more confident of her understanding of the physiology of this patient's illness. PEEP indicates an addition to mechanical ventilation that creates a positive end expiratory pressure. This helps to keep the air sacs in the lung open to oxygen even during exhalation. It is a way to force oxygen through the fine membranes in these air sacs called alveoli. The problem with PEEP, especially with high tidal volumes, was barotrauma or pressure trauma to the lungs. It could lead to a collapsed lung.

"Dialysis nurse is coming again today. Dr. Camarie is going to order the prone team to come and prone him every six hours." Jason looked expectantly at Sandy. They both knew when he started writing orders instead of the house staff, the patient was in trouble.

"You'd better go home. I know you have to come back tonight," Sandy said. "I have what I need, and I can read the rest of the chart. Have a good day."

"Okay, see ya." Jason got his backpack and walked off. He was mad at himself for being dorky when he really wanted Sandy to like him.

Sandy finished looking at the labs and radiology reports and went to get on her PPE to enter the room. The sign outside the room was now labeled airborne precautions, so that meant gown, N95, and gloves. She opened the cabinet outside the room to find three gowns, a box of medium- and large-sized gloves, and one N95 respirator mask. *Okay*, she thought, *that's enough for one entry into the room. Let me check the other cabinets.* Sandy went to each cabinet that was stationed in between two ICU rooms. When she opened each one, she found the same thing, three gowns, two boxes of gloves, and one N95 mask.

Sandy walked over to Jan and said, "Where are the N95s?"

"All locked up except for what is needed for each patient for the day."

"For the day? One N95? I need a new one for each time I enter the room. That's still the policy, isn't it?"

"Well, kinda." Jan hedged.

"What do you mean kinda? Do we have a new isolation policy?"

"Well," Jan replied. "It's coming from the CDC.[12] Or the WHO.[13] I don't really know." Jan said apologetically.

"When? What on earth are you talking about? We've had endless trainings on proper isolation technique. We get hammered for the slightest deviation from that." Sandy was trying not to sound too irritated, but this was, to her, almost heresy. You never, ever reused a mask.

"Dr. Camarie has ordered this patient proned,[14] and that will require at least seven people. That means seven N95s. Our supply is not going to last." Jan looked sheepish, having to impart a new rule that was so against years and years of practice.

---

[12] Center for Disease Control and Prevention.
[13] The World Health Organization.
[14] Proning refers to turning a person facedown. This position allows the back part of the lungs to fill more fully and help oxygenate the blood.

Sandy thought, *I'd better get into Ray's room and make sure he is ok. I'm sure this is some kind of mistake. They'll get it fixed and send the supplies to the unit.*

What Sandy would later find out is that the entire supply chain of the manufacture and distribution of PPE had been disrupted as much of it came from China, the origin of the outbreak.

She gowned, gloved, masked, and went into the room. Sandy was not prepared to see what Ray looked like.

There he was, this tall, obviously once handsome young man, now looking swollen, arms elevated on pillows, central lines in both sides of the neck, mouth open with drool coming out of one side, Ray had a peculiar odor coming from his mouth that Sandy could appreciate even with her N95 mask on. That in and of itself was odd; the whole purpose of the N95 was to inhibit the smallest particles from being inhaled by the wearer. For her to be able to smell anything through the mask meant the odor was pervasive. Before she touched anything, she made sure the mask was tight to her face

I don't even know where to start, she thought. But she did know. She got the towel that was on his pillow to wipe away the drool. She checked the position of the oral gastric tube with the piston syringe and air as she listened to his stomach.

Oh god, so much tape on his mouth, his parents will be so upset to see this. I'll see if I can fix that later, she thought.

"Okay, remember, head to toe."

Sandy started with the train of fours. This was a small phone-size box with two wires attached to the two electrodes that had been placed on Ray's inner arm. She hooked up the wires to the electrodes, moved the setting to five, and pressed the button. She was happy to see the two muscle twitches she was hoping for. If it had been more than two, she would have had to increase the Nimbex drip. If it had been less, she would have had to titrate down. The train of fours, Sandy knew, assessed the level of neuromuscular blockade offered by the Nimbex.

Okay, adequate. Sandy was making mental notes as she could no longer bring the computer workstation (and all her access to looking at and writing in the chart) into the room. Sandy touched all of Ray's extremities to assess temperature. She then felt for the peripheral pulses in each extremity to make sure blood was getting to the ends of the arms and legs. As she was doing this, she was always aware of the monitor and all the data that was displayed there. *Blood pressure, normal. But on pressor,* Sandy thought. *Pulse 103, tachycardia. He has a temp.* Meaning a fever or elevated temperature. A Foley catheter with a temperature probe had been inserted, so the temperature of the bladder (consistent with the core temperature of the body) was showing on the screen as 101.0 Fahrenheit. Sandy made a mental note to see when he had last received Tylenol.

Pulse oximetry with a waveform was next. Sandy saw Ray's oxygen saturation was 90 percent. She knew 90 percent was not a great sat with all that ventilatory support.

Sandy looked at all his lines to see what was available in case of emergency. He had a port open on the triple lumen. *Good,* she thought.

Sandy listened to his lungs anteriorly. *Not much to hear,* she thought. Sandy tried to put the stethoscope behind his shoulders to listen to his back, but it was difficult without another person. Most of the evaluation of lung sounds came from listening at the back. *I wish Ethan was here,* she thought. *Hope he comes on at three.*

Next, Sandy attached the in-line suction to the port on the endotracheal tube. What she saw was shocking. Thick, tan blood-tinged secretions came up through the catheter. *Eeww, what's that about?* she thought. Sandy knew she needed to go out and look at the medication list and start Ray's medications. *But what about my N95 mask? Am I going to get another one? Should I throw it out? What should I do with it?* She was in a quandary. With one mask, she could not do as she was taught, to discard all used PPE when doffing, or removing, it.

Before she removed her PPE, she waved over to Jerry to come over to the room.

"Hey," Jerry said as he stood outside of her room. "What's up?"

"Did you hear what we are supposed to do with our masks, since there is only one in each cabinet?"

"Yup, I did. I'll be right back."

Jerry came back with a plastic biohazard bag and opened it. "You have to drop it in here and tape it to the wall right here." He pointed to the glass door that could be reached from inside the room.

Sandy's eyes widened. "Seriously?"

"Yup, that's what we were told at the last staff meeting yesterday. Here, I'll tape it up for you, then you just drop it in as you come out."

Sandy shrugged. "Okay, I guess." She removed her gown and gloves, discarded them in the container by the door, then removed her mask and carefully placed it into the biohazard bag Jerry had taped up for her.

Sandy looked at her medication list. Ray had received doses of antibiotics at 6:00 a.m., so there was nothing until twelve and later. She looked at his oral medications. She would have to put them into the tube that entered through his mouth and went down onto his stomach. It was called an OGT, or oral gastric tube. *Good, he's on a probiotic, vitamin D, folic acid,* she thought. *That ought to help his immune system.* Sandy had noticed that the OGT was clamped, and Ray was not receiving a tube feeding. *I'll have to find out about that. Maybe he had been vomiting or not absorbing anything,* she thought.

Sandy filled out all the required documentation, such as the sedation scale and the Braden scale. The Braden scale helped to assess the patient's risk for getting a bedsore. Ray did not require restraints since he was chemically paralyzed. She was grateful he did not need restraints since that required every fifteen-minute documentation. Sandy began her head-to-toe documentation. *Thank God, it's mostly a check-off, or I'd be writing all day,* she thought.

Suddenly Dr. Camarie was standing over her.

"Are we proning soon?" he asked.

"Yes, just waiting for the team."

"Well, young lady, I am part of that team."

Sandy gulped. "Oh, okay, great." She did not want Dr. Camarie to know that this was her first time proning. "I want to get him on his belly, then I will go and speak with his parents. Let's get this going, shall we?" Dr. Camarie picked up his phone. Within five minutes, six people were surrounding the room, residents, interns, an anesthesiologist, Denise, the respiratory therapist, two nurse anesthetists. "Okay, let's get everyone dressed." Dr. Camarie walked over to the cabinet and opened it. "Where is everything?"

"I have to get Jan," Sandy said meekly.

Sandy saw Jan standing at the nursing station on the phone. She was obviously arguing with someone. Sandy tried to speak, but she waved her away. "I know, but we have that young guy, he is a one-to-one," Sandy heard her say. Jan slammed down the phone.

Sandy pointed over to Ray's room. "Oh!" Jan said. "What do they want?"

"They want PPE to go in."

"Come with me." Sandy walked behind Jan over to her office. Jan punched in the code and motioned for Sandy to come in.

There sat boxes of gowns, gloves, face shields, and N95s. Sandy could not contain her surprise.

"Why is all this stuff in here and not out where we can use it?"

"Other units have been stealing this stuff, so we were told by the higher-ups to keep it locked up. I hate this, I can't even get to my desk anymore. So how many people need?" Jan said, "I can only give out one set for each person."

"Well, There's Dr. Camarie, Denise, Keith, two residents, two CNAs, and me."

"Well, you already have yours." Sandy rolled her eyes. "And Dr. Camarie knows he has his own in his department for him and the residents. So I'll give you three sets."

"Wait, what? You want me to tell Dr. Camarie, the medical director of this unit, he has to go and get PPE for him and his two residents and Keith? I don't think so. You can tell him."

Jan thought for a moment. "I don't want to get in trouble for this." She handed Sandy four more sets of PPEs.

"Thanks." Sandy grabbed the pile and went back to the room.

When Sandy arrived back at the room, she found Dr. Camarie holding a brief lecture on proning. Sandy had wished she had been there from the beginning *If only the PPE had been where they were supposed to be—in the cabinets outside the rooms—I wouldn't have missed this valuable lecture.*

"This position is especially helpful in compromised patients. It allows for better expansion of the dorsal [back] lung regions, improved body movement, and enhanced removal of secretions which may ultimately lead to better oxygenation. Okay, let's get ready."

Sandy began to put on her PPE. She carefully took the mask out of the biohazard bag that was taped to the glass. The others, Keith, Denise, Charles, the CNA, Dr. Werman, the anesthesiologist, and Dr. Camarie, quickly donned their PPE. It was clear that Dr. Camarie was going to run the show.

Everyone performed hand hygiene. They all saw that Dr. Camarie was watching intently. "Sandy, please make sure the OGT is in place and secure. Please clamp it unless there are excessive gastric secretions."

"Of course." Sandy got out the piston syringe, and her stethoscope pushed air into the OGT and nodded. It was in place. She clamped it off, tying a knot in the tubing.

"How many pillows do we have, Sandy?"

"Seven, Dr. Camarie."

"Okay, that ought to be enough. What was his last train of four?"

"Two twitches."

"Okay, good, he is properly paralyzed. Remember," Dr. Camarie told them, "crown, significant facial, and lip edema can develop when this young fella is on his belly. We want to minimize airway compromise while oxygenating his dorsal lung regions. Dr. Werman, can you please confirm the lip line?" This was to ensure that the endotracheal tube did not move. "Of course," Dr. Werman said as he moved to the head of the bed to manage the airway. He moved the overbed table with him to the head of the bed.

"Okay, Charles and Denise, you both go to the right side of the patient, please. Keith and Sandy, please go to the left." Everyone quickly took their places. "Okay, everyone, let's do a time-out procedure." This is a technique to make sure they were doing the right procedure on the right patient. "Sandy? Would you do the honors, please?"

Sandy was trying to hide her nerves. "This is Raymond Jackson, age twenty-five, date of birth September 24, 1995." She double-checked his ID bracelet. "The procedure is proning the patient." She looked at the team members in the room.

"Agree," said almost everyone at once. Finally, Sandy said, "Agree."

Dr. Camarie nodded. "Please remove the electrodes from his chest and have new ones ready for his back. Then place the first pillow across his chest."

Sandy already had them in her pocket, anticipating this. "Got it."

"Make sure that the lines are going upward towards the head of the bed, please." Sandy did that expertly. "Good job, Sandy. Okay, Charles and Denise, you are going to start the roll towards you, then, Sandy, you place the electrodes on Ray's back so we can get him back on the monitor. On my count, please." He paused. "One, two, three, roll."

Charles and Denise began to roll Ray with Dr. Werman holding the head stable. "Make sure the pillow stays under his chest to keep it elevated. Denise, please place another pillow under his iliac crest." This is to support the person's midsection.

"Okay, sure."

"Keith, place a pillow underneath Ray's shins."

"Got it."

The team did not make a move without Dr. Camarie. Sandy was absorbing every moment, knowing that she would have to do this again.

"Sandy, as Denise and Charles begin to roll a bit more, I want you and Keith and I to pull the bottom sheet towards us so he can go all the way over and stay centered in the bed. Dr. Werman, please make sure his head is turned toward the ventilator and have his arms over the table."

It seemed like hours, but within fifteen minutes Ray was on his abdomen and looking quite comfortable if one could ever look that way in these circumstances.

"Denise, please assess for bilateral breath sounds."

"Of course, Dr. Camarie."

"Dr. Werman, Ray's airway is good?"

"Absolutely." He confirmed.

Sandy made sure to check all the lines and the drip rates. "Dr. Camarie, I'll do another train of four since we switched his position."

"Yes, Sandy, please."

Everyone looked at the monitor. Ray's heart rate, although fast, was stable, blood pressure was within his normal limits, and sats were acceptable.

"Okay, everyone may doff their PPE, wash out, and leave the room."

The entire team removed their PPE and threw it in the garbage can on the way out.

"Sandy, let Keith know if he maintains his sats on these settings. Also, see if you can get him off the Levo. Keith, get a gas, please."

"Sure thing, Dr. Camarie."

"I am going to go and speak to his parents."

Everyone left the room except Sandy. She made sure his face was not pressing on anything, cleaned his mouth, suctioned him gently, made sure he was covered, went down a bit on the Levo. She gave one final look before doffing her PPE. Sandy was about to throw her PPE in the garbage, but Jan was now standing outside.

"You let everyone throw their PPE in the garbage?"

"What did you want me to do?" Sandy said, throwing her arms in the air.

"I gave you seven sets of PPEs. They are meant to be reused."

"I'm sorry, but I am not the PPE police. Here, see I am putting my mask back into the biohazard bag for the fourth time this shift. What do you want me to do? Go through the garbage and get everything out?"

Jan walked away, obviously angry.

I don't know what this is all about, thought Sandy. *We are supposed to have enough supplies for one-time usage of all PPE. This is so weird.*

Sandy knew she did not have time to obsess about it now. Ray's parents were on their way in. Dr. Camarie walked back toward the room with Ray's parents. Sandy looked at both of them and was shaken by how sad they looked. They both had obviously had no sleep and had been crying. They stood outside the room as Dr. Camarie explained the reason behind the proning. "You see, the lungs are in the back of the chest cavity, and when a person is lying on their back, those spaces are farther away. When we turned Ray on his belly, we can get oxygen to parts of the lung that can't be reached the other way. I know it looks strange, but this will help get much-needed oxygen to his lungs so he can begin to get better."

Lloyd and Darlene nodded. Sandy, at the computer, looked sympathetically at both of them. "Hi, I'm Sandy, Ray's nurse today. I promise I'll take good care of him. It's just me and him together all shift." Sandy was referring to the fact that she just had the one patient for this shift. "I'll still be able to assess him, give him medications, and make him comfortable this way, and when Dr. Camarie writes an order, we will turn him on his back again."

"Yes," said Dr. Camarie, "Sandy here is one of our up-and-coming experts in this."

"So do we know what's causing this?" Lloyd, Ray's father, said. "He's a healthy young man. All he had was some asthma, it wasn't even that bad, and now all this?"

Sandy looked at Dr. Camarie, waiting to see if he was going to say what she was already thinking.

"Well," said Dr. Camarie, "it is possible that this pneumonia and respiratory failure is being caused by a new virus that is spreading around called SARS-CoV-2."

"You mean the Chinese virus?" exclaimed Darlene.

Dr. Camarie nodded. "I'm afraid so. From the reports we have heard from other countries through the WHO and CDC, and Ray's presentation and rapid deterioration, we think this might be from this virus."

Darlene looked like she was going to collapse. Sandy quickly grabbed a chair and sat her down.

Darlene was thinking. "He didn't get measles or mumps, he didn't get meningitis, he didn't get HIV, he didn't get a girl pregnant, he didn't get shot in the street. We kept him safe for twenty-five years, and now he gets this?" She felt as though she was losing her mind.

"But what is the treatment? And where did he get this? He hasn't traveled," asked Lloyd, trying to be stoic.

"Well, right now the care is supportive in nature. We are treating this pneumonia with antibiotics, monitoring him every minute, maintaining his blood pressure with medications, his kidneys with a slow form of dialysis. We will lower his ventilator settings based on his blood gas results, and basically take this day by day, even hour by hour. We don't know quite where he got this, but from an infection control standpoint and from the epidemiology experts—the ones who tell us how infections travel from one person to another—we know this is a rapidly spreading virus, and it is likely everywhere. Why Ray got it, we don't know, and we won't know anything until the sample gets back from the CDC."

"Can we go in?" asked Lloyd.

"No, Lloyd," said Darlene, "we'll just peek in. I can't see my boy like this." She burst into tears.

"I must go to see my other patients now," Dr. Camarie said gently. "I'll be back to check on Ray within the hour. He's in good hands with Sandy."

"Thank you, Doctor." Darlene pulled herself together.

"Sandy, when you get the gas, you or Keith call me, and maybe we can make some vent changes."

"Of course, Dr. Camarie."

As Sandy was sitting at the desk doing some charting, she overheard Darlene and Lloyd talking.

"You know the Marksons from church?"

"Of course."

"Well, someone from their family is sick. I think it's Eugenia, the grandma. I overheard someone saying she was quite sick. And they haven't been bringing her to church the last few weeks."

"I don't remember Eugenia."

"You know the sweet old lady that brought Reverend James her special lemon cookies?"

"Oh yeah, her? I remember her. That's right, she hasn't been in church for a while."

"I think we should call Reverend James. We should tell him that Ray is sick and ask if anyone else from the church is sick."

Darlene started to think back to the previous Sunday. Many members of the choir were missing, and the church wasn't as full as usual. "Yes, I'm going to call Reverend James…" Sandy continued her charting until Keith came back with the blood gas. "Looks good, Camarie said we can go down on the PEEP first. Let's make it 5."

"Okay, I'll call Denise."

Sandy stepped over to the Jacksons. "Ray has a good blood gas. That means that he is oxygenating better, and we can take down one of the settings that has been on the high side. It's called PEEP."

"Thank the Lord!" Darlene said and hugged her husband. "We are going to go back to the waiting room and let you take care of our son," she said with tears in her eyes. "Please, Sandy, please, let us have our boy back. We are going to pray for you."

Tears stung Sandy's eyes as she went to put on her same PPE for the fifth time. *Yes, please pray for me too*, she thought.

Ethan came in at his usual time of 3:00 p.m. He immediately went to Sandy. "You're not gonna believe what just happened— school and clinicals are canceled. They just pulled us out! They don't know what they're gonna do—and I paid for this semester for clinicals and everything. I have to graduate—I'm so close to becoming a nurse. This is so fucked up." He looked close to tears.

"Calm down, Ethan, please." Sandy rubbed his arm. "They'll figure something out online for all the students. It'll be fine, really." She decided to get him busy so he wouldn't have to think about it. "Come in with me to Ray's room, please. Help me bathe him, and we can talk."

"Okay," Ethan said as he started to speak in his normal cheery voice, "let me go sign in and take my vitals on the unit, then I will come in with you."

Sandy sat back a moment, took a deep breath. *What's going to happen now?* she thought.

She looked around the unit at all of her coworkers. *How are we all gonna survive this?*

Sandy started to think about her recent days off. Her mother called and said, "I'm going to Costco, you want to keep me company?" She hadn't seen her mother in a couple of weeks, and so she agreed. Her mother, a maniac overbuyer of everything, insisted that Sandy get loaded up with supplies too. "You're doing so much overtime, when will you have time to shop?" That was a good point for Sandy because she really hated shopping, so it was good to get it out of the way all at once. While they were shopping, her mother insisted they both have carts, and by the time they were done, both carts were full to overflowing. "How will we get all this into the car?" wondered Sandy aloud, but she knew her mother would figure it out. Back at Sandy's apartment, she was glad they had luggage carts in the lobby, or she never would have finished getting all the items up to her apartment. She surveyed the closet after it was all put away and realized she was now the possessor of more cans of black beans than she could—or would—ever eat.

She was lucky to be in one of the large doorman buildings in Forest Hills, quite close to her parents. She had been able to buy the apartment with a legacy from her grandmother who stipulated that she use it to buy real estate. The apartment was a modest one-bedroom but had two features that made it an excellent buy: it had its own washer/dryer, an amenity not often found in any New York City apartments, even in the boroughs, and it had a huge extra closet that Sandy's father had outfitted with shelving and which she used as a pantry/linen closet. It was most often empty except for linens, but after this trip, it was completely filled. Sandy, with the help of her dad, had fixed the apartment up, so it was perfect for her. The kitchen was just a small open galley, but there was room for a decent table opposite the kitchen. Sandy had painted the cabinets white and changed the knobs to glass. She and her father retiled the backsplash, and she was able to replace the aged range. There were lots of windows, so the place was light and airy. There was a place for everything, and she felt safe and comfortable there. It was a perfect haven for her.

Her mind then wandered to Jon-Anaica. Jon-Anaica was look-ing for a table in the crowded cafeteria a few weeks after Sandy joined the staff, and Sandy waved that there was space at her table.

"Oh gosh, thanks! I thought I was going to have to eat standing up!" Sandy smiled and replied, "I hate eating alone anyway, so it's a good thing you came along." They had seen each other in the hall, but this was their first conversation. Jon-Anaica was tall and very dark and wore her short hair in locks, which gave her a friendly but slightly exotic look. This was amplified by her almond-shaped eyes and high cheekbones. She was quite striking, the kind of woman people would stop to look at twice. Sandy had wondered who she was since the first time she saw her. She introduced herself to Sandy. When Sandy commented about her unusual name, she said, "It's a combination of both my parent's names—Jonas and Anaica. Usually, people call me Joni for short." They talked about their jobs (Jon-Anaica was a super-visor in the special hematology lab), their hobbies, their shared guilty pleasures (science fiction and first-person shooter games—especially *Doom*), and their parents. Sandy found her amazingly easy to talk to. Since that time, they had lunch together whenever they were both working. Soon they started seeing each other outside of work. Sandy helped Joni fix up the rather worn bathroom in Joni's house. "You know this is gonna need new tile and backer board. The grout has been missing for so long, I'll bet it's very icky back there," Sandy said when Joni asked for her opinion. "Lucky that tiling is one of my best skills." Sandy's father was a general contractor, and Sandy had always been fascinated with tile work. First, fascinated, and then proficient. Her father always brought her along to tiling jobs, and Sandy had learned from the best artisans. Joni was skeptical about being able to afford it. "Don't worry, I can get the tile wholesale, and I can do the install myself. There's another bath in this house, right? It'll be tight for a week or so, and then it'll be okay."

She didn't say that sometimes opening a wall also opened a can of worms, but she was hopeful.

Luckily, there were no surprises, and Sandy and Joni and Joni's brother Evens got it all done in a week. After that, Sandy was a welcome part of Joni's family. That worked out well for both of them, since they had started falling in love.

Sandy snapped back to the present and looked at Ray again. She wondered when the hospital administrators and managers were going to tell the staff what was going on. *Why don't we have a plan?* She turned her attention back to Ray. *Let me please save this man, please, God, let me save at least him.*

Sandy was in the room with Ray when Ethan appeared in his PPE. "You know, Jan gave me a set of this stuff, one mask, one gown, and told me I had to keep it and reuse it."

"I know, that's what we all have to do now."

"What changed so suddenly? First, my school closes and no one knows what's happening, and now this."

Sandy said gently, "We knew this was coming." She remembered the note from Joel the month before. In fact, she had saved it. "Remember that patient Mrs. Cantor with the son from California?" Ethan nodded. "Remember the note?" Ethan nodded. "Well…it's here, now we have to do what we have to in order to save these patients and protect ourselves." She turned to the patient.

"Ethan, look at this guy," she said, referring to Ray. "He didn't deserve this, and we are going to do everything in our power to save him. He's not much older than you. So let's get to work." Sandy filled the basin with warm water and got out the towels and soap. "We are going to make Ray look so comfortable, as though he is just sleeping like a baby. Then his parents won't sob every time they peek into the room. That's what we can do right now."

"I'm with you, beb," Ethan said.

Ethan thought back to when he first met Sandy. He had been on the unit for many months before she transferred in. He got along with all the nurses but kept things low-key and to himself; he'd had enough exposure to homophobia, and he didn't like to invite those sorts of comments. A lot of the staff made all sorts of remarks about other staffers or patients, and he didn't want any part of that. When Sandy arrived, she seemed sweet, and was genuinely nice to everyone. She looked like Susie Straight with her blonde hair and California-girl athletic looks. Ethan noticed that she was very modest in a way that a lot of young women weren't.

You never saw cleavage or anything tight on her, and she didn't wear jewelry or makeup. She was never flirtatious with any of the guys. It all became clear to him one day when she got dropped off to work by what he could only describe as a stunningly beautiful, slightly older woman than Sandy. She had long dark silky hair and a beautiful full-lipped face. She was wearing a very low-cut shirt that revealed her breasts perfectly. The kiss they exchanged in the parking lot was so passionate that when Sandy turned, she looked almost short of breath. She composed herself before entering the hospital and didn't see Ethan.

Ethan almost ran up and shouted at her, "That's the model from Bebe'! And you're kissing her!" Which he didn't, of course. He didn't really know who the woman was, but he was thrilled to find another gay person in his workplace. Ethan started thinking of her as Bebe', instantly shortening it to beb. He was always shortening words—too much to say and not enough time to say all those tiresome syllables. Later that day, he got up the courage to bring up the exchange with Sandy.

"I see you didn't drive in yourself today," he opened, pausing with a smile.

"Now don't come all over the gossipy queen with me, Ethan. I don't want people around here to know about my personal life. God. Especially Maureen."

"I totally hear that," Ethan replied, realizing that Sandy's gaydar was definitely turned on. She certainly had his number. "She'd have your whole history printed on the front page of *Newsweek* if you let her. Still, she's okay when you get to know her."

"I'll bet, as long as she doesn't know me. I've heard her talk about queers and dykes." Sandy had actually heard Mo say something about Ethan, but she didn't reveal that. Mo was just cranky about everyone.

So it was established in that moment that they would know what they knew but watch each other's backs. All these months later, Sandy knew Ethan had never said a word, even when she broke up with Bex (who, incidentally, was not a model but a physicist who worked developing MRI technology) or when she started seeing Joni. She never heard a thing about herself from other staff members. If she heard someone gossiping, she made it clear she was not taking part. Sandy and Ethan spent the better part of an hour washing, drying, doing range of motion, and oral care on Ray. Sandy changed the tapes on all the tubing and moisturized his face and lips.

When they were finished, Ethan said, "He looks good, beb."

"Well, as good as anyone could look with all these tubes and lines and pumps. But you're right, he does look surprisingly good." Over the last few hours, Sandy was able to wean Ray off the Levo and maintain a normal blood pressure. The latest blood gas was looking better, and vent setting changes were made by Dr. Camarie.

I don't want to be too hopeful, Sandy thought, *but this one might make it.* Out loud, she said, "I'm gonna talk to Camarie about weaning off the Nimbex."

Sandy and Ethan removed their PPE, washed out, and put their N95s in the plastic biohazard bags just outside the doorway.

Someone else called for Ethan to help. "Gotta go, beb, see ya later."

Sandy sat down at the desk in front of the room to chart. Jan approached her. "So Mo called in sick again for tomorrow. What do you think about coming in? I'll give you this same assignment."

Sandy thought about it for a moment. She did have plans with Joni, but this case was too interesting not to see it through. "Okay, I'll work." Sandy would have to break the news to Joni when she spoke with her later.

"Thanks." Jan walked back to the nursing station.

Sandy began the arduous process of charting again. She wondered, *What's wrong with Mo? I know she talks about how much she hates her job right now, but she always comes to work.* Sandy put it out of her mind and finished up her charting.

Sandy finished off her shift feeling quite accomplished. Dr. Camarie had decided to wean off the Nimbex (paralytic drip) that Ray was on. He was kept on the propofol and Versed drips for comfort. But he was beginning to breathe on his own. When Sandy gave report to Jason, she was able to tell him that Ray's vitals were stable off the Levophed, he was off the Nimbex, and the FIO2 was beginning to be weaned down.

"They are beginning to discuss a trach[15] and PEG[16] with the family. I think they are gonna go for it, given his great progress so far. The proning schedule really helped." She paused and waited for Jason to make a few notes.

I hope when I come back in, they have continued to make progress, Sandy thought.

By this time, the ICUs in New York were filling up with patients with COVID or suspected COVID.

Everyone was in PPE all the time, but supplies were in short supply, so they had to be rationed. The CDC had amended their guidance to optimize the use of N95 masks and other personal protective equipment. They even posted a "burn rate" calculator to help hospitals know how long before they "burned" through their current supplies. They also amended rules for contingency and crisis situations, which meant all the rules would be changing. Things that would never be considered in conventional times—such as using a mask for more than one entry into an isolation room—were completely acceptable in contingency mode and mandatory in crisis mode. To get all the staff to buy in to this radical change was difficult, if not impossible. It left everyone feeling unsure of how best to practice, afraid their exposure to CoV-2 would be greater, and distrustful of a system that could pivot away from what was considered gospel in normal times. For Sandy, it was as strange as if someone told her the sky would be pink from now on.

---

[15] Trach is shorthand for tracheostomy, a surgical procedure that puts an opening into the windpipe from the neck. This bypasses the mouth and pharynx and causes less complications than an endotracheal tube causes. It can be surgically closed when the person recovers.

[16] PEG is a tube that goes directly into the stomach through the wall of the abdomen. Like the trach, this method of feeding puts no pressure on the mouth and esophagus and so has fewer complications than prolonged feeding through the nasogastric approach. It can be surgically closed when the person recovers.

For good or for ill, all the usual regulations and behaviors were changing. It left Sandy very worried.

Sandy got home to her apartment, and Joni was waiting for her. They opened a bottle of wine and turned on the news.

Chapter 9

The Emergency Room
March 2020

March 11, 2020. The WHO declares a pandemic of COVID-19, the disease caused by the novel coronavirus.

Michael came back to work after a stretch off. As soon as he entered the ER, he knew there was something different happening. All the staff were in surgical masks. There was an IV pole hanging in front of the critical care room, trauma room, and main room with obviously used isolation gowns. They all had names written in Magic Marker on them. There were paper bags taped to the wall by the nursing station with names written on them. Michael thought, *What's going on around here?* But he already knew. COVID-19 was here.

Over the loudspeaker came the usual *"Safety huddle main desk, safety huddle main desk."*

Michael grabbed a surgical mask and walked over to the main desk. Even Helen was wearing a mask with her street clothes and lab coat. But this time, Dr. P was standing with her. Dr. P started the meeting. "The WHO has declared a pandemic of the novel coronavirus, also known as COVID-19. We are preparing to handle the load of patients we think may be coming in for care here. We will have two screeners in triage. They will be wearing a surgical mask only. There is no need for everyone to wear N95s at this time. Patients will be asked if they have had any travel to China or any part of Europe. They will be asked if they have had a cough or a fever. If those answers are yes, we will give the patient a mask to put on. That is the important thing. Put a mask on the patient. They will be put in beds 10 through 20 as PUI [persons under investigation]. If we require more space, we will move into SSA [same-day surgery admit area]."

"So where are the masks?" said Melissa "And where are the N95s?" said Catherine, a new PA in the ER.

"I think Helen can do a better job of answering that. Helen?"

Helen cleared her throat. "Of course, you will all be protected when you care for your patients." As the meaning of this double-talk became clear to those in attendance, a ripple of muttering started. Michael heard bits and pieces come through. "What the fuck?" "You gotta be kidding." "You can't be serious…"

Helen ignored all of this. "We have of all our PPE locked up in the supply room. The code has been changed since most of the hospital knows it by now. Each department is responsible for giving out PPE to their own employees. We will not be supplying everyone that comes down here to see a patient." Another round of muttering accompanied this extreme change in policy.

"Do the other departments know that?" came a voice from the crowd.

"You mean to tell us that when radiology comes to do an x-ray or sono, they have to come with their own masks?"

"They always take a mask from the cabinets before going into the room."

"Yes," Helen said, "the director of the department has been notified."

"I see disaster written all over this," said another voice.

"What about visitors?"

Dr. P. stepped in. "Patients will be allowed only one visitor each. They must wear a mask. I do not care about Press Ganey[17] scores right now. Our responsibility is to keep patients and staff safe."

Helen chimed in, "Of course, we will be courteous to the visitors and explain everything we are doing." This elicited even more

---

[17] These satisfaction surveys are sent to patients after any hospital encounter. Hospital administrators are overly concerned with the results of these surveys, as they indicate direct patient feedback.

mumbles from the crowd. "They say that now, but wait until someone complains…" "Of course, now we'll get stuck trying to explain this bullshit to the families…"

"What are all those paper bags for?" asked Michael. "Why are there gowns hanging from IV poles outside of critical care and trauma? Have they been used? They have names on them."

"Well, we really have to keep tabs on our supply right now, so yes, we will be reusing gowns and masks unless they are visibly soiled."

"What?" said almost every person simultaneously. This went against everything they were taught without exception. Everything was always single use only. If you got caught not changing between patients, there were serious consequences. Now all those previously chiseled-in-stone rules were out the window. It felt completely surreal.

Michael sighed. *The world is coming to an end*, he thought. *Let me go see my assignment.* Michael saw he was assigned to the trauma room. *Okay, not bad, should be okay in there.* He went to take report, but the room was empty. He began to take stock of what he needed for the shift. Michael checked the carts, the cabinets. He checked the rapid transfuser (for giving blood rapidly in emergency situations), and he checked that each bay had setups for oxygen masks, nasal cannulas, and intubation sets.

He sat down, took a sip of water, and signed on to his computer to look at the emergency room census. The emergency room which held fifty patients exclusive of critical care, trauma, and pediatrics had twenty-six patients so far. He scanned their admitting complaints. What he saw surprised him. Fever and cough, fever and cough, chest pain and cough, chest pain, abdominal pain, and cough. Gone were the rule out appendicitis, rule out cholecystitis, fall, fracture, rule out CVA, it was all respiratory and chest complaints. Michael felt as though he had been slapped hard upside his head. He was beginning to think this was some sort of bad dream.

He continued his preparations for the shift. As he was finishing up the stocking of the trauma bays, over the loudspeaker came *"Trauma code east—trauma code east parking lot."*

"What the *hell?*" Michael said. Before he could even think, he was out the door to the ER. The front parking lot, used to drop patients off for the ER only, was full, but through the front row of cars he saw an elderly man on the ground. "Shit! I don't have a mask."

Michael tossed this one back and forth in his mind for a second or two and continued on to the distressed man.

"Hey, guy, what's your name? What happened?"

"Harry" came back in a whisper.

"What happened, Harry?" Michael's assessment skills were in full gear. *Doesn't look like a trauma, no obvious signs of bleeding, moving extremities.* Michael noticed some bruising of his hands, but that did not seem to be the main issue right now.

A team started to form in back of Michael. Someone passed him a surgical mask. He put it on.

Someone had a stretcher.

"My wife is back there in the car. I didn't want her to walk, so I got out of the car after I parked." His voice was so weak, Michael could barely hear him.

"You drove here?"

"Yes."

"What brought you here?"

Harry raised his hands slightly. There were purplish bruises and blisters all over his fingers.

"What happened to you, man?" Michael said. He had never seen anything like it.

"I don't know. I woke up with this. I felt weak when I got out of bed, so Dorothy said we should come here." He paused to catch his breath. "I didn't want to bother with an ambulance. They are so busy, so I drove myself here."

Suddenly Harry's eyes rolled back. Michael knew he was arresting.

"Call a STEMI." Although he did not have an EKG to confirm, this seemed like a typical heart attack to Michael.

Michael started compressions. "Someone get the code cart. Someone get the intubation tray." It seemed as if the entire ER staff was now in the parking lot.

Dr. P was outside as well. "Check for a pulse." Since Michael was on the ground, he ripped through Harry's shirt to feel the carotid. Kim was on the ground next to him in full PPE, opening his pants to feel for a femoral pulse. Melissa had the electrodes on his chest and was hooking him up to the portable monitor/defibrillator.

"No pulse—continue CPR," said Dr. P. "Can someone please intubate?"

Michael looked down at Harry's face, saw the bluish tinge he was so familiar with, and looked up at Dr. P. "This guy is gone."

Dr. P leaned down to look closer at Harry. "I concur." He felt for a pulse, and he listened with his stethoscope. He shook his head.

"Melissa, can you run a strip, please?" Melissa pressed the button, and a strip came out with asystole (flat line) on it. Dr. P looked at his watch. "Time of death, 9:04 a.m."

Michael got up off the ground. "He has a wife, Dorothy, somewhere here sitting in a car. Someone has to find her."

Michael had never seen anything like this in eighteen years in the ER. He was staggered. He was even more upset to see Melissa start to cry; she was a pretty tough person. Michael had never felt so helpless.

"Hey, Dr. P, look at his hands." Dr. P looked down and saw what Michael had earlier, the purple blister-like formations.

"They look like microemboli—maybe he had a PE." PE is short for pulmonary embolism, a blood clot in the lungs which can be fatal.

Months later, they would learn that these would be called COVID hands, which were actually microemboli but were also present in the lungs.

Michael was trying hard not to shake or show emotion. As he came back into the ER, he was greeted with applause from his colleagues, which he waved off. "Just doing what had to be done."

Then came the admonishments. "Why did you go out there without PPE?" "I wouldn't have done that." "He wasn't wearing a mask?"

Michael started to get that cold feeling in the pit of his stomach, the one that meant he had made a huge mistake.

Dr. P came over and patted Michael on the shoulder. "I know you did what most nurses would do in this situation, but I want you to know that what you did was extremely brave. I want you to take every precaution to protect yourself going forward—as I would all the staff. We don't know what we are dealing with here." Dr. P wandered off to make rounds.

Michael went back into the trauma room. He started to worry about how much he was exposed. *Is there a way I can get tested for this virus?* he thought. *What about Pam and the kids?* Then *I'd better read up on the CDC recommendations.* He started to rationalize. *This guy probably had a PE or a heart attack. No one knows if he had COVID. What about his poor wife sitting in the car, what if she is sick?* Michael made a mental note to follow up on Dorothy, but he didn't even have her last name.

About four hours into the shift, he was out by the ambulance bay, taking a break, when he heard a ruckus near the entrance. He wandered over and asked a cop that was there what was going on.

"Someone found a dead woman in a car in the parking lot. They said she was starting to get stiff already."

Michael could hardly get his phone out of his pocket, he was shaking. He had to talk to Pam. Later, Michael spoke briefly with the police, finding out that Harry and Dorothy had been living with their daughter, Lois. Lois had been away on business for a few days when Harry began to feel sick. Lois checked in daily with her parents and was concerned when her dad had developed a bad cold. She wanted to fly home right away. Dorothy said no, they would be simply fine. When Harry began feeling worse, they decided to go to the local emergency room just to check things out. Michael thought about their poor daughter. *What she must be feeling, I can't imagine… and those blisters…*

When Michael got home that night, Pam was waiting for him, glass of scotch in hand, poured and ready.

Her hospital had now been affected, and the labor and delivery units were now closed off to all visitors except the spouse. One of the patients that had just delivered a baby went into respiratory distress and was intubated and now in their ICU. Her spouse had gone home for one night to shower and change, and he was now in another ICU intubated and sedated. Michael took a sip of the scotch. "Maybe you should quit." He was serious, but Pam just laughed.

"Our bank would just love that." They were almost at the end of their mortgage, but not quite. She admitted to herself that she was exhausted and scared, but she kept that to herself. The last thing she needed was for Michael or one of the boys to pick up her fear. She put her hand on the back of Michael's neck. "We'll get through this. It'll be all right." She leaned over and put her cheek on his. They sat that like for a minute, and it calmed Michael down.

After he ate, Michael sat down at his desk in the den and opened his emails.

There was an email from Dr. P, one of several that would be sent to the staff during the COVID-19 crisis.

Intubated patients pending care goals discussion, non-intubated patients with poor prognosis? he read. *What does that mean exactly?* What used to take days or even weeks with a palliative care nurse consult was now a discussion that was happening in the emergency room.

Never in my career have I seen something happen so quickly, he thought. He continued to read the email. It summarized what was going on throughout the institution.

COVID UPDATE—Monday March 30, 10:00 a.m.

1. MICU, SICU, Neuro ICU, Peds ICU, PACU (post anesthesia care unit), 4B all filled with intubated pts
2. 3B now filling up with intubated pts
3. Next up for conversion to COVID unit: Cath lab recovery room
4. Total census: 234 COVID positive pts; additional 55 PUIs
5. 6 COVID ICU beds available; 7 non-COVID ICU beds available

6. 19 beds are available for noncritical COVID admits
7. 73 patients intubated...67 COVID positive: 7 PUIs

Note: All intubated COVID patients should be *admitted to observation*; pending care goals discussions; likewise, non-intubated pts with poor prognosis.

Of all patients intubated, approx. 63 percent have been in ED, the rest on the floors

Please extend well wishes to our hospitalist Dr. Peter Jappnone, currently hospitalized with COVID pneumonia...he is stable.

Beginning today, we will have additional physician coverage for non-COVID patients in the Main area...7:00 a.m. to 7:00 p.m., Monday–Thursday: Dr. Steve Greene; Friday to Saturday: Dr. Preston Drillman

ED tent opening today...will be staffed by a physician and a PA/NP

We will begin working in Physician-PA/NP teams in each patient care area

Hospital has adequate supply of PPE at present

Of note, New York Times article today: just arrived from China yesterday, for distribution to NY, NJ, CT: 130,000 N95 masks; 1.8 million face masks and gowns; ten million gloves; thousands of thermometers

Please make sure to review the FAQs below:

FAQ:

If I feel unwell, when must I stay home from work?

If you feel unwell, you should not come to work. If you are experiencing fever, cough, or

flu-like symptoms, please call employee health (9:00–5:00 p.m., Monday–Friday). A physician will review your symptoms and, if indicated, order a COVID-19 test. For health concerns outside of these business hours, or if you are working from home and develop flu-like symptoms, please use *Virtual Urgent Care*.
LP March 30, 2020

Michael pushed himself back from the desk, closing his laptop. Dr. Jappnone was one of their anesthesiologists. *He must have gotten a face-full during an intubation*, he thought. He was shocked by the numbers. He had no idea the incidence was so high and that so many people were in the ICU. He was getting agitated again. He felt he had to do something—anything—or he was going to explode. He went to the garage where he had a corner set up with his weights and started an aggressive workout. An hour later, sweaty and exhausted, he took a shower and crawled in next to Pam. He gathered her up in arms and fell asleep with his face buried against her neck.

Michael was happy to be off for a few days. He needed to recover from the shock of the last shift. As he was having his morning coffee, he turned on the news.

March newscasts:

Ten New York City playgrounds are being closed due to overcrowding, the mayor said. Queens, Staten Island, Bronx, Brooklyn playgrounds will be shut down.

Nonessential construction work must end immediately, while essential construction is still a go. Those in nonessential construction who do not cooperate will be fined and closed down immediately.

He then went to his email for updates from the ER medical director:

COVID Update—Wednesday, April 1, 10:00 a.m.

    1.   MICU, SICU, Neuro ICU, Peds ICU, PACU, 4B, 3B, Cath recovery room,

2. M.S.E. conference center, Endoscopy, 1 Porter all dedicated to COVID pts
3. There is now only one floor in hospital available for non-COVID pts (2 WEST)

Census

- 306 COVID positive pts; additional 88 PUIs
- 9 COVID ICU beds available (there are currently 111 ICU beds)
- Next ICU area: OR (8 beds)
- 2 beds available for non-critical COVID admits
- Next non COVID area: TBD I anticipate additional tent for ED patients Michael scrolled down to the next email:

As of April 1, 9:00 a.m. (testing began March 4)…

- 1601 pts tested for COVID
  - ○ 815 positives
  - ○ 688 negatives
  - ○ 98 pending
- Total expirations: 44

A bit of good news, 2 patients were extubated in the past 24 hours. We have received total 68 vents from national stockpile

BEGINNING TODAY, COVID TESTS WILL BE RUN IN HOUSE… TAT (TURNAROUND TIME) APPROXIMATELY 2 HOURS

Regarding the tents:

FAQs:

- Are there HEPA filters connected to those negative pressure hoses?
  Yes. But please keep an eye out when walking from trauma bay to the tent. There is no need to walk directly in front of the vents.

- Should we be doing VBGs[18] and blood cultures on COVID patients?
  No. They should be reserved only for non-COVID patients who meet sepsis criteria.
  JP March 31, 2020

April newscasts:

"Record unemployment: unemployment claims surged by more than 1,000 percent in New York last week to nearly 370,000 initial claims. 6,648,000 people applied for unemployment in one week. This is now the largest ever documented by the weekly jobless claims report by the Labor Department. More people have filed for unemployment over the last 2 weeks than live in New York City" (ABC NEWS Channel 7).

Michael went back to work, and only now there were tents outside the emergency room. They started with one tent; later on, there would be three. *The hospital must be full to capacity. We are working in a MASH unit now*, Michael thought ruefully. He remembered watching reruns of the hit show *MASH* with Pam. Now here he was in his own MASH unit.

Michael saw he was assigned to the tent where patients with suspected COVID would be cared for. Patients were triaged outside the emergency room by the entrance to the hospital, then they were walked or put in a wheelchair and brought into the tent.

The tent held only ten chair slots and filled up immediately. Several were in various stages of desaturation, but many were still chatting away on cell phones as their families were waiting outside. They were not allowed in the tent.

Michael and the other nurses were quickly getting patients into geri chairs, checking their vital signs and oxygen saturation. He was working with two strangers, both out-of-state volunteers working through an agency.

---

[18] Venous blood gases: Less invasive than an arterial stick, these still give a lot of information about a person who may be septic.

Michael quickly knew that many of the patients might have to be intubated within hours. But where were all the ventilators? The stretchers? He called respiratory therapy, "Hey, we're going to need vents down here in the tent."

"We're doing the best we can, but you know if a patient needs to be intubated, they can't stay in the tent."

Dr. P walked in to look at who was in the tent. "Can we have a small huddle here?" he said to Michael and the other two nurses.

"Listen, guys, we have to re-triage all these folks. We can't intubate them all. We can't even give them all oxygen. We can't bring them all inside. There is just no room. We don't even have oxygen set up in the tent because there is no oxygen feed. We have to keep stable patients only. So let's round and figure this out." He paused and repositioned himself, so all four were facing one another.

"We have to FaceTime their families and discuss goals of care."

"Wait, what? You mean a DNR discussion on the phone?" Michael felt the wind knocked out of him. "Perhaps a goodbye on the phone? Who is going to make these calls?"

"I will. But I'm going to need your help, Michael."

Dr. P walked over to each person in a chair and looked at them. He reviewed their vital signs, looked at their makeshift charts, which held a little information about each one.

"Can anyone fill me in here about PMH on any of these folks? Did any of them get chest x-rays yet?"

"Nope."

"Blood gas, coags, CMPs?"

"Yes, all of them."

"Michael, please walk with me. And let's call someone from anesthesia. Let's try to get Murray Stein."

They walked around to all the patients in the tent, reviewed their sats and vital signs. Dr. P asked each one about their medical history.

"Okay, let's have another huddle here."

Dr. Stein came down. "Hey, Jack, what do we want to do here?"

"Well, I'm sorry to say we need to consider who should be intubated or put on HIGH-FLOW and sent inside and who should be sent home."

"Oh god, I never thought I would have to make these types of decisions in my own hospital."

"Murray, could you go have a look at these patients and tell us what you think?" Michael, Dr. P, and Dr. Stein went to each chair.

The first patient, a forty-year-old man, John Masterson, an electrician at an apartment complex in NYC, was talking excitedly on his cell with his wife and daughter that were outside the ER. "Honey, it's okay, they are taking good care of me." John's sat was 88 on 100 percent non-rebreather mask hooked up to a portable tank that was soon to run out.

"He needs to be inside," said Dr. P. "Hi, John," said Dr. P, "this is Dr. Stein from anesthesia, we need to talk to you."

"Where's respiratory?" Stein said to Michael.

"I'll call," Michael replied.

"John, your oxygen saturation is pretty low, which means your body organs are not getting enough blood supply to function. It is possible that you will require a ventilator, a breathing machine, soon to make sure your body is getting enough oxygen."

"Okay, Doc, what are you saying to me? I'm gonna die without a breathing machine?"

"We will do everything to avoid that, but I have to be straight with you. It is possible, I'm sorry to say."

John's wife, Melissa, was on the other end of the phone. "Honey, let them do what they have to do. We can't live without you," she said with desperation.

"Will I come off the breathing machine?"

"I can't say for certain."

"What do you mean? You can't tell me whether I'm gonna live or die?"

Melissa was crying on the other end of the phone. "Doctor, please save my husband." The staff could hear her clearly. Dr. P picked up the phone to see Melissa pacing outside in the parking lot, holding on to their daughter's hand. She was distraught, crying hysterically. "Can't I please come inside? I need to see my husband."

"I am sorry, but it is just too dangerous to have visitors in here now. We are not sure yet how fast this virus is spreading, and we don't want you to become ill."

"Oh my god, how can this be happening?" Melissa said, crying. "How can we talk about this now? On the phone!"

"Melissa, this is Murray Stein, the anesthesiologist." Dr. P handed the phone over. "We are going to try to put your husband on something called HIGH-FLOW oxygen, where we give him a high content of oxygen under pressure through nasal prongs. We will see how he does. We are also going to turn him on his belly to see if we can get some more oxygen in his lungs. And we will hope for the best."

"Hey, Doc, I'm turning over already," said John, as he tried to turn over on his belly in the recliner chair. "I really don't feel that bad right now."

Michael jumped in. "Let's put your phone on its charger so we keep it running. I want you to stay quiet for a while on the HIGH-FLOW, preserve your energy for breathing." He spoke to the phone. "Melissa, you talk to your husband, but just talk to him, play him some music, let him rest and breathe." Michael called into the main ER, "I am bringing John Masterson in. He needs HIGH-FLOW."

"Well, we have no room" came the reply. "Well, make some damn room, 'cause he's comin' in." Michael transferred John into a wheelchair and quickly wheeled him into the main ER area. There were chairs and stretchers everywhere. Every available space was now a makeshift slot of a patient.

"We all will be with you in here. Right, Stephanie?" Michael winked at her in a knowing way.

"Sure," said Stephanie soothingly. "We will be here with you." To herself, she despaired, how could she be there for all of these sick people?

Just then, Joseph from respiratory came in with the HIGH-FLOW setup.

"Put him on 30 L," said Dr. Stein. "Let's see if we can get him past this crisis."

"Okay, Doc, but just so you know, we don't have many HIGH-FLOW machines left."

Dr. P, Dr. Stein, and Michael went back to the remaining seven patients in the tent. They looked at the blood gases, vital signs, history, anything that would tell them if these patients were candidates for mechanical ventilation and whether they needed it imminently.

"Can we get x-ray down here?"

"Sure," said Michael, "I'll call Kyle. He should be covering down here today."

When they were done rounding, Dr. P, Dr. Stein, and Michael stood in the center of the tent out of earshot of all the patients and talked.

Michael was exhausted already. He had made rounds on eight patients whose life hung in the balance. *Fuck this, who am I to decide who gets to live and die?*

Kyle came in with the portable machine. "I don't have requisitions for all these people. Are they all wearing name bands?"

Michael chuckled. "It's just like you, Kyle, to keep things real. I'll make sure they all have name bands on." Michael went to each chair to make sure they all had proper identification. "Okay, Kyle, all good, shoot away."

Kyle went to each chair and introduced himself and asked to check each patient's name band.

"Kyle, please call me with each film?" Dr. P asked.

"Sure, Doc."

Dr. P and Murray Stein continued to confer about the patients. Michael joined them. Kyle brought each x-ray up on the portable screen. Out of the current eight patients in the tent, it was decided that only five should be admitted and monitored if they needed it, intubated. The other three patients just had too many comorbidities or were too old to survive possible intubation, sedation, initiation of pressors, central lines, etc. They would have to talk to these families waiting outside the emergency room about taking them home.

Of those, one was the hardest for Michael. She was a seventy-year-old retired teacher who lived with her husband nearby. She had preexisting cardiomyopathy and poorly controlled diabetes. She desaturated dangerously every time she talked, but she had also made up her mind to die at home.

"I'm more scared of all of this than dying in my own bed, my own home. We've talked about this, Larry and me. We're ready. I can feel it's time." In fact, Larry was outside the tent and even had a small portable oxygen tank ready. Where he got it, no one had time to ask. But based on this woman's x-ray and blood gas, she would not be needing it for long. Michael thought she had only hours left rather than days, and his heart went out to Larry. It was another uphill struggle to find an ambulance to get her home—they were all so busy bringing patients in, but Michael and Dr. P managed.

Dr. P, along with Murray Stein and Michael, picked up each patient's cell phone to FaceTime their relative that was either pacing outside or waiting in their car.

Dr. P was gentle in approach and spoke eloquently and calmly. "Your family member seems surprisingly well at the moment," he would say. "I think it's best if you take him/her home right now and let them be comfortable in their own surroundings. They really are not right for admission to the hospital at this juncture." He spoke about isolating them whenever possible. He did get pushback from some, but most people were happy to take their family member home. They thought it was a sign that they weren't sick at all, which was not the case. Michael felt he needed to explain to some of these family members, but there wasn't time. He let the physicians do the talking.

Michael and Kyle stood and overheard some of these conversations as they did their work, knowing that some of those same patients would be back perhaps within hours. Or maybe not at all. They looked at each other, not knowing what to say. They just witnessed patients and their families being told in so many words that they were going home to die.

They nodded at each other; Kyle went on his way. Michael put on his game face and went back to work with the patients who needed him. He felt desolate. All he could see was Larry standing outside in the parking lot with that little green tank, thinking he was getting his wife back.

Chapter 10

The Orthopedic Floor
March 2020

Fran's phone rang. It was a nurse from the step-down unit calling for report on Mrs. Cobb. By this time, it was after 5:00 a.m., and Fran was getting tired. She knew she had a full day ahead of her with Robby and Lilly.

"So what's up with Mrs. Cobb?" said the voice on the other end. "I read most of the notes. Your ortho PA Annie already talked to the medical PA over here. She is thinking post-op pneumonia."

Fran was hesitant to say what she was really thinking. "Thanks for that," said Fran. She went over the details of the shift she spent with Mrs. Cobb. "It doesn't seem like she has a surgical problem any longer. Whatever is going on, it is medical, and she needs care that the orthopedic service is not prepared to give. She is a genuinely nice woman, and I am hoping the best for her," Fran said as she hung up the phone.

Fran called for transport, packed up all of Mrs. Cobb's belongings, and promised to call her family to update them. She was hoping that Annie remembered to call Dr. Gregorio about all of these findings. After all, he was the attending.

Fran looked at her watch, 5:30 a.m., a little too early to call the Cobb family. "But what if Annie never called Gregorio? What if the family comes in early and sees she's not here?" Fran's conscience could not allow her to not let this family know the status of their beloved family member. "I'll wait until 6:00 a.m. then call," she decided. She wrote down the phone number of the son on her report sheet.

Fran went on her last set of rounds, started her early morning finger sticks, offered pain medication to her patients she knew would be having early physical therapy, and ordered the early breakfast trays. Fortunately, everyone was doing well this morning. As she walked around the unit, she noticed the isolation signs again. *What is with all this?* Fran pulled up the names of a few of the isolation patients on her computer to see if she could get some information on their isolation status. Mr. Jackson, eighty, right knee replacement, awaiting rehab placement, temp spike two days post-op, chest x-ray with patchy infiltrates, being treated for pneumonia.

Mrs. Sommerstein, seventy-six, status post-fall at home with left hip fracture, left ORIF, complained of shortness of breath three days post-op, fevers, chest x-ray normal, awaiting CT scan of the chest.

Fran stopped looking. Her heart sank. She knew.

At 6:00 a.m., she called Mrs. Cobb's son. "Hi, this is Fran. No emergency—I just wanted to tell you that we moved Mom to the step-down unit for closer monitoring."

"What?" said the voice on the other end. "What happened?"

Fran recognized Mrs. Cobb's son's voice. "Well, it's possible she developed a pneumonia, which sometimes happens when an older person has anesthesia and doesn't move around a lot. I am sure Dr. Gregorio will call you to explain in more detail. I just did not want you to come for a visit and not find her here. She is now in room 379, 3 North."

"Thanks for the call, we really appreciate it," said the voice on the other end.

Fran gave report to the day shift. She was glad to have the next three days off.

Fran arrived home and removed her scrubs, shoes, and underclothes outside in the back before running into the shower. She put them in a big plastic garbage bag for laundering later. She made herself a cup of tea and picked up her tablet to read the news on her iPad.

"WHO calls on industry and governments to increase manufacturing by 40 per cent to meet rising global demand. The World

Health Organization has warned that severe and mounting disruption to the global supply of personal protective equipment (PPE)—caused by rising demand, panic buying, hoarding and misuse is putting lives at risk from the new coronavirus and other infectious diseases."[19]

Fran got up, looked at her kids sleeping peacefully in the other room, walked into the bathroom, and looked in the mirror. She thought she looked pale. Inside, she was afraid.

The next bunch of days, Fran busied herself with the kids and taking care of the apartment. She went shopping with her mom to stock up on supplies. At all the outlet stores, paper and cleaning products were in short supply. In fact, there were shelves in Walmart and Costco that were empty. *What? Even large diapers?* She went to the store manager to see if there were any in the back. Fortunately, he was able to come up with a box.

"That's all?"

"Sorry."

"Ma, we're gonna have to try another store."

Fran needed large diapers for Robby. They went to the local supermarket where things were more expensive, but what choice did she have?

The day before Fran was scheduled to go back to work, she received a call from her charge nurse.

"Hi, Fran, Laura here. How are you? I'm calling because the hospital has canceled a lot of the orthopedic surgery for the next two weeks, so we will be taking medical patients here."

"Oh okay." Fran replied.

"Okay, see you tomorrow. Have a nice night."

What was that all about? Fran thought. That was very weird. Laura never called her. Why would she call about a change in surgery schedules?

She turned on the nightly news.

"The United States confirmed 272 additional cases, bringing the total number to 1,272, seven more deaths were reported, bring-

---

[19] World Health Organization March 3, 2020, news release, Geneva.

ing the total to 38. As a result, the NBA suspended the entire season after the night's games."[20] She changed the channel.

"One week later, the United States confirmed 1676 new cases, bringing the total number to 6,135, with 25 more deaths reported, bringing that number to 112. The Brooklyn Nets announced that four of their players tested positive, including Kevin Durant."[21]

Fran now knew what Laura was trying to tell her. Things on her floor were going to change in a fundamental way. She remembered the supplies she had bought a month ago at Costco. *Time to keep them in my car*, she thought.

Fran arrived at work at her usual time of 6:30 p.m. She walked into the locker room. The first thing she noticed was the garbage can filled with masks and gloves. *I wonder what that's all about?* she thought. *Why wasn't this emptied?*

She arrived on the floor and looked around. She noticed the signs on the first set of rooms. Droplet precautions, contact precautions, airborne precautions. All signs were up on every room. *Well, which one is it? And, what on earth is going on around here?* She walked to the desk to see the day shift sitting in gowns, wearing surgical masks and gloves. This went against everything she was taught in school and during her orientation on infection control.

"What's going on?" she asked Laura, who was sitting at the main desk in full PPE.

Laura handed her a bag. Inside were three gowns, one N95 mask, and three surgical masks. "Put the extra masks in your locker. This is now the PUI—persons under investigation—unit. All of these patients are waiting for the results of their COVID tests. They are here for various complaints. Wear your N95 and a surgical mask over it. You have two more surgical masks to wear over your N95 for your three shifts this week."

"Are there no surgical patients still left?" asked Fran, reeling.

"Yes, down at the end of the hallway, they are PUI, too, unless they get discharged." Fran could tell Laura was angry. In fact, there

---

[20] Reuters, March 11, 2020.
[21] CNN, March 18, 2020.

was anger in everyone, the way they were all speaking with one another. It was as though they felt someone was at fault, but they did not know who.

She overheard bits and pieces of conversations of the day staff. "They must have known." "Where is all the PPE being stored?" "Why don't we have access to everything we need?"

Fran was surprisingly calm about all of this. She had heard from friends in Italy and family in Greece, and she had been following the news. She knew this was to be expected. However, it felt different to be on her unit now. There was an aura of fear that was palpable. Everyone was in a bad mood.

Chapter 11

Critical Care
April 2020

NYPD Reports 10th Death from Suspected Case
of Coronavirus

New York Police Department Auxiliary
Police Lt. Pierre Moise died on March 28 from
complications due to coronavirus, according to a
daily coronavirus report from NYPD.

Moise was assigned to the 71st Precinct in
Brooklyn and became an NYPD Auxiliary Police
Officer on August 21, 1994, the NYPD report
said. He is the 10th NYPD death from a suspected case of coronavirus.

On Friday, 6,698 uniformed members of
the NYPD were out sick, which accounts for 18.5
percent of the department's uniformed work-
force, according to the daily NYPD coronavirus
report. Currently 1,775 uniformed members and
260 civilian members have tested positive for
COVID-19, the report says. (CNN, Laura Ly,
April 4, 2020)

Sandy took out her iPad and thumbed through Instagram.

MLB Pitcher Justin Verlander and his wife
Kate Upton to donate MLB paychecks to
coronavirus charities

Huston Astros pitcher Justin Verlander and wife Kate Upton announced on Instagram that they will be donating Verlander's weekly MLB paychecks to coronavirus charities.

@kateupton and I have decided to donate those funds to a different organization each week so that we can support their efforts and highlight the great work they're doing during the COVID-19 crisis.

Joni was trying to stay away from her family by essentially moving in with Sandy. In her household, she had both her parents and two brothers, but also her mother's mother who was in her eighties. Joni had to go to work every day in the lab, and although she didn't have direct patient care, she was cognizant that her risk for exposure to CoV-2 was higher than either of her brothers, who by this time were working from home. They were not quite at the moving-in stage yet, but Sandy agreed Joni should isolate from her grandmother. Luckily, her apartment was big enough. Half the closet was empty, so there was room for Joni to settle in without living out of a suitcase.

Their schedules were rather different, because Sandy worked three twelve-hour days and Joni worked five days a week, Sunday to Thursday. Sandy always tried to get Fridays off so at least they could be sure of one day off together. This week was propitious because Sandy was off for both Friday and Saturday.

"Though what we can do, I have no idea," she said to Joni. "We can't go to the movies or to dinner or visit with anyone." This was really the early days of social distancing, but both of them were determined to follow the guidelines. In some ways, Sandy felt weird about being so careful to stay away from strangers when her highest risk was what she did every day at work.

"How about *Doom Eternal*?" Sandy asked Joni.

"Fuck *yeah*!" Joni said, only partially kidding.

They spent time exploring it. "It's so different than 2016," Sandy said happily. "Look, the chain saw is just a button now... You don't have to fool around taking it out..." They finally took a break after two hours to go shopping for food and stretch their legs early on Friday afternoon. They spent the rest of the weekend watching the news in horror, calling family and reassuring them, cooking, and napping, and too soon, Sunday morning rolled around.

When Sandy returned to work, she requested to take care of Ray again. But she looked around the unit, and it seemed to have changed overnight. All twenty beds were filled with patients that sounded exactly like Ray. In fact, Ray was doing the best out of all of them.

"Sure, Sandy, you can have Ray, but he comes with two other patients," said Jan.

"You mean I am tripled? With vents and drips?"

"Not just you, everyone is. Your PPE is in this drawer." Jan tapped one of the drawers outside the room to the side of the computer. "We have had a bunch of sick calls throughout the hospital."

Sandy looked around. *Is this really happening?*

Everyone in the unit was on a ventilator, the glass doors were shut, and the vents were facing the doorway so one could look in and see the vent setting without having to go into the room. The attendings had requested that the pumps be outside the room with extension tubes so that drip rates could be changed without having to go into the room.

That meant that even though the IV sites and central line sites were on the other side of the bed, they were draped across the patients so they could monitor the pumps from outside. *Where am I?* Sandy thought. She thought back longingly for her grandmother and the days when they watched *The Wizard of Oz.*

Sandy looked in her PPE drawer. There were six pairs of gloves, one gown, one N95 and two surgical masks. *WTF?* She walked across the unit to Nero, another nurse. "What have you got in your drawer?"

"Same as you." He shrugged. "I can use six pairs of gloves in an hour on one patient."

"We are wearing the same mask, gown, and gloves between patients? This is nuts! This is contrary to everything we have been taught! I never heard of such a thing!"

"Me either," said Nero. "This is beyond anything we have ever learned about infection control." Sandy went back to her assignment. She saw Dr. Camarie coming around the corner to make rounds. He was in scrubs instead of his usual spotless shirt and tie, and he was wearing a long isolation OR jacket, N95 with face shield, and gloves.

How come he gets a face shield? Sandy thought. *What does he know, and who does he know?*

Sandy took a deep breath and went to start her day. She put on her PPE and went into Ray's room.

She noticed that he was off the propofol and Versed drips but getting PRN (as needed) doses of Ativan and Dilaudid.[22] He now had a tracheostomy and a PEG. Gone was the dialysis catheter, and she could tell by the Foley catheter his urine output was normal. She saw the tube feeding going.

Oh my god, he's tolerating feedings! she thought.

"Hey, Ray, it's Sandy." Ray's eyes fluttered open. "You're awake! Hey, buddy, you've been out for a while, but you are getting better! It's so good to see you awake." Ray nodded slowly. Sandy could see that he was trying to mouth words. She tried hard to make out what he was trying to tell her. He had mittens on his hands, so Sandy assumed that he had been pulling at his lines. She bent down close to his face. "What are you trying to tell me?"

"Mom," he mouthed weakly.

"Oh, your mom, I'll go check and see where she is."

What Sandy did not know was that all visitors had been banned from the hospital just days earlier.

"Let me finish checking you out, and I'll go and see." Ray nodded and went back to sleep. Sandy looked at his vent settings. *Almost in the weanable range.* No longer was he on a high level of PEEP, his FIO2 was down to 35 percent, and his respirations were within normal range. In fact, she had seen orders for CPAP trials today for two hours. CPAP is where the ventilator is set for some pressure sup-

---

[22] This would lessen the amount of sedation he had on board but would prevent him from being in pain or becoming too anxious.

port and PEEP, but no breaths are delivered by the machine, so the patient is doing all the breathing on their own.

Sandy suctioned him, noticed his secretions were not as dark as they had been, and she checked his PEG site, tube feeding rate. She did oral care with the chlorhexidine swabs that were in the room. *My god, he's so thin*, she thought. *But he's awake, and that's a good thing.* Sandy suddenly realized she had two more patients to take care of and could not afford to spend all her time with Ray. She went to doff her PPE, but suddenly realized that there was not another set to put on. She stood at the doorway for a moment and looked across the unit.

She saw Nero coming out of his patient's room and, with the same PPE, go into the next room. Sandy was horrified. *What in the world is going on here?* When nurses are taught isolation technique, one of the most important parts is getting rid of all the PPE used with one patient and careful hand hygiene and donning fresh PPE for the next patient. To share PPE from one patient to another is so antithetical, it is practically surreal.

She walked out and into the next room. She was not prepared for what she would see. Peter Murphy, thirty-eight, was already proned. He was admitted the night before with cough, fever, rapid desaturation requiring intubation, and chemical paralysis. He was on propofol, Versed, and Nimbex, the cocktail for those who had been hard to sedate. He was on Levophed to maintain his blood pressure, had a central line and dialysis catheter for CRRT. Sandy had read in his chart that he had recently had his first baby, a son, only weeks earlier. Peter was a police officer, NYPD, stationed in Queens. He had been feeling sick for a few days but had not wanted to seek medical attention as his wife was home with their newborn. His wife, Cindy, had taken him to the ER where she was not allowed in but had to leave him there. She had heard from Jason that there had been quite a commotion down in the emergency room when Cindy was told she could not stay. Sandy noticed there was a cell phone next to his bed.

Sandy began her usual system assessment, train of fours, listening to his lungs, suctioning him, doing oral care, reviewing his medications, calibrating the CRRT machine, when the cell phone rang.

It was a FaceTime request. Sandy picked up the phone and immediately saw a young woman, obviously distraught on the other end.

"Hey, are you Pete's nurse?" said the voice.

"Yes! Hi, I'm Sandy."

"Can I please see my husband? Please just flip the phone and let me see him. I just have to see him." The woman sounded desperate.

So this is what we're doing now, Sandy thought. *No visitors, so we are doing it by phone.* Even for Sandy, brought up in the cell phone world, this seemed like a stretch. "I just want to tell you he is on his belly. To better oxygenate him. He is a bit puffy looking, so don't let that alarm you."

"Please just go up to his face so I can talk to him." Sandy knew she still had a third patient to get to, but she couldn't not honor this request. "Okay, I am going up to him now." She turned the image around.

Sandy heard a scream. She turned the phone back around.

"What's wrong, Cindy? I told you to expect to see him on his belly."

"It doesn't look like my Peter, are you sure you are in the right room?"

"Yes, Cindy, I am in the room with your husband, Peter. I am so sorry you have to see him like this, but this will only be temporary, we hope. Do you want to try again?"

"Yes, please," she said, crying outright now, "I want him to see our son, Jared."

"Okay, let's go."

Sandy turned the phone around again near Peter's face. She heard the voice at the other end. "Please, Peter, wake up! I have Jared here. Our son! Please wake up, we need you. I need you. I love you so much!" Cindy was hysterical. Sandy did her best to explain everything that was happening, particularly that Peter could not wake as he was heavily sedated.

"I can't believe this. We were just talking last night, we were finishing up the nursery, then he didn't feel well. He wouldn't go to the emergency room because he didn't want to leave us." Cindy was talking and crying at the same time.

Sandy said gently, "Cindy, let me get back to taking care of Peter again. We can talk again later when I'm back in the room." Cindy was sobbing. "I need to be with my husband. I need to be there. Please let me come. Please."

"I am so sorry, but this is for your protection."

"When will you be back in the room?" Sandy knew it would not be for a while.

"I'll tell you what, when I come back in, I'll FaceTime you and you can be on the phone when I'm taking care of Peter."

"Please don't let it be too long, I don't know what to do with myself."

Sandy could hear the desperation in her voice. "I promise, Cindy. Now let me go and care for him, and we'll talk later."

Sandy was in tears when she hung up. Her N95 was rubbing against her face and was wet inside from her own tears. Sandy could feel the flexible metal piece cutting into the bridge of her nose. Suddenly Sandy felt like she could not breathe. She walked over to the door and lifted the N95 up slightly and took a breath of the stale hospital air, but it was better than nothing. She glanced up at the monitor. *Vitals stable for now.* Sandy wondered how long that would last.

Sandy put Purell from the dispenser on her gloved hands. It felt slimy, it felt weird, it felt wrong.

She walked into the next room.

The loudspeaker wailed, "*Code blue ICU, code blue ICU.*" Sandy looked across the unit, it was Nero's patient. She ran across the room. She stopped at the door. Inside was Nero, Dr. Camarie, and Denise, the respiratory therapist. She looked up at the monitor. The heart rate of this patient was in the 20s. Denise was bagging the patient; Nero was standing on a stool over the patient's chest ready to start compressions. The sat was reading 63 on the monitor.

Dr. Camarie put his hand up. They all waited. The patient's heart rate went down and then to asystole. Dr. Camarie listened to the chest. Denise stopped bagging.

"Time of death—11:28 a.m."

Jan was suddenly standing there. "We need the bed."

Sandy whirled around, angry. "What about his family, what if they want to—"

"Stop!" yelled Jan. "It's Maureen, she's in the ER. They are intubating her, she needs the damn bed."

Sandy felt the room start to spin.

Sandy had to sit down. The small kernel of nascent fear she walked around with all the time suddenly blossomed into a near full-on panic attack. *One of our own,* she thought. *How could this happen?* Sandy racked her brain. Had Maureen looked sick the last time she saw her? She couldn't actually recall when that was.

Sandy thought back to all the times they had worked together, side by side. She thought about the patients they took care of and how no one was on any isolation precautions. *Could some of those patients with sepsis and ARDS have had undiagnosed COVID? Could we have been better prepared?* And then the thing she was avoiding all along, *Oh, shit, am I gonna get this now?* and the corollary *Could I have given it to Joni?* She started to think of the rest of the staff, especially Ethan. *He hasn't even finished nursing school yet.*

She shook herself up. *Sandy, get a grip—there are other patients who need care.* Sandy knew that this bed, now reserved for Maureen, was Nero's admission. She so desperately wanted to take care of Maureen. Nero was a capable nurse, but somehow Sandy thought she was better. She was chosen to take care of Ray, one of their first (so they thought) cases of COVID, and she had the experience with Dr. Camarie and proning and sedation and all that. Sandy just felt she could do a better job.

Maybe I'm taking myself too seriously, she thought. *All these patients deserve care, but this is Mo. I really need to be the one.* Sandy knew she would not stop until she did everything—and anything—she could to save Maureen's life.

Nero and another nurse were preparing the body of the last patient to take down to the morgue. The family had been called, and since the hospital was no longer allowing visitors, they had to arrange the services from home.

When Nero was done, he called transport, and Jason, a new transporter, was sent up to assist with taking the body downstairs. Nero had to go since they only sent one person.

The room was cleaned and prepared for the admission. Denise got the ventilator ready. Nero got back from downstairs. He was sweating. "You're not gonna believe this!" he said aloud. "There's no space in the morgue! We had to go outside. There is a truck out there, for bodies." Sandy was in with her third patient, on a vent, sedated, the usual cocktail of drips, wearing the same PPE as she had in the other rooms. She looked down at the sedated woman knowing she was going to have to prone her in another hour, looking at the Levophed drip, the fentanyl, propofol, Versed, insulin. *Who is this woman? She is someone's mom, grandma, wife, sister. Will she make it off the ventilator? Is any of this going to work?* Sandy sighed. *I have to try.* Sandy also had to go back to Peter Murphy, where his wife was anxiously waiting for another FaceTime call. *Oh god, a man with a new baby, then there is Ray, a kid himself, not much younger than me, waiting for his mom who can't come. He's never gonna understand that.* She was busy trying to figure out her work priorities, finally realizing she was stuck. *What do I do first? This is not safe care,* she thought. She wondered how long the nurses would have to work under these weird and dangerous circumstances.

She walked out of her room without doffing her PPE, despite that it was against her training and instinct. She felt she was trailing germs wherever she went without changing the protective gown and gloves. She was just in time to hear Nero's remark about the truck outside.

"What? There's a truck for bodies outside?"

"Yup." Nero looked as though someone had slapped him.

"How many are in there?"

"Couldn't really see. But a lot. They are just piled up on top of each other. It's just awful."

"Oh god, I hope I never have to go down there. Was there a lift or something?"

"Yeah, it's like a refrigerated moving van. There is an electric lift, and we had to lift the body onto it then pull it inside and on top of someone else. It's disgusting, dehumanizing—I hope the families never have to see this."

Nero went to wipe down the IV poles and infusion pumps. He then got extra IV tubing to set the pumps up outside the door, set up the sequential compression devices, and get the hypothermia blanket ready for Maureen to come up.

The emergency room was calling to give report.

The entire staff of the ICU lined the hallway as Maureen was brought up. She was accompanied by Dr. Camarie, who was on his cell phone talking to Carly, Maureen's daughter. Also helping the transport was Dr. Werman, the anesthesiologist, an ER nurse, and Ethan, who had been sent down to help.

Everyone overheard Dr. Camarie speaking to Carly. "I know, I know, we don't know how it happened, but it did. Yes, she was likely exposed here. We are doing everything in our power to help her get better. Yes, she will have the best team. Okay, Carly, yes. I will have your Mom's cell phone in the room, and we will FaceTime you when we get her settled."

Everyone gathered and walked behind the stretcher like a procession. The staff were all crying.

Maureen did not look good.

Nero was in the room waiting to transfer Maureen to her bed. All the supplies were perfectly set up. Propofol was already primed and ready to replace the one from the ER. The fentanyl drip was already in the pump ready to go, as was the Levophed. He had the overbed table at the head of the bed ready to prone her. Dr. Werman wrote the orders for the vent settings. Sandy looked over his shoulder at the settings: AC 18, TV 400, FIO2 80, PEEP 10. *Lots of support*, thought Sandy, wondering how bad her arterial blood gas results were.

Everyone went into the room.

"I know we all want to be here," said Dr. Camarie gently, "but we have enough people to prone her, so some of you need to step out. I will help prone her now, and we will get a gas and see where we are. Stan"—referring to Dr. Werman—"will you please manage the airway?"

"Got it, Henry."

Denise, Ethan, Nero, Sandy, Jan, Dr. Werman, and Dr. Camarie stayed in the room. "Let's try to get her from the stretcher right onto her belly." Maureen was a tall thin woman. But her appearance shocked Sandy, who thought, *My god, she has lost so much weight!* She wondered how long Maureen had been sick. She couldn't remember the last day they had worked together.

"Sandy!" She snapped back as Dr. Camarie ordered the staff to take their places.

The stretcher was set up next to the bed. Ethan was down at the foot of the bed holding the stretcher and bed together. Sandy and Ethan locked eyes for a moment. Both of them were thinking how grim this looked. They each thought, *I wonder if I'm next.*

Dr. Werman was at the head of the bed ready to go. Denise and Nero were on one side, Sandy and Jan on the other. "Okay," said Dr. Camarie, "one, two, three." Denise and Nero pulled Maureen on her side while Sandy and Jan held on to the sheets so she would land perfectly in the bed. Jan had the electrodes for her back. Dr. Werman draped Maureen's arms over the overbed table, which Nero had cushioned with a pillow.

Nero expertly hooked up all the new tubing to Maureen's central line, pumps out of the door. He also clamped her oral gastric tube, careful to put a gauze pad underneath so it would not leave a mark on her cheek. Sandy thought, *What do we do now?* but she was impressed with how detail oriented Nero was being and realized he would take excellent care of Maureen.

I guess I should go back to my assignment and call Cindy Murphy. I did promise, she thought. Sandy walked away, turning around at almost every step to look back at Maureen, tears running down her face. The inside of her N95 was wet, but she no longer cared. *We will all probably get this sooner or later.* She briefly thought about her will, which her father insisted she make when she got her apartment. She thought about leaving everything to Joni now, and then her thoughts leapt to fear about her bringing this illness home to Joni. She thought about how devastated her parents would be if she died, and then thought about her grandmother. She was thankful her grandmother didn't live to see this mess. All of this went through her mind in the time it took her to do "hygiene" on her gloves.

She went into Peter Murphy's room to call Cindy. That was not going to be an easy call. She was exhausted, totally spent. She realized she had not eaten or had anything to drink since she got out of the car at six thirty this morning. It was 4:00 p.m.

She pressed the button for FaceTime. "Hi, Cindy, it's Sandy."

Sandy felt like she was just going through the motions of talking to Cindy. She knew that she deserved her full attention as she was so devastated about her husband's illness while taking care of a newborn. But Sandy could not get herself to focus on the conversation. She found herself saying "I know" and "I am so sorry" and a lot of "Uh-huhs." She was thankful for once about having the mask on. *At least Cindy can't see my face.*

Her mind was on Maureen. In fact, her mind was racing with thoughts of Maureen, her daughter Carly, and how they could get Maureen the best therapies. She realized she could call her friend's aunt who was a research nurse practitioner at Weill Cornell Medical College. She realized she had no idea if there was anything experimental going on that could help. She vowed to read all the research when she got home that night and reach out to her friend to get the aunt's email.

Sandy walked to the garage almost begrudgingly; she was hoping she might be asked to stay and do overtime so she could keep an eye on Maureen. She checked to see who was assigned to Maureen that shift. It was Jason, someone she had only minor confidence in. Ever since he tried to flirt with her, his appeal as a nurse diminished in her eyes.

She walked to the parking lot in full PPE, changed into a first set of clothing in the garage, and bagged up her PPE with her scrubs. When she arrived home, she sprayed down her gown with Lysol spray and put her N95 out in the back to air dry. It was full of sweat and tears from the day. Joni was there to greet her, but Sandy was only in the mood to research COVID-19.

Meanwhile, Joni, after hearing the news about Sandy's colleague Maureen, had already started the research. They read together but didn't get any idea of how to access anything. Sandy did email her friend Kia who replied almost immediately with her aunt's phone and email. Sandy didn't think she could call so late, so she sent an email. Almost immediately, even though it was nearly eleven, her phone rang.

"Sandy? It's Vanessa from Cornell. Kia called me to say one of your friends has COVID and is on a vent."

Sandy became very emotional and started to cry. "Yes, and it's not looking good…"

"We are doing both the remdesivir and sarilumab studies here, but we can't accept a transfer in and there is no mechanism to get the drugs outside our institution as of now. I'm so sorry. I will see if there is any way your friend could get compassionate access. I'll call you as soon as I find out anything."

It was a long time before Sandy and Joni could sleep.

Sandy came into the unit early in the morning to check to see if Nero was back, the usual courtesy being if you had an assignment the day before you would have the same one the next day. Nero was off, but she saw that Jerry, a veteran nurse, was assigned to Maureen. She had her same assignment as the day before. Ray, who was continuing to improve, Peter Murphy, and the older woman, Joan Marino, who was not doing well.

Ray was now being Hoyer-lifted[23] out of bed into a chair daily. He was off sedation, on a tracheostomy collar of 35 percent oxygen. However, he was weak and deconditioned. Physical therapy was coming up to see him daily now. Sandy was hopeful they would be able to stand him soon, prepare to remove his tubes—including the tracheostomy tube—and possibly send him home. Sandy was ecstatic for Ray and his parents with whom she FaceTimed daily, but her mind was still on Maureen. Ray was constantly pointing to his cell phone when she entered the room. Sandy knew he wanted to hear his parents speak to him, but she had little time for that, so she

---

[23] A Hoyer lift is a hydraulic assist device that allows one person to move an immobile person from the bed to a chair or back again. It uses a sling that is placed under the patient and hooked to the sling lift mechanism.

asked Tom, the physical therapist, to FaceTime the parents when he was in the room. *Problem solved*, she thought.

Cindy was a different story. Peter was still sedated, with a proning schedule, and on a high level of ventilator support. Sandy was hopeful he was young enough or some therapy would be available to help him, but at this time, she was doubtful.

She still called Cindy every time she was in the room, but often tuned her out. Cindy was always telling Peter to look at the baby, not really understanding why he could not. "Sandy, if only you could just stop the sedation for a few minutes and let him see his son, I know he would get better." Sandy understood Cindy's logic but had a hard time explaining to her that it would not be beneficial to Peter's care.

Her third patient, Joan Marino, a retired MTA employee, was in the worst condition of all. She had multiple medical problems, making her a poor candidate to recover. Still, she had the proning team come by, but by then almost every patient on the unit had to be proned, so some patients' schedules had to change. There were just not enough hands to do all the work. Since the cardiac cath lab had stopped operations and there were minimal surgeries being done, the nurses that had worked in those areas were floated to the critical care areas to help with the sickest patients. There was still not enough PPE, and there became a war over who was to provide it. Jan was adamant, floated nurses had to bring their own from their respective departments. The nurses coming down from the recovery room and the cath lab insisted they did not have any, and they were not going into the rooms without it.

Jan called the managers of those departments but only ended up with an argument. So the nurses ended up standing around a lot and running for supplies for the nurses in the rooms who did have PPE. This ended up being helpful because it was nearly impossible to foresee every contingency before entering the isolation room, and it was increasingly necessary to have someone on the outside to do that running. The recovery and cath lab nurses at first felt dismissed and demoted, but as the days went by and the workload only increased, they found a way to work efficiently together.

Sandy gave report to Jason. Report became mundane since everyone was the same. "Just keep 'em alive for the next shift," they all said.

Sandy went to her car, changed out of her PPE in the parking garage, double-bagged everything, and drove home. She was exhausted, physically and emotionally. Joni was waiting for her. Sandy had two much-needed days off. She had to do food shopping, some chores around her apartment. She was grateful for Joni being there all the time. The next day they went to Target, to stock up on much-needed items: food, hygiene products, cleaning supplies. When they got there, a line had formed outside the door. There were only a certain number of people allowed in the store at any one time, and the security person was quite strict about it. Everyone in the line was wearing a mask, and many were wearing gloves. As they approached the entrance, a large sign read: "EVERYONE MUST BE WEARING A FACE COVERING." When they looked around the parking lot, Sandy was astonished to see the ground littered with masks and gloves, even N95s. "Where are people getting N95s?" she said to Joni. "We need them so badly in the hospital, and there they all are in the fucking parking lot." They got inside, and many shelves were bare. No toilet paper, paper towels, Clorox wipes, virtually no cleaning supplies. They settled on a can of Comet for cleaning and bought the remaining two sponges on the shelf. People were panic buying all around them. "Jeez, do you think that couple needs all that cereal?" They watched an elderly couple sweep all the boxes of dry cereal into their cart. "Who needs thirteen boxes of Cheerios?" They laughed. They went up and down every aisle just in case they saw something that could be repurposed for the things that they needed. They bought a set of kitchen towels that could be used as dustrags. They were able to find a few protein bars and pretzels for Sandy to take to work as pocket snacks.

There were no vitamins, Tylenol, nasal spray, nor any form of over-the-counter medications for minor injuries or illnesses.

"It's a good thing we don't need diapers," said Joni. The children's supply aisle was bare.

They continued walking. There were no cases of water, no milk, no orange juice. They saw people with carts filled with soda instead.

"We will have to drink tap water."

"Fine by me."

"Or wine."

"Even better."

The final laugh for Sandy and Joni was watching a fight between two women over condensed milk cans. As one woman reached down to pick up a can of condensed milk, another woman just swooped in, grabbed the entire box of twenty-four cans, put them in her cart, and hurried off.

They stood there in disbelief. They looked at the woman who was trying to get only one can and laughed, but it was difficult to read anyone's emotions with masks on.

They went to another supermarket, only to find the same situation.

"Maybe we'd better order things online."

"We can try."

The next two days flew by. Chores were accomplished. They ate, watched TV, and researched more about COVID. Sandy tried hard not to think about Maureen, but Mo was never far from her thoughts. Joni knew when to be silent and sit with Sandy, and she knew when Sandy wanted to talk. Their relationship was stronger than ever.

Sandy packed for the next day at work. She wrapped her gown in plastic. Her N95 had been hanging on the terrace in a bag. Her cousin had sent her some homemade cloth masks from North Carolina and a decent version of a face shield that she packed.

Sandy felt like she needed a suitcase to go to work now. Since there were no water bottles, she packed a thermos of water with ice, a baggie of pretzels, and some protein bars since she knew there would be no time to eat.

Sandy was determined to take care of Maureen. She got there early and spoke to Jan.

"Maureen helped make me the nurse I am. Please, I would really like to take care of her today."

"Okay, but she is not your only patient. She comes in a doubled assignment."

"That's fine."

Sandy went first to the locker room where she remembered she still had the extra N95 that Keith had given her. She put it in her pocket. She went into the break room. There were pizza boxes, sandwiches, fruit, doughnuts, and all kinds of cakes and cookies. There were bottles of soda and water. There were napkins and paper towels. There were many thank-you cards and letters from surrounding businesses and restaurants that had sent over food and supplies. Sandy took two bottles of water and put them in her lunch bag. All that food in the morning was very unappealing, but she knew it would be gone by the end of the day. She went to take report. Stephanie was waiting for her. She looked exhausted. She was wearing her blue isolation gown, her N95, a surgical mask over it, goggles, and a plastic rain poncho with *Giordano's* written on the back. *What's with that?* Sandy thought. Stephanie had been a night nurse on the unit for over two decades. She knew Maureen well. Sandy could tell she had been crying.

"Who's gonna be next? I have grandchildren. My kids won't let me see them. I have to FaceTime my own grandchildren." Sandy let her vent for a few minutes.

"Well, it is a good thing FaceTime was invented. At least you can see their faces. It's better than just talking on the phone."

Stephanie nodded "I guess so." Sandy looked around to see who was on with her today. She saw Nero, and they nodded at each other. Then she saw Pete.

Over his gown, he was wearing a plastic rain poncho, again, with *Giordano's* written on it. *What* is *with that?* Sandy thought. She said to Stephanie, "We have rain ponchos for PPE now?"

"Oh yeah, Giordano's restaurant had them made up for us somehow." She opened the drawer. "Here's one for you."

"I can't wear a rain poncho over all this stuff."

"Well, you might want to use it so your gown doesn't get soiled." Sandy took the folded-up rain poncho in its plastic packet and put it in the side pocket of her scrubs. She thought about it; Stephanie was right, but it seemed so inappropriate to be advertising food in an effort to protect herself.

"Okay, let's get started."

"Who do you want first?"

"Give me Joan first," said Sandy.

"Well, she's not doing so well. In fact, she's a hot mess. She is only being proned every twelve hours now. She is up to 100 percent FIO2, PEEP of 12. They lowered her TV to 300 and upped her rate to 28. Her gasses suck." Sandy looked at her latest ABG on the computer. It was as bad as Stephanie said.

"She's still on Levo. We switched her over to a morphine drip at 6 milligrams per hour."

"No wonder she needs all that Levo."

"Well, there is no more propofol in the pharmacy, extraordinarily little Versed and fentanyl. Anyway, Joan is poorly responsive, so they are saving the other drugs for other patients that need more sedation. We have prn Ativan push orders."

"So I'm guessing we have enough Ativan?"

"For the moment."

"What are we really doing for her?"

"Waiting for the family to make her DNR. She has a history of heart disease. She is a diabetic, and has lots of comorbidities to make this a poor outcome." Sandy just nodded. Her thoughts went right to her grandmother, for whom she would have moved the world for just one more day. Her grandmother would not have wanted this, however much Sandy wanted her to stay. She realized there was no answer to this question, and she was happy not to have to be the one who decided to get treatment and who was left to die.

"Okay, on to Mo." Sandy had Maureen pulled up on her computer, already looking at her latest labs. "So she had a pretty uneventful night. I was able to go down on her Levo to .02 micrograms per minute."

"That's great, she came up on 1 microgram per kilogram. That's real progress."

"Her vent settings have stayed constant. AC 18, FIO2 80 percent, TV 400, PEEP 10."

"Lot of support."

"Yes, can't get her down past that, still paralyzed on Nimbex, train of fours two out of four twitches, Versed at four milligrams per hour, fentanyl at ten milligrams per hour."

"No propofol?"

"Nope—can't get it. Proning every six hours. She is tolerating her tube feeds, urine output adequate, hasn't had a bowel movement, so we put her on MiraLAX[24] daily until she has. Right subclavian central line, site benign, getting a bit of fluid fifty cubic centimeters per hour. Maybe that's helping her blood pressure."

"No dialysis?" Sandy said after reviewing her labs. "I see she bumped up her BUN and creatinine."

"Carly says no."

"Really?"

"Yup she told us last night on FaceTime that Mo said, 'Don't you ever put me on dialysis.' So she is quite adamant about that."

"Do we have a DNR status?" Sandy said, remembering what Mo had said many times when a hopeless patient came in.

"Well, Carly is her proxy. Her mom is a DNR, no compressions, but do everything else, for now."

"She's been intubated a little over a week now, are we thinking tracheostomy?"

"Not sure Carly will go for that. I have her on FaceTime every time I go in. Carly wants to see everything."

"Okay, got it. Steph, go home, get some rest. There's food in the lounge. Take some home so you don't have to cook."

"I think I will. Take good care of our Mo."

"You can count on it."

Sandy got right to it. She went into her charts, wrote down any pertinent labs she wanted to remember on a folded-up piece of paper. *This way I don't have to come out just to check on labs.* She saw there were a few nurses from the EPS lab standing around. "Does one of you want to come in here and help me turn Mo?"

---

[24] A laxative.

The three of them looked at one other and back at Sandy. They were dressed in their gowns, surgical masks, and they even had their ponchos on, but *no* N95s.

Tamara said, "*If* you get me an N95, I'll come in." Sandy thought about the extra N95 in her pocket but thought against it. "Forget it, can you just get me some ice packs, please, Mo has a temp." Indeed, her temperature by Foley catheter probe was 102.8. Sandy knew she had been given Tylenol earlier, so it was not time. "So where are the ice packs?" said Tamara. "We don't have any of those crushable ones you have upstairs, so you have to make me some."

Sandy was very frustrated because it seemed they could not think or problem-solve for her when she was stuck in the room. She was trying hard to be pleasant and not sarcastic. "Please go get a bio-hazard bag from the front desk in the top drawer, then go to the ice machine in our lounge and fill it up and bring it to me. In fact, get me at least four of them, thanks." Sandy could sense her frustration building and did not want it to interfere with her care of Mo or the phone call she was about to make to Carly.

Tamara was standing outside the door holding the four bags of ice, appearing as if she did not know what to do with them. "Uh, Sandy, I have them."

"Can you just toss them on the chair by the door, please? Thanks. And, Tamara, can you please check on Joan's pumps next door, they are outside the door, and call the pharmacy if I am running low on anything, please and thank you." Sandy turned to look at Mo.

The iPhone was ringing already. It was Carly. "Hey, Carly, it's Sandy. I know it's hard to tell faces through all the PPE we have to wear."

"What's going on with Mom now?"

"Well, she has a temp, and she has had Tylenol already, so I am having ice packs brought in to cool her down."

"Have you been able to go down on the Levo? The vent settings? Anything positive?"

"Well Stephanie was able to go down on the Levo during the night. I will see if I can shut it off later. Your mom's blood pressure is staying stable."

"Oh, that's good."

"Yes, it is, I will let you know my progress as the shift goes on. She had a bath already, but when Ethan comes in at 3:00 p.m., we will give her another bath."

"Okay, Sandy, thank you, can you call me the next time you are in the room? I know Mom is doubled with another patient."

"Yes, she is, and I will go check on the other patient now and be back in a bit. I'll call you as soon as I get back in the room."

Sandy went into Joan's room. It was clear that Joan was deteriorating. She required more Levo to maintain her blood pressure. Her level of responsiveness was such that she required little sedation. Joan was no longer being proned because it was not helping. Sandy did the perfunctory assessment. She did her oral care, changed all her dressings, and suctioned her. She was acutely aware that Joan was someone's beloved grandmother and wife. She deserved what minor comforts could be afforded her.

Sandy's mind was on Mo all the time. She and Joni had read up on all the latest research and therapies they could find. Mo was now on heparin, an anticoagulant, as it was now known that COVID caused clots to form in the lungs and impair the oxygen transport into and out of the small units called alveoli where oxygen and carbon dioxide exchange takes place. Mo was also getting steroids to decrease any inflammation caused by the virus. She was on maximal support with every medical intervention available. Dr. Camarie came in and stood by the doorway. "Sandy, any change?"

"Well, almost off the Levo, BP's stable."

"Good, good."

"Dr. Camarie, don't you think she needs dialysis?"

"Yes, she does, but that, Sandy, is up to Carly, and right now, she is refusing that therapy."

"I know, I know, maybe I can convince her to at least try it," Sandy said hopefully.

"You certainly can talk to Carly, but don't push her too hard. I have already explained that to her, but she will not consent, so let's go easy on her. This must be so difficult on her too. And honestly, I am not sure that putting in another central line is in her best interests since she has been so febrile and requiring so much ventilator support. If we could lower her vent settings, perhaps that might be a better time to speak to Carly."

"What about a trach?"

"We're not there yet, Sandy. I know we are all desperate for Mo to survive this, but we all have to face the reality that she might not. We all know what kind of person and nurse Mo is, and I am not sure she would want any of this. And Carly knows this too." He paused.

"Just do the best you can right now to get her off the Levo. We'll see if she can tolerate lowered ventilator support. We will continue to prone her, keep her comfortable. And thank you, Sandy."

Dr. Camarie went to round on the other ICU patients.

Sandy sat down. *Mo's not going to make it*, she thought.

Chapter 12

The Emergency Room
April 2020

COVID UPDATE—Saturday, April 4, 10:00 a.m.
1. MICU, SICU, Neuro ICU, Peds ICU, PACU, 4B, 3 B, Cath recovery room, M.S.E. conf center, Endoscopy, OR all ICU-COVID pts (total 146 ICU beds)
2. Next up: Trauma bays (4)
3. One floor remains open for non-COVID admits
4. 96 percent of hospital volume now COVID
5. Nearly all of Main ED now negative pressure
6. Tent with additional 24 beds opening next week
7. The hospital does NOT have a shortage of vents.

Census 7am
- 418 pts:
- 389 COVID positive
- 29 PUIs
- Vented pts: 105
- 7 COVID ICU beds available
- 55 beds available for non-critical COVID admits

Total tested: (data pending)
Past 24 hours:
- 2 patients were extubated
- 42 COVID pts discharged
- 6 mortalities

FAQ:
How do we keep nurses from having to go back and draw labs a second or third time? Order everything admit team needs at the outset. So *please use COVID order set.* These patients need studies we would never have ordered in the past (Ferritin, Interleukin levels, etc.)...but they need them now. JP April 4, 2020

*****

Michael came into work. He felt tired. He felt overwhelmed. He had all his PPE which he had disinfected to the best of his ability in his garage. He had been able to obtain a pair of goggles from Pam's brother who worked in the automotive repair industry. He put everything on in the hospital parking lot. As he walked into the ER, he could no longer recognize anyone. Everyone was wearing PPE. No one was taking it off.

He went in to find out he was in the trauma bay. It was no longer the trauma bay, it was all COVID patients on ventilators. It was just him and an ER tech. *How am I going to take care of all these patients?* he wondered. He thought about Pam and the boys. His oldest son came home from college to finish classes online. Michael was relieved, although having all three boys home all day was tough. Pam would not tolerate sloppiness, so at least they could not mess up the house. With all of them trying to do classwork from home, there was a fair amount of squabbling. *At least he is home where he is with us.* In truth, Michael was thinking, *If something happens to me, at least the rest of my family is all together."*

Michael saw Kyle coming into the trauma bay with requisitions. Kyle was in a gown and surgical mask, no N95. "Can I have an N95 please?"

"Sorry, buddy, but your department is supposed to get you that."

"That's funny, my director told me to get it from here. Well, it's actually not funny," Kyle said. "We were told our department doesn't have any more."

Michael knew that some of the nurses stashed a few N95s underneath the sink behind where they kept the rapid transfuser.

"I got you covered, man," Michael said. Michael moved the rapid transfuser, a rather large machine on wheels, out of the way. He opened the cabinet under the sink. There he saw the urinals put there by Sam. He moved them to find a box labeled blood culture bottles. Inside that box were the N95s stashed by Sam. He took one out.

"Don't tell anyone where you got this." He handed Kyle an N95. There were only three left underneath the sink, but Michael didn't care.

"Thanks, man." Kyle proceeded to do chest x-rays on all four patients in the trauma bay.

"Where are you going next?" Michael asked.

"Up to the ICU."

"With the same PPE?"

"You got it—I'm holding on to this mask."

"Take care, man."

"You too. Give my best to Pam and the boys." Kyle was off.

Dr. P walked into the trauma bay. "Michael, let's round."

"Okay, Dr. P, I've just got these four patients. They all came in at some point yesterday, and all required intubation within hours of arrival. All their chest x-rays look similar. They all have bilateral patchy infiltrates and ground glass appearance opacities. They all are requiring high FIO2s. They all have PEEP above 10." Dr. P paused to review all the x-rays with Michael on the computer.

"The patient in bay 3 should be proned," Dr. P announced.

"On a stretcher?" Michael asked, surprised.

"Yes, we have to do the best we can, and there are no ICU beds right now. I'll have to speak to the intensivist to see if there are downgrades so we can move this gentleman up. Okay, thanks, Mike. I am going to do oxygen rounds on the rest of the ER."

Oxygen rounds? What the hell is that? Michael thought. Michael did not have time to think about it then, but he would soon find out what that meant.

Michael looked out the glass doors into the trauma holding room (which was where patients were kept pending discharge). He had not noticed before, but all eight stretchers were occupied. Patients who were on these stretchers all had oxygen masks. He counted at least five had 100 percent non-rebreathers on. Michael looked to the left of the stretchers to see chairs lined up and filled with patients sitting attached to portable oxygen tanks, with nasal cannulas or masks in place. These patients were not on a monitor. There were portable NIBP machines, and the patients were attached to the saturation monitor only, which gave a reading of their pulse as well.

This area was not designed for patients on oxygen or to require monitoring. He thought, *Who is back there with all these patients?* He then saw Kim and another ER tech there. Kim waved to Michael. He noticed Kim was wearing a gown, her N95 with a surgical mask over it, and goggles.

Michael thought about it, *Do I need to be protecting my eyes? Is this spread by a splash exposure? At least I have intubated patients so there will be no aerosolization here.*

Michael started to feel the beginnings of fear in his stomach. He again realized he could acquire this illness himself and bring it home to Pam and the kids. He thought about being the instrument of their illness and broke out into a cold sweat. He'd known for years how much his happiness—no more—even his existence, depended on his family. Especially Pam. He could not imagine life without her. He shook himself back to the present.

"How many patients do you have back there?"

"Including the ones in chairs? Eighteen."

"You have all those patients?"

"For the moment, yeah. They're trying to get more staff in." Michael shook his head.

"This has disaster written all over it." He had not even seen the rest of the emergency room.

He turned to Sam, his ER tech. "Let's get started."

"What do you want to do first?" Sam asked.

"Can you get temps on everyone, please?" Not everyone had a Foley catheter with a temperature probe.

"Sure."

"Just let me know who's febrile."

Michael began to look at the orders on each patient. There were bloods to draw, all at different times. Two out of the four were on Nimbex, so train of fours had to be done.

Next, Michael saw orders for the one patient to be proned. Michael picked up his phone and called respiratory.

"Respiratory, Joe speaking."

"Hey, Joe, it's Michael, I'm in trauma bay. I have a patient that Dr. P wants proned."

"What the—? In trauma bay? That means he's on a stretcher."

"I know, but Dr. P says we have to try. He's a young guy, only forty. He's not a huge guy, so we probably can do it."

"But we need, like, seven people. I am the only one covering the ER right now. I have a load of vent changes to do, oxygen tanks to change out. I'll try to get there, but you have to get some more people."

"Yeah, I know. And there's one more thing, you have to come in your own PPE." But Joe had already hung up.

Dr. P was roaming through his ER, stopping to talk to all the physician assistants, nurse practitioners, and nurses.

"Good job," he would say as he passed by. "Hang in there, we've got this."

But he was looking for ways to combine tubing so that patients could be hooked up to wall oxygen from the same flowmeter. He had oxygen extension tubing in his pocket. He had squirreled away some of the plastic connectors in his pockets. *Jeez, how are we going to do this?* Suddenly he went back to the trauma bay. "Hey, Mike, do you have any of those Y connectors for chest tubes?"

"Yeah, we have them, but I have to charge them to a patient or Helen will have a fit."

"No, don't do that, just take them out and give them to me. I'll handle the charge business." Michael gave him four out of the five chest tube Y connectors. He wondered what Dr. P wanted them for, but he had too much work to do to think about it.

He turned again to Sam. "I am going to call the pharmacy. I need four bottles of propofol. Can you run and get them for me?"

"Sure, anything to take off this mask for a minute."

Michael picked up the phone and called the pharmacy. "Hey, Don, it's Michael in the ER. I'm going to need at least eight bottles of propofol up here in trauma bay, two for each patient. We're going through them like water."

"Sorry, Mike, can only send you one at a time. We are running low in stock, so we can only give out one bottle per patient at a time. The ICU is asking for them too."

"Are we going to get more in?" Michael asked, incredulous.

"We're trying."

"Okay, I'm sending Sam down to pick them up for me."

"Sure thing."

"Okay, Sam, they are only going to give you four. But it's better than nothing."

What are we going to do if we run out? Michael thought, then he thought some more. *What are we going to do when we run out?* He thought about decreasing the doses and made a mental note to ask Dr. P about that.

The next eight hours flew by. Michael was titrating drips, drawing blood, turning people on stretchers with Sam to the best of his ability, suctioning endotracheal tubes, starting tube feedings, giving meds down NG and OG tubes, and doing train of fours on the paralyzed patients. He even managed to prone the one patient Dr. P wanted proned. He did it with only four staff since Dr. Jamison was rounding to put in central lines and assisted with the airway.

He started to feel light-headed around 5:00 p.m. and realized he had not had a sip of water or been to the bathroom all day. The bridge of his nose was starting to feel sore. *I'd better start putting a Band-Aid on it,* he thought. He knew he needed a break. He also knew there was no one to relieve him. He had sent Sam on a break earlier.

He called out the glass doors to Kim who was in a similar situation, except she had received another nurse who came in for overtime. Still, two ER nurses for eighteen patients? That was unheard of. Kim came over to the door. Michael could tell she had been crying. "What happened?"

"We just lost a forty-year-old woman."

"What? I didn't hear the code called!"

"We didn't call it."

"Wait, what? A forty-year-old and you didn't overhead it? Was Dr. P there?"

"Yes, he was the one who called it." Michael had no words.

"Yeah, so this woman was brought in by her husband. She said she had not felt well for a few days…"

"Wait, she said? She came in speaking?"

"Yes, she said she was feeling like the flu, so she stayed in bed, did the usual, Tylenol, drank fluids, then she woke up with chest pain, took some more Tylenol, and tried to go back to sleep. She woke her husband up at 6:00 a.m. and said she needed to see someone. The pain had not gotten better. She got here and looked okay. Her husband checked her in and went to park the car. He had their seven-year-old daughter with him. He knew he was not allowed in, so he was pacing outside for hours. She was talking to me, and her sats were in the 70s. She also had her husband and daughter on FaceTime so they could see she was okay." Kim started to cry again. "Dr. P said her x-ray didn't even look that bad. He wanted to send her for CT scan, but when we started to move her, she brady'ed down—real slow, like twenty beats per minute. We tried to resuscitate her for twenty-four minutes—she went asystolic, we couldn't get her heart rate back. After Dr. P called it,[25] I realized her phone was on FaceTime the whole time. Her husband heard and saw the entire thing."

Michael realized he was also close to tears. *Imagine being outside and seeing your wife code on a cell phone. This is horrible. What is happening to everyone?*

He looked around. "Hey, Kim, I really need to get out of here for a few minutes, I have to pee and get a sip of water. These guys here are stable for at least ten minutes. Could you please stand here and watch the monitors?"

"Why not? I've had eighteen patients most of the shift and a code, what's one more thing." She winked at him. "Please go take a break, drink something, get a bite. I'll watch from here." Michael realized there was no longer any need to remove his PPE, so he walked out of the trauma bay into the main ER. Half the unit were ventilators, others were on HIGH-FLOW, and several patients were proned and on HIGH-FLOW. He peeked into the triage area.

There, sitting in chairs, were patients on nasal cannulas hooked up to one oxygen tank using the Y connectors and extension tubing that Dr. P was carrying around with him. Two patients, one tank. *So that's what Dr. P was talking about, oxygen rounds.*

He went to the bathroom, took down his N95, and saw that the bridge of his nose was red and angry looking. *I think I have a pressure injury.* Michael could do nothing but laugh. Michael decided to take a few minutes to go up to the ICU and check on James. He knew there were no more visitors allowed, and he thought about poor Will, who must be home and frantic.

He figured he would check on Irene and Maria as well. He was surprised he remembered everyone's name at this point. Everything was so jumbled up in his mind. *There are some things I will never forget*, he thought. Maria, Irene, Sonia, James, Harry, and Dorothy would be embedded in his brain forever.

Michael got up to the ICU and looked at the census board. In the rooms that had Irene and Maria were new names he did not

---

[25] Meaning calling the end of the code and pronouncing the person dead.

recognize. He walked by the rooms and saw a now familiar sight, a ventilator facing the hallway, multiple pumps now outside the door, the usual fentanyl, Versed, propofol. *I wonder if they have their own stash of propofol,* he thought, thinking about his conversation with the pharmacist earlier.

He got to James's room. There he was in a RotoProne bed. That is a bed that was designed to turn a patient over without requiring so many staff; to use it, one places a series of pads on top of the patient which becomes the support when the bed flips over. It was originally designed for multiple trauma injuries but was often used for ARDS. Michael saw James had a tracheostomy, and he could see the central line peeking out from under the massive cushions surrounding James—on his chest, abdomen, and lower body. He looked around for Will before remembering he would not be there.

I couldn't bear it if Pam were here and I couldn't be with her. I wonder if he has a cell phone in there for FaceTime. Jasmine, the nurse manager, walked by. "Hey, Jasmine, how's it going?"

"How's it going? Well, I'll tell you how it's going. We have no staff. We are all tripled. Everyone here is on a vent. We have two on ECMO. We have this guy James on the RotoProne. So it is easy enough to prone him, but now they decided there aren't enough RotoProne beds in the world to rent for these people that are going to die anyway! I don't know why this guy is still on it. It costs a fortune, and is probably not going to do him any good anyway." She looked defeated. She continued. "We are reusing PPE. All the propofol you see hanging is the very last of it. Pharmacy says we have to start mixing up morphine drips for people that need extra sedation. They say Precedex is too expensive, so we can only use it if there is a chance to extubate. You guys down in the ER keep calling for beds we don't have. Some of my staff is out sick. I have no idea if they have this virus or not, and we all don't know if we have been exposed. That's how it's going." She gave a sarcastic grin. "How are you?"

Michael felt like he should either hug her or slap her. "Jasmine, I know how it is. We are holding intubated, proned patients on stretchers downstairs. We have no PPE, staff are making stuff at home, trying to buy stuff online. It's a shit show everywhere."

"I know, I'm sorry to have unloaded on you. I know it's bad everywhere. We are all so exhausted. Everyone is doing overtime. The families want to FaceTime us constantly. In fact, all the cell phones by the bedside are ringing constantly, and we just can't keep up. They were supposed to send PACU nurses up here to help out. They were supposed to send cath lab and EPS nurses here, but since they opened the conference rooms as patient care areas, they are all there. Imagine caring for ICU patients in a conference room? I haven't even had a chance to go down there so see what's going on. And since they are considered ICU patients, technically I am in charge of them, scheduling, supplies, everything. I don't know how much more of this we can take. Administration is nowhere to be found. They are all working remotely, whatever the fuck that means."

Michael knew he should get back downstairs, but he felt the need to call Will since he had said he would check on him again, and unless he called, Will would never know he did. "Do you mind if I go in and see James and call Will?"

"Who is Will?"

"His boyfriend."

"Oh, I didn't even know the name of his boyfriend. Sure, knock yourself out."

Michael stepped into the room and picked up the phone. He saw all the missed FaceTime calls from Will; he pressed the call back button.

Will came on immediately. "Who is this? Have I seen you before? Are you the nurse for James?"

"Will, it's Michael from the ER. I came up to check on James and thought I would take a moment to call you."

"Oh my god!" He started to cry. "Thank you so much. Since they kicked us all out, I don't know what to do with myself. I can't sleep, I can barely work from home. Please let me see him."

"Sure, but I want you to know he is in a special bed that rotates him. He was the first one to get this bed, it's a rental, but they are letting him stay on it because they believe it will help him."

"Oh, thank God, anything that will help him, I can't live without him!" Will sounded so desperate, Michael was beginning to think he would never be able to get out of there.

"Will, I am still in the ER. I only have a few minutes. Let me flip the phone and you can talk to James, then I have to go."

Michael flipped the phone, so the image was on James. He heard Will on the other end crying. "Please, baby, please get better. I miss you, I love you, I can't do this life without you. Molly misses you. She walks around meowing all day. She smells your clothes. She sleeps by your shoes. Honey, we love you. Please come home." Will was sobbing. Michael hated to tell him he had to go.

"Will, I have to get back to the ER. I'll try to come up again in a few days and call again. Take good care, and hang in there, we are doing everything we can."

Michael rushed down to the ER. As he walked through the A section, he was amazed at how many people were crammed into a space meant for ten patients. He had to walk sideways through the crush of stretchers which were stacked two deep and into the hallways. Every available portable oxygen tank was in use, often with Dr. P's Y connector so two patients shared one tank. The place was also crowded with staff trying to take care of the patients. It was worse than Grand Central Station at rush hour. It was unbelievable.

Kim was walking by the trauma bay. "What happened to you? You were gone so long."

"Sorry, I went up to the ICU to visit one of the first people I took care of before—and I had to call his boyfriend."

"Okay, I didn't do much, but you're running out of propofol on all of these patients." Kim walked away.

Well, I guess it's now morphine, Michael thought. *I should call the pharmacy and tell them to prepare four drips.* He knew they weren't going to be happy to hear from him. They weren't. Michael went home, undressed in the garage, scrubbed himself in the shower twice, put up a load of laundry, and checked his emails before going to bed. He saw that he had missed a few.

Nothing but bad news, he thought, but he was drawn to the statistics.

COVID Update—Friday, April 10, 2020, 10:00 a.m.

1. Current ICU areas: MICU, SICU, 4B, PICU, NICU, MWE CONFERENCE ROOM, CATH LAB RECOVERY, PACU, ED ICU
2. Next stop: 1 PORTER has opened
3. Approx. 70 percent ICU admits now coming from floors

Census 7am
- 458 COVID pts: 435 COVID positive; 23 PUIs (decreased from yesterday)
- ICU pts: 124
- Vented pts: 123
- 11 COVID ICU beds available

Past 24 hours:
- 4 mortalities
- 54 COVID pts discharged
- 54 COVID/PUI admits

Discharge/admit ratio better than yesterday

Since March 4, 2020
- Total tested: 3557
  - Positive: 1630
  - Negative: 1927
- Mortalities: 122

FAQs: How do we prevent asymptomatic (likely, not tested) COVID positive patients, admitted for non-COVID related problems, from residing on a non-COVID unit?

All medicine and neurology admissions should be COVID tested, regardless of admission diagnosis. Bed 11 has been set aside for swabbing pt.

JP April 10, 2020

COVID Update—Monday, April 13, 2020, 10:00 a.m.

1. Current ICU areas: MICU, SICU, 4A, PICU, NICU, MWE CONF RM, CATH LAB RECOVERY, PACU, ED ICU, 1 PORTER
2. ICU's: majority of consults coming from floors
   a. 7 upgrades last night.
   b. 3 admits from ED

Census 7am

- 451 COVID pts: 428 COVID positive; 23 PUIs
- ICU pts: 129
- Vented pts: 142*
- 13 COVID ICU beds available

Past 24 hours:

- 10 mortalities
- 40 COVID pts discharged
- 38 COVID/PUI admits*

*Although admissions seem to have peaked, number of patients requiring intubation remains high, and unfortunately rising

FAQs: What are we doing with the tents?

It is likely, hopefully, that we will not need to use the big tent.

Weather permitting, we will continue to use the smaller tent in lieu of North Campus corridor.

JP April 13, 2020

Michael put his face down on his arms and tried hard to think of something, anything, that wasn't COVID. He drifted off a bit to the day he first met Pam, back when the world seemed full of endless possibilities. He was much more reserved back then. He hated all the pickup lines and posing he heard other men using. Some women did respond to that kind of attention, but he wasn't that guy. Yet the first time he saw that slow smile, he was intrigued, and in his careful way, he made her know he was interested. Later, she confided in him that his reserve is what attracted her, and his heart skipped a beat, so happy that she liked who he was. That was well over twenty-five years earlier, half his life. He realized he was not at all prepared to die. He didn't have a will or a power of attorney. They still had a mortgage on this house and schooling costs for the kids. He had paid off his car, but hers was newer, and when their youngest started driving, the insurance would go up yet again. He sat straight up and made a list of things to do on his next day off. The number one item was to find a lawyer for making his will. He added eight more things he wanted to check on. Finally, exhausted, he went up and crawled in next to Pam. She did not wake when he pulled her into his arms and fell asleep with his face up against her back. Michael got up early the next day, made a fresh pot of coffee, and went to the den to look at his emails. He was tired of the updates from Dr. P, but he was compelled to look to see if things were getting better. *At least I am off a few days to decompress*, he thought.

COVID UPDATE—Thursday, April 16, 2020, 10:00 a.m.
Yesterday's Volume
- Total: 103
- Adult: 100
- Peds: 3
- Total adult admissions: 41
- COVID admits: 39
- ICU admits: 3

Yesterday's COVID Dispositions
- DISCHARGES: 36 (total >500)
- MORTALITIES: 6 (total 176)

Today's COVID Census 7:00 am
- Total: 406
  - Confirmed: 390
  - PUIs: 16
- ICU pts: 132
  - Vented pts: 113
- Bed availability:
  - COVID ICU: 35
  - Non-COVID ICU: 1
  - COVID floor: 35
  - Non-COVID floor: 9

FAQs:
What are Dr. Donald Thorson's findings at autopsy?

Diffuse alveolar damage both early and late phase—very textbook and similar to other diseases

Microthrombi (means small clots) are prevalent regardless of prophylactic or therapeutic AC (AC means anticoagulation)

D-Dimers seem to correlate with macrovascular thrombosis (thrombosis is clotting)

No myocarditis seen (myocarditis is inflammation of the heart)

JP April 16, 2020

Michael tried to look at the numbers and come up with a trend that made things look better to him. Try as he might, the numbers seemed worse.

Microthrombi? So they were bleeding and clotting in the lungs? That's not textbook ARDS. Michael remembered Harry from the parking lot. *We were right, those were microthrombi, and it must have been in his lungs as well. It seems no matter how hard we work, cases just keep coming in, and they are sicker and sicker.* Michael ruminated on how best he could protect himself, Pam, and the kids. He thought about his kids going to school. They were all doing work online for now, and he was happy to have his oldest, Russell, home for a while. But he worried—would this interfere with their education? Would they all graduate with enough experience and knowledge that they would get if they were actually in school?

He had to call an attorney and get his will drawn up and get that detail organized. He sipped his coffee and thought about his life with Pam and the kids. He tried to be as engaged in his family's life as he could be. He felt he tried to be present every moment, as much as anyone could be. But this scare woke him up to how short life really is. Going forward, he would be looking at things with more gratitude than ever before.

He thought of James and poor Will at home wondering if the center of his world would live or die. He could not think of anything more terrifying.

Pam had to work today, so he would be home with the boys. That included seeing that they did their schoolwork. Then, he thought about getting outside with them. He remembered fondly they used to play that four-way game of catch and running bases. He hoped they would still want to do that. It was still early; Pam would be getting ready for work. She would come down to get her coffee and go back upstairs to dress and pack her things. He would not interfere with her routine, although he desperately wanted to talk to her about the boys and their education. He decided not to burden her with that just yet.

He turned on the news.

Governor on phased reopening: "'We're going to turn the valve on reopening, and then watch the dials,' Governor Andrew Cuomo said. The coordinated and slow reopening of some services would be dependent on the hospitalization and infection rate. NY PAUSE ends on May 15th, but only for areas where the regional hospital rate is in decline for 14 days, according to federal guidance from the

CDC. The governor said that the state will leave some extra medical centers built by the Army Corps of Engineers in place to deal with flu season and a possible second wave of COVID-19" (ABC NEWS, April 17, 2020).

He changed the channel. "New York auto dealers in the metropolitan area are donating 500,000 masks to New Yorkers in need" (CNN, April 17, 2020).

Michael went back to ABC NEWS.

"Governor Cuomo says there has been a sharp increase in demand for food and supplies at food banks He said that he would like to start funding and philanthropy funding. He said there are farmers upstate who can't sell their product and dumping milk. His administration is starting a special Nourish NY Initiative. They will work with industries in the state to get excess milk to people who need it." Michael turned off the TV. Pam had come down to get her coffee and finish getting ready for work.

"Plans today, hun?" she asked.

"Hoping the boys will want to hang out with their old dad." Pam kissed his cheek gently. "Of course, they will, but boys will be boys." Pam went upstairs to get her things and leave for work.

The boys were still sleeping. Russell had a while before he had to be online for his first class. His younger two, Miles and Joseph, had to be up soon to get online for their high school classes respectively. Michael decided to go into the garage for a workout but set his iPhone alarm to make sure everyone was up for their virtual school.

As Michael was in the garage doing some bench presses, he thought about everything that had been happening in the world. He thought about what he wanted to plan for his next two days off. *I want to try to stay away from the news*, he thought, but he knew he would not be able to. Michael finished his chest set, then went on to do biceps and triceps. He thought about doing squats and lunges but thought he would save that for tomorrow. When he was done, he felt tight and ready for the day. He went to shower. Pam had left for work. It was just him and the boys.

COVID UPDATE—Friday, April 17, 2020, 10:00 a.m.

Yesterday's Volume
- Total: 106
- Adult: 100
- Peds: 6
- Total adult admissions: 46
- COVID admits: 45
- ICU admits: 3

Yesterday's COVID Dispositions
- DISCHARGES: 49 (many on home O2) …total > 600 discharged
- MORTALITIES: 6

Today's COVID Census 7:00 am
- Total: 381
  - Confirmed: 361
  - PUIs: 20
- ICU pts: 136
  - Vented pts: 109
- Bed availability:
  - COVID ICU: 30
  - Non-COVID ICU: 0
  - COVID floor: 42
  - Non-COVID floor: 6

FAQs:
How are things looking overall? Better…

ICUs remain terribly busy, but many pts are going home.

Much more bed availability for COVID admits and ICU downgrades.

Planning underway to begin opening ORs.

Volume of non-COVID ED pts increasing.

JP April 17, 2020

Michael went back to work. He put on his PPE, his N95 now showing signs of wear after several attempts at disinfecting. His gown was torn in a few places. His cousin had managed to get him a suit used in the automotive industry, so he decided to wear that instead. *At least I can wash this better.* At this time, PPE was being donated to hospitals, and everyone was wearing whatever they could get their hands on. Michael shook his head when he saw that some staff were actually wearing large plastic garbage bags over their gowns. Some staff had received eye shields made by various local industries recruited for this purpose. Communities had rallied around and began making homemade masks and headcaps. Michael was the recipient of a full set sent from one of his cousins. Each set had a headcap and four matching cloth masks made with ties. He used the cloth masks to reinforce his N95. He was grateful to have them.

There was quite an array of colors in the emergency department now.

Dr. P was in a hazmat suit he managed to obtain from overseas. *He's well protected*, Michael thought. *I wish he could have gotten more from wherever he got his stuff.*

The emergency room was in total chaos. The beds on the north side had been designated for vented COVID patients. The pediatric emergency room was full of vented adult COVID patients. There were now three tents outside to screen potential patients.

There were new faces he had never seen before. Public outcry had agencies scrambling for workers to come from other states to help out in New York. Many nurses answered that call, and of course, the agencies were being well compensated for this. Nurses came from North Carolina, Texas, and Tennessee as Michael would find out. They were making upward of $100 per hour with hotel rooms paid for and stipends for food being given. They brought their own PPE.

There was donated food every day from local restaurants, tons of pizza, doughnuts, sandwiches, soda, and water.

Michael was appreciative for the help and the food.

"Safety huddle main desk, safety huddle main desk" came again over the loudspeaker. Helen was not there; she had been working remotely from home. There were lots of comments from the group.

"Of course, why should she come in?"

"But isn't she an essential worker?"

"Figures."

There was Dr. P in full hazmat gear leading the meeting. "Thank you all for your persistence and dedication. This does not go unnoticed. Although we are still seeing an upward trend in COVID cases, we can be happy that we are actually discharging some patients. In fact, the hospital has now decided to play the Beatles song 'Here Comes the Sun' whenever a patient is discharged. So if you hear a portion of that song on the loudspeaker, please congratulate yourself on a job well done. It means someone is actually going home."

Applause came from the crowd.

Dr. P continued, "We are thankful that local businesses have been donating food and making some supplies for us. We are happy that so many nurses came from other states to join us in this fight against COVID."

More applause.

"Some patients are being extubated and transferred to a step-down or floor level of care."

There was applause from the crowd. Michael looked around at all the new faces or what he could see behind all the masks, hair coverings, goggles, glasses, face shields. He felt like he was in a war zone.

Michael just could not bring himself to applaud, not with what he was still seeing.

Chapter 13

The Orthopedic Floor
April 2020

"The United States Reports a Total of 31,002 Deaths from the Corona Virus, the Highest in the World" (Rasheed, Zaheena; Stephansky, Joseph, Live Updates, April 16). Fran looked at the assignment. She had five patients and two empties. The usual assignment, with no adjustments made in staffing despite that there would be additional time needed for assessing these patients for symptoms.

Wait, Fran thought, *we are using the same PPE for everyone. How can that be safe?* She sat down next to the day nurse, Stacy, to get report. Stacy was still in her gown, mask, and gloves. Fran was not yet wearing anything. *What is wrong with this picture?* Fran thought. "Are you going to take that stuff off before report?"

"No way, I am not going to take this off until I get to my car. Then I will throw the gown and gloves in a garbage bag and put the mask in my paper bag. Then we have to take this stuff home, try to clean it, and wear it again. I swear I didn't sign up for this shit."

Fran did not want to be confrontational, nor did she want to show fear or support for Stacy's anger, so she sat there and waited for her to start report.

Fran took report on all her patients. She got up and went back to her locker and put on her PPE. She had two gowns left. She put on one, put on her N95 and a surgical mask over it. She then went to her workstation on wheels and signed on to look at her patients' labs. She reviewed the previous vital signs of her patients. *Not too bad*, she thought.

Okay, Mr. Pearson, what have we got here? she thought as she looked through his labs drawn this morning. She saw his hemoglobin was low, indicating anemia. She also saw his coags were abnormal, meaning he was having trouble getting his blood to clot properly. That was always ominous—it could indicate a potential for a blood clot in a vein that could go to the lungs, but equally dangerous was a potential bleed. The seeming paradox of this was something Fran had only begun to understand. Some of the things needed (called fibrin split products) for proper blood clotting got used up in a "bad" or dangerous clot, and so those blood products were not available when needed to prevent a real bleed. She also saw the results of inflammatory markers although she did not understand how important they would be.

Gee, he is anemic for someone that came in for gastroenteritis… What is this Interleukin 6 thing? I never heard of it. She decided to take advantage of the link to UptoDate,[26] an online medical reference. Fran was feeling way out of her depth; she felt she had just mastered the art of nursing in orthopedics. She was not sure she had the competence to take are of such sick people.

She pulled up a radiology report on Mrs. Roth. *Ground glass opacities, I've been seeing that a lot. I wonder what that means?*

She decided to do what she always did, start at the top and work her way down the list. At least she had Lisa with her, and she could always count on Lisa to help.

She walked by each of her five occupied rooms. All of her patients were on nasal cannulas or aerosol masks. *They should all be on a continuous sat monitor*, she thought. *How am I going to know if there is a problem with only one NIBP machine?*

Fran pulled up orders on each patient as she walked by. There were orders for titration of oxygen, IV antibiotics, Protonix, heparin, labs, nothing like the few and far between orders of a typical orthopedic patient. *Am I prepared for this? Ugh! I should have tried to get right into pediatrics. It would have been better than this.*

---

[26] UpToDate, an online medical reference database providing evidence basis for medical practice, continuously updated, and published by Walters Kluwer.

Lisa had started vital signs already. "Mr. Pearson has a temp of 102.2."

Fran quickly looked up to see if he was due for Tylenol. He was not. *What do I do now? Think… Maybe ice packs.* Out loud, she said, "Hey, Lisa, can we get some of those crushable ice packs we used for the ortho patients?"

"Love to say yes, but we are out of them."

"Seriously? Well, I guess we'll just have to make our own." Fran looked at her orders for Mr. Pearson. "Call for temp over 101.6." She picked up her hospital phone and dialed the number of the on-call PA. She prayed it was not Annie.

"This is Liz."

"Hi, Liz, this is Fran on the ortho floor. I have a patient, Mr. Pearson, he has a temp of 102.2, not due for Tylenol yet."

"Did he get cultured?"

"I see he has had multiple blood cultures since he has been here, and they have been negative."

"Well, get another set just to be sure."

"Look, Liz, we know this is COVID, and we want to avoid having the phlebotomist exposed any more than necessary. There is a shortage of PPE, so can I just give him some ice packs and we will check a temp later?"

"So why did you call me if you don't want to do what I say?"

"Because it says call MLP for temp over 101.6. If you don't want to be called, change the parameter." Fran hung up. Why were the PAs so horrible? Fran was proud of herself for standing up to that nonsense. She felt it was right to say what was on her mind to avoid risking unnecessary exposure of health-care workers. Fran refreshed her computer and saw the order was now "call MLP for temp > 102.5."

"Lisa, let's get some gloves if we have any. Fill them with ice and put them underneath Mr. Pearson's neck and under his armpits."

"I'm not sure we have extra gloves to do that."

"How about biohazard lab bags, do you think we have any of those, or are we supposed to send blood in a paper bag now?" Fran could not help but be sarcastic. Lisa knew she was joking and just laughed.

They managed to get some ice onto Mr. Pearson until it was time for his Tylenol.

Fran's other patients were in various stages of discomfort and deoxygenation. Since she had titrate orders on oxygen up to 50 percent before she had to call the MLP, she used them to the best of her ability. Patients who were on two liters nasal cannula went up to four or five. Patients who were on 35 percent or 40 percent aerosol masks went up to 50 percent as necessary.

She gave out Tylenol to practically every patient, either for fever or body aches. She asked patients that could to prone themselves as she had read about proning online.

Fran thought, *Maybe I am making a difference here*, when a patient said they felt better when lying on their abdomen.

The last patient of her five was Mr. Gomez, a forty-year-old construction worker. He had a wife and two young daughters. Fran had remembered him from her last shift when he had been a PUI (person under investigation). He was now a documented case of COVID and had his room changed from the back into Fran's district. Mr. Gomez had known he was exposed at his construction site when some of the other men had come down with the virus. He knew he was next. He was right. He was always on his cell phone talking to his wife and comforting his young daughters. "Daddy will be just fine. I just have to stay here for a little while." He was proning himself every two hours. When Fran went by, he was often lying on his belly with his arms stretched over the bedside table in a Superman pose so when he spoke to his daughters, he could tell them that he was, in fact, Superman. Fran felt her eyes well up as she entered his room to see two beautiful little girls talking to their daddy, telling him he was Superman now. She thought of her own kids and wondered what would happen if she got COVID. What would she tell her children?

Mr. Gomez was stoic and hopeful. He took all his medications, he wanted to know his oxygen saturation at every chance he could get, and often, that was his request when he rang the call light. Lisa knew what he wanted, and it was a small request, so she did her best to honor it. With his 50 percent aerosol mask in place, he always hovered around 90 percent. When he talked too long on the phone, it went down to the low eighties. He would say, "Daddy has to go fly like Superman for a while, so I will call you girls later."

He did not have a DNR on his chart, but he would not talk about it. He was determined to get better on his own. Fran decided to talk to him early that morning when she found him awake at 3:00 a.m., prone, but obviously short of breath.

"Mr. Gomez, you know if you require more than this 50 percent aerosol mask, we will transfer you up to a step-down or the ICU unit for more monitoring."

"No," he said, "I am okay here, I know what to do. This prone position always seems to help me."

"I know it helps you now, but I am looking at your saturation, and it is barely making 90 right now. I may have to call the MLP and have them order more oxygen, but then you won't be able to stay on this floor."

"I like this floor. I know all you girls. You take good care of me."

Fran had a bad feeling. "Okay, but I am very worried about you and would like to see you get better."

"Don't worry, honey, I have God to watch over me, and I will ask him to watch over you too. Do you have children?" he asked.

"Yes, I have two, a boy and a girl."

"Well, I will ask God to look over them too."

"Thank you, Mr. Gomez, I appreciate that."

Fran made another set of rounds and was just sitting down to get some charting in when Lisa came running up to her. "Mr. Gomez, his sat is 79."

"Leave the sat monitor on him." Fran grabbed a 100 percent non-rebreather from the respiratory cart and told Lisa, "Call an RRT."

Fran ran into the room. Mr. Gomez had a bluish tinge around his lips. He had purple blisters forming on his hands. Fran put the 100 percent non-rebreather on him as the RRT team congregated outside. Fran waved them in. "What's his sat now?" called Liz.

"It's eighty-two."

"Tell him to take deep breaths."

"That's what I have been doing." Suddenly Fran realized that no one wanted to come into the room. The team made a show of adjusting their PPE.

"Don't you have any more surgical masks for us?" one MLP shouted.

"Whatever we have is already out there." Fran called back. Lisa came back in the room. "What do you want to do?"

"Let's sit him upright and see if he can cough."

"Mr. Gomez!" they both shouted. "Breathe, take a deep breath!" Finally, the intensivist in full hazmat gear came into the room.

"Why aren't any of you in here with this patient? He obviously needs to be intubated." The team idled around pretending to be looking at something on the computer or their phones. "Call a full code!" Suddenly, over the loudspeaker, *Code blue 2 south, code blue 2 south* could be heard.

Most of the team was already there since the RRT team was also the code team. A nurse, Janet, arrived from ICU and immediately got the code cart and went into the room, expertly got out the intubation box, and set up for intubation. Janet called out to the team, "Someone better get their ass in here. In fact, all of you better get your asses in here now. This patient is coding, and we need help. Someone start compressions." Janet began directing the activity of the code with the intensivist. "You," she said, pointing at Liz, "take over compressions. You," she said, pointing at another MLP, "what's your name?"

"Uh, Todd."

"Well, Uh Todd, get in here and get ready to help Dr. James intubate. What the fuck are you all doing on the RRT team if you're going to do nothing but stand around and look at your pagers and phones? You," she called out yet to another MLP, "what's your name?"

"I'm Joe."

"Well, I'm Joe, come in here and take over compressions so Liz can put in a central line. Liz, you do know how to put in a central line now, don't you?"

"Sure, I do."

"Well, don't just stand around fiddling with your phone, put one in!" Janet said as she was opening the central line kit.

Janet looked at Fran, shook her head, and said, "Good call, lady." She looked at Dr. James. "We've only got one bed in the ICU. Are we taking it for him?"

"He's forty, he goes."

Fran was awestruck. Here was this superintelligent nurse, not afraid of anything coming down here and telling all these people who are supposed to know what to do, what to do. She was so grateful someone knew what to do. She hoped she would be like that one day.

Mr. Gomez was intubated, sedated, and moved up to the last bed in the ICU. Fran packed up his belongings and paused as she saw the FaceTime call come in with a picture of his daughters.

She could not answer the call.

It was almost 6:00 a.m. Fran barely had enough time to chart. She gave report in her full PPE. The nurse who relieved her came in her old PPE. You could see the wear and tear on the N95s now. Fran got to her car, removed all her PPE, and put everything into her two big garbage bags. She prepared to put her mask into the paper bag she had brought for it. She had also made a spray bottle with 70 percent alcohol, and she sprayed the outside of the mask before putting it in the bag. She felt the N95 was the only thing between her and the certainty of getting COVID, and she protected it carefully. She then did hand hygiene with her last small bottle of Purell. Fran drove home and showered. When she looked in the mirror, she saw all the marks the mask left. She puttered around in her kitchen and looked at the space fondly. She thought it would be time to put up the lighter curtains soon. She looked at some of the photos on the refrigerator while the water heated up. She made tea, consciously using her favorite china, the set with pink roses. She wanted the comfort of her favorite things. Despite trying not to think about work, her shift just replayed again and again in her head. She sat down on the sofa with her cup of tea and began to cry.

Soon the kids would be up, and it would be time to start the next part of her day. She was grateful to have her mom there to lighten some of the load. She needed to shop again for the house since she would be on another three-day stretch after these days off.

Fran was exhausted. She knew she needed sleep, but that would come later. She had to make it to Costco to make sure she could get supplies for her apartment and the kids. She needed diapers for Robby, food, and cleaning supplies if there were any to be had.

Since Robby was growing constantly, she needed adult-size diapers now. She sighed. *How am I going to keep this up?* she thought. Then she remembered the plan. Fran got lost in the thought of her dream home in upstate New York, lots of Robby-friendly property for him to roam around. A place for her, Lilly, her mom, and Robby to live out their lives while she worked in a local hospital. She had already looked into upstate hospitals that had pediatric departments. She just needed a bit more medical and surgical experience and a whole lot more money for a down payment. She would sell the co-op, but unfortunately, she had re-mortgaged it twice to pay for living expenses. Whatever was left in equity she would use to buy her forever home.

As she was lost in thought, she heard the familiar children's song "Shark Shark, My Little Shark." That meant Robby was up walking around with his iPad. She got up to put out finger foods for him on the table so he could grab things as he walked endlessly around the apartment with the same song playing over and over.

Three days flew by. Fran got what she could from Costco. She had to go to several stores to buy the adult diapers as most places were out. She played with the kids, and she cooked chicken nuggets and baby potatoes for Robby. She ran to McDonald's drive-through to get Happy Meals for the kids on one of the days. That was a luxury she could barely afford, but Lilly loved the toy in the Happy Meal and Fran needed to give her a treat once in a while.

Fran rarely went on social media although she had created a Facebook page for the sole purpose of connecting with other moms with disabled children. Fran was so frustrated that she even made a Facebook post about it. "Please folks, at least leave some of the diapers those of us who need them."

Fran was getting ready for work on the third evening. She was still tired. Robby had gone to sleep early on the sofa, and she did not want to move him. Her mom was fine with him sleeping on the sofa as well. She packed all her PPE, a few granola bars and pretzels for her pocket, and set off to work.

She arrived to the new normal. Most of the staff were unrecognizable in their PPE. The schedule was lying in the notebook on the desk as most administrators were working remotely. *How does a nurse work remotely?* she thought for a moment. Fran looked at the schedule. She did not like what she saw. Her vacation for the first week of May had not been approved. There was no one to speak to about this. She would have to wait until the morning to speak to someone in charge. Fran had been waiting for this vacation for months. It was her first week off since she started there. *How could they not give it to me? No one else had requested it.* Then she looked up at the bulletin board by the nursing station. ALL VACATIONS ARE NO LONGER APPROVED DUE TO CURRENT CONDITIONS.

Shit.

Fran took report from Laura again.

Report had become mundane and repetitive, but what she heard next was perplexing. "Okay," Laura said, "everyone in the district has oxygen titrate orders. They all have prn Tylenol. They are all febrile at some point. They all have abnormal labs. Okay! Be safe." Laura walked off the unit, leaving Fran in disbelief.

Fortunately for Fran, she knew many of the patients from the last time she worked. The bed that was empty had been filled. Another COVID-19 patient. Same story, same symptoms. Fran kept up the best she could. She medicated for fever, for pain. She titrated oxygen up and, sometimes, miraculously down. She gave IV fluids and antibiotics, and she FaceTimed with families when she was in the room. She held hands through her gloves and tried to smile with her eyes at relatives on the other side of the phone. Fran tried to convey hope when she knew there was none. She and Lisa bathed patients that were too weak to move. There were tears in her eyes after every encounter. Fran felt beaten, frustrated, useless, tired.

What more can we do for these people? Death was an every shift occurrence, but Fran could not get used to it. She heard children screaming on the end of the phone. "Please don't go, Daddy, please don't leave Mommy." It was the same with all of them. Grandmas, grandpas, uncles, aunts, cousins, sisters, brothers, all succumbed to this illness. Fran tried to be gentle on the phone. She cried with them, the tears soaking through her mask. She worried about that. If her mask were wet, would that leave her more vulnerable to this?

What about my children? she thought. *How could they live without me if I got this?* The morgue was filled, so yet another refrigerated truck had been brought in to house the casualties. She knew that when transport left the floor with another body, it would be piled on top of another in a refrigerated truck and would sit there.

Deceased patients' belongings were piled up in plastic bags with name tags in utility and supply rooms on the unit. No one would come into the hospital to pick up any property. People were too frightened.

Fran was able to take a short break after she finished charting. She went into the utility room.

She saw the bags upon bags of property with name tags on, names she recognized.

Ms. Rosen, Mr. Pearson, Mrs. Roth, Mr. Gomez. *Oh my god, they are all gone!* Mrs. Edna Cobb. *Oh no, not her too.*

Fran felt defeated. She went out to the nursing station.

She saw a few of her colleagues with extra PPE she had not seen before. *What the fuck,* she thought. *My mask is soaking wet, and they have new stuff.* She asked Lisa, "Where is everyone getting N95s?" Lisa motioned for her to follow. They went back into the utility room. There, in the property bags of deceased patients, were plastic bags of N95s, gowns, and gloves. Even bottles of Purell.

Fran felt like she was going to faint. "Lisa, people are putting PPE in the property of deceased patients?"

"Everyone is just trying to survive, and no one would think of looking in there, so it's a great hiding place. Go take some stuff for yourself, you need it."

Fran took an N95, a gown, and a few pairs of gloves. She also took one small bottle of Purell. She went back to work, finished her charting. As she was giving report, she started to notice that more of her colleagues were, in fact, wearing new N95 masks. Fran never let on that she knew.

Fran also had the worst headache of her life.

Chapter 14

Critical Care
May 2020

Sandy was back in her assignment again. Mo and Joan. Joan was continuing a slow deterioration. However, her family would not make her a DNR and consider a compassionate wean, which would mean that Joan would be put on a morphine drip, taken off the ventilator, and allowed to pass away peacefully. Joan's family still held out hope that recovery would be in her future even though they had multiple conversations with Dr. Camarie on the futility of continued care.

Mo was making slow progress toward coming off the ventilator. However, her kidneys continued to deteriorate, and Carly was steadfast in her refusal of dialysis.

As Sandy was sitting at her desk doing her charting, a familiar voice sounded, "Hey, Sandy, how are you?" She turned to look at a gaunt, pale, much smaller version of Keith.

"*Oh my god*, what the hell happened to you? Where have you been?" Sandy had been so wrapped up with researching treatment for Mo and her relationship with Joni, she had never realized that Keith was not around. She suddenly felt guilty.

"Well, I got COVID."

"Wait, what. You got COVID? You got better. You beat this?" She wanted to get up and hug him but thought better of it. She remembered the state mandate of social distancing precautions. "So how? When? What was it like?" Sandy really wanted to know exactly what had happened, and that blunted her tact somewhat.

Keith sat down at the desk, obviously a bit weak and winded. Sandy pushed her chair back. "It's okay, I tested negative, and I am allowed back to work."

"I'm glad you're back, Keith." She paused and smiled, though he couldn't see because of the mask. "How do you think you were exposed?"

"Look around."

Sandy nodded. "I guess. But we were in PPE."

"Well, I think it was that kid that came in. What was his name?"

Sandy gestured across the room. "Ray, he's still here. Doing well, actually, he should go to rehab soon."

Keith looked into the other room. He knew the occupant was Maureen, but he was not prepared for the sight.

Sandy looked up at him. He had tears in his eyes. "That Mo, she is one tough bitch, but she sure does know her shit. I learned a lot from her."

"As did I," Sandy said.

"How's she doing?"

"Off Levo, maximal vent settings still, needs dialysis, but Carly says no, that Mo would not want it." Sandy really wanted to change the subject. "Tell me what it was like to have COVID."

"You can't even describe it," Keith said. "I started with body aches, then came the fever, twelve straight days with over 101. Even my skin hurt."

"You didn't come to the hospital?"

"No, what were they going to do? I wasn't short of breath—thank God." He paused. "I drank, slept, tried to eat, I actually proned myself! I waited, I sweated, I lost weight, and finally, I recovered. I just couldn't stay at home anymore. I had to wait for two negative swabs, and here I am. Back to work. I hear the PPE is impossible to find."

"It really is. We are all getting three sets of stuff that has to last as long as possible." Sandy turned her head so Keith couldn't see that her eyes were welling up with tears. She wasn't sure why she was feeling so emotional.

"What's with the ponchos?" Keith asked.

"Donated by Giordano's. A bit bulky, but if we have nothing else…"

"And a little advertising for them too." Keith laughed.

"And they have been giving us food almost every day. At least no one has to cook anymore."

"So Camarie wants me to round on half the unit now. So I thought I'd start with you."

"This one is Joan"—Sandy pointed to the room—"is not doing well. Her family refuses DNR or compassionate wean. Levo requirements keep going up. I think we'll have to add another pressor soon. Not requiring much sedation anymore, she's pretty unresponsive. A boatload of vent support."

"'Nuff said," replied Keith, taking brief notes. "I know how Mo is doing. Dr. Camarie told me to keep an eye out, so call me if you need. I know you know what you're doing." Sandy was surprised that he seemed to have more trust in her. She felt satisfied for the first time after an interaction with him.

Sandy looked across the unit. There sat Ray, up in a chair playing with his cell phone. She knew he was trying to call his parents. Sandy knew he was still disoriented, probably could not understand why his parents were not with him. She motioned to Tamara.

"Do you mind going in to help Ray call his parents, please?"

There were still not enough N95 masks in the hospital, or so everyone thought. There was a secrecy about supplies, where they were kept and who had access to them.

There were unwritten rules now about which patient to spend the most time with and who got the most nursing care hours. Tamara didn't want to go into Ray's room.

"Tamara, please."

"He has been fiddling with his phone for most of the morning and afternoon when he is not sleeping." Sandy knew that Tamara was not going in the room without the N95. She reached into her pocket and pulled out the extra one Keith gave her weeks ago and gave it to Tamara.

"Where'd you get that?"

"Doesn't matter, just go help Ray. He's a kid, he needs to see his parents. Please stay with him and help him with the conversation. He still has a trach. Even though it is being capped, he can't speak well enough for his parents to understand. I have to go into this other room now and take care of Mo, and Nero, who has Ray today, has two other patients."

She saw Tamara put on the N95, put her surgical mask over it, put on the "COMPLIMENTS OF GIORDANO'S" poncho, and went in the room. Sandy just sighed.

Sandy looked at the clock; it was almost time for Ethan to come in. She was relieved because he was a friendly face and he wouldn't push back with every request.

She wanted to bathe Maureen with Ethan and FaceTime Carly. She knew that with the both of them in the room, they could keep Maureen's dignity intact and give Carly a chance to see her mom being lovingly cared for.

Sandy heard the pumps beeping next door outside Joan's room. She went over to the room and saw that the Levo was almost out and the IV piggyback was empty.

Sandy walked across the unit to see Tamara in with Ray holding the phone for him. Sandy thought, *That's the one thing that Ray can do is hold the phone. I wanted her to help Ray communicate, reassure his parents. All she's doing is standing there.* She didn't grasp that her expectations about Tamara were not entirely realistic.

Out loud, she said, "Excuse me, Tamara, did you order more Levo for Joan?"

"I called the pharmacy."

"And?"

"They said they would send it up."

"And did they? Because she's out."

"I didn't check—you told me to come in here."

Sandy walked away. She went to the front desk where there was a bag of Levo labeled with Joan's name on it. How long it had been there, she would never know.

She hung the bag and reprogrammed the pump. Sandy put up another bag of IV fluids. She peeked in the room to make sure

Joan did not need suctioning or oral care. Joan looked okay for the moment. Sandy saw Nero coming out of one of his vented patients' rooms. They nodded to each other.

The staff of the ICU had become so much closer, even though there was little to say. They all just knew how each other was feeling.

Ethan came around the corner with his usual bounce of energy. Sandy watched him go to the desk and sign in. He came right over to her. "Waz up?"

Those words were comforting. "I know you have vitals and other stuff to do, but when you are finished, could you come help be bathe Mo? I want to have Carly on FaceTime so she can see Mom is being well taken care of."

"Sure, beb." Sandy smiled under her mask. Sandy could count on Ethan to lower her anxiety, even just a notch.

Ethan went off to do his afternoon routine.

Sandy gathered up all the supplies she would need for Maureen's bath. She had even brought in some lavender-scented body wash to keep in her room. She had everything on the desk outside the room when Keith came by.

"Camarie wants to try Mo without Nimbex. Wake her a little and see if she can breathe a little. I'm putting in the orders."

"Sure thing. Ethan and I are going in to bathe her, so we will be in there a while and can see how she does."

Sandy walked into the room and put down all the supplies. She walked over to the head of the bed. The tears started to flow. *Mo, don't you do this. You need to fight this.*

Ethan came in and walked up to Sandy, put his hand on her shoulder. "How's virtual school?" Sandy asked.

"Well, I'm gonna be a nurse with my only experience being here. But my grades are good."

"That's not such a bad deal."

"I know, I've learned a lot watching you and the others. And of course, my Mo. Mo always told me to go to nursing school. And here I am almost to graduation, and I wanted her to see it. I want her to see it." Ethan held back more tears.

"Let's get started," Sandy said gently. "I want to FaceTime Carly."

Ethan and Sandy carefully removed Maureen's gown and covered her up with a bath blanket.

They got the basin of warm water and the lavender body wash out.

"I want to try to wash her hair and tie it back."

"Yes, beb."

Fran then walked over and disconnected the Nimbex drip.

Fran pushed the FaceTime button. Carly jumped on. "Is Mom okay?"

"Yes, we have taken her off the Nimbex to see if we can begin to wake her up so she can breathe on her own. Ethan and I are going to bathe her now. This way we will be in the room to see how she does off the Nimbex."

Sandy picked up the bottle of lavender body wash and showed it to Carly.

"I brought this in for her."

"Oh, thanks so much, Mom loves the scent of lavender."

Ethan began to gently wash Maureen's face. He had put on his cell phone to the Spotify app for music. "Hey, Carly, any song in particular your mom likes?"

"Oh god, yes, Mom loved the music from the seventies, let me think a minute. Oh, oh, oh, I know, can you put on Seals and Croft 'Summer Breeze'?"

"Sure thing."

"Sweet days of summer, the jasmine's in bloom..." The song went on. Carly started to sing on the other end. "Mom loved this song and the other one by them, too, 'We May Never Pass This Way Again.'"

"Okay, we'll play that next. I'm going to put the phone down and position your mom's phone so she can hear you singing to her."

Sandy and Ethan continued the bath, careful not to expose any part of Maureen's body. They gently turned her and washed her back, Sandy moved the iPhone slightly so Carly could not see that part.

Carly was busy singing to her mom. Ethan and Sandy could hear her crying in between the lyrics.

"We are going to wash her hair now."

"Oh, God…thanks so much. I know Mom never did much about her hair anymore, but it was always long, thick, and beautiful."

"Yes, her hair is still beautiful, and once we wash it, it will look that way again. I brought a band to put it in a ponytail, so it doesn't get all over the place."

Sandy gestured to Ethan to look at Maureen. She was beginning to take some shallow breaths on her own. Before Carly could see, Sandy titrated up on the Versed so Maureen would look comfortable. It was clear to Sandy that Maureen would become asynchronous with the ventilator when off the paralytic agent. That was not a good sign.

"Can you shut off the music a second, please?" Carly asked. "I want to talk to Mom. Can you put the phone by her ear?"

"Of course," Ethan said.

They put Maureen's iPhone up on her pillow, and they both stood there to hear Carly talk to her mom.

"Mommy, please tell me what to do. I'm lost. I know you wouldn't want any of this… I'm not going to let them dialyze you. You said you would never want that. I know you said no ventilator, but it happened so fast." Carly was sobbing in between words. "Please, Mommy, tell me what to do for you now. I don't want you to suffer, but I can't lose you."

Ethan and Sandy both were tearing up. They looked at each other. They thought they knew what was coming next.

"Mommy, I'm not going to let this go on much longer. I'm not gonna let them do a tracheostomy. So please just breathe, please just breathe. Listen to Seals and Croft, Mommy. Summer breeze makes me feel fine, blowin' through the jasmine in my mind." Carly was singing in between sobs.

"Sandy, are you there?"

"Yes, both Ethan and I are still here. Her bath and hair are done, and we are going to get some more people in here to put her on her belly for a while."

"Is it okay if we call you a bit later after we do that? Please promise me you will."

"Of course, we will, Carly."

"Thank you, Sandy, Ethan, you both have been so good to me and Mom. I know you both love her too. She is one crazy sarcastic nurse. She was that way at home, always sarcastic, but that's the mom I know. This, the way she is now, she would kill me."

"Of course," Sandy said, choking back her sobs. She nodded to Ethan to go out and assemble the people to perform the proning.

"Call you later, Carly." It was all Sandy could do to control her voice.

Sandy knew that Maureen needed to be back on Nimbex by her rate of respirations. She picked up her phone and called Keith.

"Mo's not gonna make it off the Nimbex. She's breathing way too fast and ineffectively."

"Shit. Put it back on."

"Okay." Sandy hooked back up the drip, did the train of fours, and increased the drip until there were only two twitches.

She went out of the room to chart.

Sandy knew that Dr. Camarie would have to speak with Carly about the goals of care for her mother.

Sandy left that night feeling like she failed Maureen. She was still young enough to believe she could save people, and her skill was key in the rapid recovery of many cases. But no one had the tools in April of 2020 to fight the SARS-CoV-2 virus. Sandy and the team performed flawlessly, and it made no difference. She could not make sense of that.

Maybe we should have lowered the Nimbex instead of turning it off, maybe we should have proned her more often, maybe if we started steroids earlier... She knew her thoughts were rambling. She was glad that Joni was there for her when she got home. They ate dinner in silence and went to bed. Joni held her all night as she cried. Sandy finally fell asleep. She had to be back at work the next day.

Sandy came in to find that Joan had coded during the night and did not make it. "It was a slow code. She was already on maximal support of everything. There was nothing much to do," Stephanie was on and told her.

"How was the family?"

"Horrible. They couldn't even come in to say goodbye."

"I thought we started letting family in when it was imminent."

"It happened too fast. There was no time to call them in. And we had to get the body out and ready for another admission."

Sandy looked into the room." "Is there someone waiting to come up?"

"Not yet."

"You have to pick up Ray today. And guess what?"

"What?"

"He's leaving for rehab today!"

"Oh my god, wait, what, he's actually leaving the hospital? Virtual hug!" said Sandy, and they both put their arms out in the air as if to hug.

"Okay, tell me about Mo."

"Well, I don't have good news. She is, of course, back on the Nimbex. I tried to stop it again as per Dr. Camarie, but she just can't breathe."

"And?"

"Her pressure started to drop, didn't respond to a fluid bolus, so her Levo is back up."

"Does Carly know?"

"Yes."

"So what's next?"

"Carly is trying to talk to Mo's mom, but she just doesn't understand."

"But Carly is the proxy, right."

"Yes, she is, but she feels like she has to talk to her grandma before she makes any final decisions."

"I understand."

"Dr. Camarie should be in early to FaceTime with Carly and make some decisions. We're going on two weeks now."

"Is there anything good to report?" Sandy said hopefully.

"Well, you did a great job with her hair." Stephanie tried to joke.

"That was mostly Ethan. He did a good job."

"Okay, so do you know what time Ray is leaving?"

"I think about four o'clock. Ambulette is all set up. Discharge paperwork is filled out. He just needs a set of vitals."

"Wow, I never thought he would make it, but I am so happy and happy for Darlene and Lloyd."

"I hope they will be able to visit in the rehab."

"Don't know, visitors are still restricted everywhere, especially in rehabs." Sandy already knew that from watching the news that rehab places were very underreported in terms of COVID. Many residents died and were never tested. "I'm not gonna even get into that discussion now."

"So what are we thinking with Mo? Are we up to that point now?"

"I think so."

Sandy's eyes started to well up. "You know, she was my preceptor. She was tough as nails, but I learned so much. I will never forget her. Do you think we are going to do something today? I would really like to be here."

"Well, Dr. Camarie is coming around the corner now, so you can ask him."

He looked somber as he came up to Stephanie and Sandy. "So anything positive here?"

"I'm afraid not, Dr. Camarie," Stephanie said, tearing up. Sandy started to cry silently.

"It's okay, ladies, we just have to come to terms with honoring Mo's wishes. We all knew her. We knew her ideals, values, and certainly her opinions. She was never quiet about that."

"Will Carly be able to come in to see her if we do a compassionate wean?"

"We will get her here, someway, somehow. But first, I am going to examine Mo, then call Carly."

He went into her room. "Hey, Mo, it's Henry Camarie. We had hoped things would have progressed in a different way for you, but we find ourselves in a predicament. I want you to know that every treatment we could get our hands on was tried to no avail." Dr. Camarie was beginning to cry. "Mo, you were one crazy smart outspoken nurse. I learned a lot from you, as did everyone. We have the utmost gratitude for all your contributions to this unit, sarcasm and all." He tried to laugh, but it came out strangled and defeated. "Now I have to speak to Carly, and we have to decide what to do going forward. She knows you. In fact, we all know you, so for this decision, you've made it easy for us."

Stephanie and Sandy were outside, looking through the glass, crying.

Dr. Camarie put his hand over Maureen's. "Mo, there are no words." He choked back tears. He picked up the iPhone and dialed Carly.

Carly was on in an instant. When she saw Dr. Camarie's face on the phone, she started to cry. "*No, no, no!* Not yet."

"I'm afraid so, Carly. It's time. We have done everything possible, but I'm afraid Mom is just not getting better." Sandy came into the room and put her hand on Dr. Camarie's shoulder.

"Who is that with you?" Carly said.

"It's Sandy, I'm here with your mom."

"Can you stay until I get there?"

"Of course."

"How am I going to get in?"

"Don't worry about that. Can you have someone drive you to the emergency room entrance?"

"Yes."

"I'll meet you there in, say, one hour? Is that enough time?"

"Should I bring Grandma?"

"That is up to you, but I think it would just be too much for her. We will be here with you."

"Can you make it two hours? I have to get some stuff ready and make some calls."

"Of course. Let me give you my cell number, and you call me when you have parked, and I'll meet you."

"Okay, thank you for everything, Doctor. Is Sandy still there?"

"I'm here."

"Will you be there when I get there?"

"I wouldn't be anywhere else."

"Thank you, Sandy." Carly hung up. Sandy looked at her watch. It was almost one thirty in the afternoon. She felt like she was in the twilight zone. Jan came over to the room to find out what was going on. All she had to do was look at Sandy and Stephanie, who was still there well into the day shift. She knew what was going to happen.

Sandy asked, "Is Ethan due on today? I know he would want to be here."

"Yes, he is." Sandy went out and shot him a text so he would be a little early.

"OMW" (on my way) was the text she got back. Sandy went to check on Ray. He looked good; he was smiling, and he gestured for her to come into the room. "So I hear you're going to rehab today!"

Ray nodded excitedly. He had been decannulated, so he was able to phonate (make sounds).

"Yes" came back in a soft voice. "Where's Mom and Dad?"

"Well, they still can't come into the hospital, but I'll bet they will be there waiting for you at the rehab." Ray nodded. He was still slow to respond, but Sandy knew in her heart that after a stay in rehab, he would eventually get back to normal. She was so happy for him. "Ray, I am just going to take your vital signs for your discharge paperwork, then all we have to do is wait for your ride."

"Okay," he said slowly. "Can I have the remote?"

"Of course." Sandy shook her head as she realized it had been placed just outside of his reach. She went back to Mo's room. Sandy got out linens and was going to wait for Ethan to bathe and make Mo look presentable for Carly. Ethan was already in the room, cell phone out, playing "Summer Breeze." They both started to cry as they began one final loving bath. They tried to sing along although they didn't know the words.

"This is surreal," Ethan said. "Stop it, we're going to ruin our N95s, and good luck getting us others." They both concentrated on the bath, being careful to wash her hands, underneath her fingernails, do detailed oral care, and remove all leftover tape residue. Everywhere

Carly looked would be clean and presentable. Sandy fixed all her dressings. She made sure to use the lavender body wash everywhere. Soon the room began to smell like lavender. There was nothing to be done about her near-skeletal state, however. It had been two weeks since Carly had seen her, and Sandy knew she would be shocked.

Ethan tidied up the room, put everything in the closets and underneath the sink. They had both hoped to have the environment look less hospital like, but that was impossible due to the pumps, ventilator, and monitor. Still, they did their best. They had been in there over an hour when they saw Dr. Camarie coming toward them with a person in full PPE whom they assumed was Carly. They had a chair prepared for her beside her mom. Maureen had been turned to the side, facing the chair.

"Take all the time you need," Sandy said. Carly noticed they had "Summer Breeze" playing. "Oh my god, Mom's favorite, how can I ever thank you?"

"We love your mom, our Mo," Ethan said. "Call us if you need anything." Sandy and Ethan left the room. Much of the staff on that day made it a point to pass by the room to say hello to Carly and goodbye to Mo.

They would let Carly sit there as long as she needed to. Carly put on music again and started to sing to her mom.

As staff passed by, they nodded to Carly and told her how much they had all learned from her mom.

"She taught me how to start an IV…"

"She was the best… She could get blood out of a stone, and the patient never even noticed…"

"She knew everything about chest tubes…"

"I wouldn't have survived my first week here without here…"

People did not mind donning their PPE to pay their respects to Maureen and Carly.

Carly held her mother's hand and leaned in and put her head on her chest. She was whispering to her mom quietly. Suddenly she stood up and announced, "It's time." Maureen was already on enough sedation to keep her comfortable.

The staff gathered around her room. Dr. Camarie came in, shut off the ventilator, and gently extubated Maureen. Sandy watched the monitor. Within a few minutes, Maureen's heart rate became slower and slower, her saturation became lower, and her breathing ceased. It was surprisingly quiet and all too quick.

Dr. Camarie put his stethoscope to her chest, shook his head, and spoke, "Time of death—3:47 p.m."

Chapter 15

The Emergency Room
May 2020

Michael was assigned to one of the tents for the day. Since there were now three tents, one was for ICU-type vented patients, the other for PUI (persons under investigation), and the third was for non-vented COVID-positive patients. Michael knew that there would be lots of transfers between the tents depending on the status of the patient.

Michael was in the vented unit tent. He noticed that one of the x-ray portable machines was now housed in the tent. *I guess they are keeping one machine available for the COVID patients.* There were ten vented beds in the tent, and only five were filled. For the moment. Michael was happy to see there were three nurses in the tent, because they knew there would be upgrades from the non-vented and the PUI tent.

He took report on one patient, and the other two nurses, travelers from out of state, took report on two patients each. It was impossible to get to know all the nurses that had responded from other states and come to New York to help out in the crisis, but he was grateful to see them. He saw that they were each given PPE, and there were stashes in each tent put away by the ER techs. Michael never knew exactly where it all came from, but he was happy to find spaces to keep it hidden.

Greta from Tennessee was there on an eight-week contract assignment. She had been there three weeks already, and this was the first time Michael had met her.

Clare was there on a thirteen-week contract assignment from Texas. Michael found out that Clare had been in New York for six weeks already but had been bounced around to different hospitals during her assignment.

"Thank you so much for being here today." Michael greeted each one as warmly as one could with proper distancing. What he wanted to do was give them a hug.

Michael would have loved to chat with them about the hospitals they had been at and their experiences so far in New York, but there was much to do. He went and assessed his patient. Mr. Jose Perez, forty-eight, was a construction worker from a building site in Manhattan. Several of his fellow workers had tested positive for COVID. Jose, or Joe as he was called, was the only one who got sick and intubated.

Why do some people get mild symptoms, while others just tank? he thought.

Joe was on the typical cocktail, Levo, fentanyl, Versed, Precedex. The hospital was still out of Propofol. *At least he is not paralyzed,* Michael thought. Michael reviewed the orders and was surprised to see no proning schedule. He would remember to ask Dr. P. when he rounded. Michael pulled up his email on his phone. It had been a while since he had seen the updates by Dr. P. Maybe something in the emails would tell him why not all patients were being proned.

COVID UPDATE—Wednesday, April 29, 2020, 10:00 a.m.
Yesterday's Volume
- Total: 96
  - Adult: 89
  - Peds: 7
- In comparison:
  - Bronx 109
  - Brooklyn 102

Total adult admissions: 43
Total peds admissions: 1
COVID admits: 20
ICU admits: 1

ICU upgrades from floors: 3

Yesterday's COVID Dispositions
- DISCHARGES: 25
- MORTALITIES: 6

Today's COVID Census 7:00 am
- Total: 238
- Confirmed: 214
- PUIs: 24
- ICU pts: 83
- Vented: 80

Bed availability:
- COVID ICU: 23
- Non-COVID ICU: 7
- COVID floor: 36
- Non-COVID floor: 3·

Decommissioned ICU areas:
- MWE conference room
- 2 South

FAQs:

I understand we reached a milestone today. Is that true?

Yes. The number of COVID pts is down 50 percent from a peak just 2 weeks ago.

Also, of 19,000 COVID tests at Queens Memorial, at the peak, 60 percent were positive; currently, just 22 percent positive.

And in L&D here, 25 percent delivering moms were positive; now down to 5 percent.

ALL GOOD SIGNS!

JP April 29, 2020

Michael had not realized that he had not checked his email for a while. It seemed like things were getting better. Areas that were formerly COVID only were now returning to their original purpose. He hoped that this trend would continue, but looking around, it did not seem that way in the emergency room yet.

He went back into the tent; it was time to reposition Joe. Just then, Kyle came into the tent for the morning run of portables. He meticulously wiped down the x-ray machine that had been housed in the tent.

They elbowed each other, which had replaced the handshake and fist bump as a salutation.

"I still have this mask you gave me."

"Wait, what, I gave that to you at least two weeks ago."

"I know, it's been holding up pretty well."

"Your department didn't get any PPE supplies?"

"If they did, they aren't saying."

Michael knew that they had some PPE stashed in the usual nursing hiding places underneath the sinks, in boxes labeled with something else.

"Wait here." Michael went and retrieved another N95 and handed it to Kyle.

"I don't want you to get into trouble."

"No worries, stay safe, man."

Kyle started to x-ray the patients in the tent one at a time. Each time he called "X-ray," the staff huddled at the door of the tent.

When he finished, he went over to Michael with a stack of requisitions.

"Do you know where any of these patients are? They haven't created a code for the tents yet." Michael noticed that Kyle's eyes were a bit glassy looking.

"You okay, man?" Michael felt that familiar knot in his stomach forming.

"Yeah, thanks for asking, just have been doing a lot of overtime lately. Several people out sick these days."

"You sure?"

"Yeah, I'm sure."

Michael looked up the ER census and found that the patients Kyle was searching for were all in the PUI tent. He pointed Kyle in the direction of the tent.

"So these patients are not confirmed COVID?"

"Not yet."

"Wait, I have to call my supervisor. I don't know if I can use this same machine if they are not confirmed cases. Can I use a phone anywhere?"

"Sure, take mine." Kyle called Donna only to find out he had to replace the COVID machine with a clean machine. Kyle calmly walked the machine back to the tent where Michael was in, wiped it down with a towel and spray bottle of the solution the pharmacy was making to replace the Clorox wipes, and plugged it in.

"See you in a moment, going to get the other machine."

What a waste of time, Michael thought. This is not going to make any difference in these people. It is not like the machine is touching them. He felt worried about Kyle.

Michael received the call that one of the non-vented patients in the second COVID tent was now being intubated. He set up the next slot to get ready. He got out the pumps with Precedex, ordered the Levo and Versed drips from the pharmacy.

How are things looking better? That's not what I'm seeing.

The staff from the non-vented tent came in with the patient already intubated. A respiratory therapist was bagging the patient, and the second respiratory therapist went to get the ventilator set up.

Another travel nurse, Carmela, was there with the patient. Michael had never met her either. After a quick hello, Carmela began report. "This is Mrs. Campbell, she is eighty. She has a history of heart failure on maximal medications, was being considered for a TAVR, diabetic, then came down with fever, cough, SOB, tested positive by PCR. DNR denied by the family, so here she is. Her vitals are actually stable right now."

Michael already knew that this was not a patient that would do well. He reviewed Mrs. Campbell's orders for the drips: titrate Levo as appropriate, Versed and Precedex to maintain vent synchrony. There was now an order set for the vented COVID patient. Then he saw the order for an insulin drip. He picked up the phone and called pharmacy again.

Michael shook his head. *This woman never should have been intubated with all these comorbidities. Meanwhile, Joe has no proning schedule, and they want me to titrate an insulin drip. I just don't get the priorities.* Michael made a mental note to talk to Dr. P.

All these things were running around in Michael's head when Kyle appeared with the second x-ray machine.

"Is there a Campbell in here?"

"Yes, right over here."

Michael looked at Kyle and saw he was sweating. He started to sway on his feet.

"Whoa! You need to sit a minute." Michael did a quick temp scan and was alarmed to see it was 101.2. "Hey, Kyle, you have a significant fever. I'm taking you to triage, and I'm gonna call Donna."

Kyle was so wiped out, he couldn't even argue with him. He felt awfully sick all of a sudden. Michael called out to Greta and Clare, "Be right back, I have to take this employee over to triage."

"No worries."

Michael walked Kyle over to Sheena, the triage nurse for the shift. Sheena, another traveler from South Carolina, was pleasant and cheerful.

"Whatcha got here?"

"This is Kyle, he is a rad tech here. I think he needs to be screened."

"Okay," said Sheena vibrantly. "Have a seat, Kyle, let's see what's doing here."

Sheena began with the usual questions. "Have you traveled anywhere recently?"

"Uh, just around this entire hospital," Kyle said jokingly.

Sheena scanned Kyle's forehead for a temperature. "Okay, you're hot, 101.8. You just got a free sick day!" She saw her levity was wasted because Kyle was struggling just to stay upright. She got serious again. "Any shortness of breath, cough, how long have you been feeling this way?"

Kyle, always one to minimize his symptoms, said, "Well, I've just been feeling a little tired lately, but I figured it was because of all the overtime we have put in…and I'm always sweating around here underneath all this PPE, so I didn't figure anything was up." Sheena pulled up the order set for the COVID protocol.

"I've got to get back, buddy, but I'll check in again in a few minutes," said Michael. "I'm gonna to tell Dr. P to come see you, and I will call Donna right now."

"Okay, thanks, man."

Michael walked away, the knot in his stomach tightening yet again.

"Well, let's get you swabbed, get some blood drawn, then I'll call that Dr. P for you since you are an employee. Do you have someone that can take you home?"

"I can drive."

"Not sure that's such a good idea. But let's see what happens."

Kyle was brought back to the PUI tent. An IV was started, blood work and COVID PCR swab done, chest x-ray ordered. His vital signs were normal except for the temperature and a bit of tachycardia. He was given Tylenol and a bolus of normal saline.

Just then Dr. P came in. "Hey, Kyle, how are you feeling?"

"Not bad really, just tired."

"Let's get one of your guys to x-ray you. I think we'll send you home after the x-ray. What's his sat?" Dr. P said to the nurse.

"It's 97 percent. His rapid COVID swab came back positive."

"Okay, you don't need to be admitted, but you will need to be out for at least fourteen days. Who can drive you home?"

"I feel okay to drive."

"Sorry, buddy, but we need someone to pick you up."

"My parents will be too upset. I don't want them to find out I am a patient, even just for a few hours."

Just then Michael popped his head in. "I'm gonna call Pam. She is off, she'll take you home."

"No, I don't want to expose her."

Michael bent over to whisper to Kyle. "I'll give you another N95 from the stash," he whispered, "and I'll tell Pam to wear one too. I'm not taking no for an answer."

"Let's just hydrate him, and then I'll discharge him."

"Thanks Dr. P," Kyle said.

Kyle knew he would have to quarantine from his parents. He knew they would be so upset. He would have to tell them the truth. He did not want them to have to drive anywhere to get him anything, as he was used to doing it for them.

Michael had already called Pam, and she was on her way.

Michael went back into his assigned tent. He continued to assess Joe and Mrs. Campbell. He asked Dr. P about the proning schedule for Joe. "Damn! Sorry, I meant to write that in. There is just so much craziness going on, I forgot. One of the MLPs should have seen that and written for it."

Michael waited with Kyle until Pam came driving up. "Take care, buddy, we've got games to go to when this is all behind us."

"Sure thing." Kyle turned to Pam. "I really appreciate you doing this."

"Of course." She turned. "See you later, honey," she called out to Michael, but he had already disappeared into the tent.

Michael finished his shift with more of the same, titrating drips, suctioning, turning, drawing blood, calling Joe to make vent changes, and trying desperately to get patients in a place to titrate down vent settings.

He did notice, however, that one of the tents was being taken down. *Maybe that's a good sign?* he thought.

Reading the emails from Dr. P and seeing the news, nothing seems real. I don't know what to believe. Is it getting better or worse?

Michael finished his shift. He gave report to another traveling nurse he had never seen before and drove home. He did not listen to a news station or music; he drove in silence. Michael got home, removed all his PPE, and put it all in a plastic garbage bag ready for the washing machine, but he felt too exhausted to do laundry. He wanted to find out how Kyle was. Michael went inside. Pam was making dinner. He waved, blew her a kiss, and went up to shower.

After he showered, he called Kyle. Kyle had spent the afternoon sleeping and felt somewhat better, though by no means normal. The Tylenol had broken the fever, but he had no appetite and, in fact, couldn't smell or taste anything. He loved orange juice and drank a large glass when he got up, but it had no flavor at all. His head was pounding, and the Tylenol didn't help that at all. After washing up a little, he was ready to go back to bed. He thought about the conversation he had with his parents when he got home. He called them rather than went into their section of the home. He explained what was going on and had to keep his mother from rushing in to take care of him. "Look, Ma, if you get this from me, it could kill you. How do you think I'd feel then? You gotta let me deal with this on my own. I just need to rest."

"But, Kylie, I could make you some soup!"

"Yes, Ma. But you gotta leave it by my door. Do not come in, I'm not kidding." Kyle was grateful that the in-law suite had its own full kitchen. He kept his protein drinks and juices in the fridge. He knew fluids were most important. But his mother was irrepressible, and the parade of soups and snacks would be inevitable. He didn't have the strength to argue with her, but he was not going to let her come in, not expose her more than he already had. He fell asleep again until his phone rang. It was Michael checking up on him. At the same time, he heard his mother knocking on the door then calling out that she left soup on a tray.

"Don't let it get cold! You gotta eat it while it's hot!" she called out.

"Yes, Ma!" Kyle yelled back. "She's gonna make me crazy," he said to Michael. They finished talking, and Kyle went to the door to get his soup. Even though he couldn't taste it, he felt better after eating it. Then he took more Tylenol and went back to bed.

"How's Kyle?" asked Pam when Michael went downstairs after showering.

"Well, he seemed pretty tired, pretty worried, but said he didn't have fever. He's not short of breath, or anything like that. I think he was more worried about his parents' reaction. I'll call him later."

Pam called the kids in for dinner. They sat around the table. Pam tried to make small talk, but she knew Michael was in another dimension. The kids noticed it too. "Dad, what's wrong?"

"It's okay, boys, taking care of all these sick people has just made me exhausted and worried."

"You're not getting sick, are you, Dad?" Russell said. Of all the kids, Russell was the one who worried the most, and was also the one who was tuned in to how other people felt. He was extraordinarily sensitive.

That snapped Michael to attention. He did not want to worry the kids, who also had so many changes to deal with. "Look, Russell, I'm fine. I'm just a little worn out with all the overtime. I'm taking care of myself, and I will be fine. You've got nothing to worry about." He looked directly at Russell as he spoke. He was amazed to see Russ's shoulders relax. He knew he had said the right thing.

Inside, Michael wondered if he really was going to be fine. He wondered if anything would be fine again.

Two weeks later, Kyle had tested negative for COVID and had recovered enough to return to work. When he showed up in the ER, Michael started to think things really were improving.

Chapter 16

The Orthopedic Floor
May 2020

Fran went home, and she knew something was not right. She kept her mask on when she got home. Her head was pounding. Her joints ached, especially her knees and hips. She knew she had a fever. She used Robby's forehead scanner thermometer. Sure enough, her temperature was 102. She called employee health.

"Come in for a COVID swab." Not "How are you feeling?" or "I'm so sorry." Fran knew she could not drive at that moment. *This shows how they really feel about their employees. If we ever got caught talking to a patient in that peremptory way, we'd get written up.* She felt scared in the moment, but also deeply resentful. She felt as though she had fulfilled her obligation by going to work and taking care of sick people, but her supervisors were oblivious to the danger to her. They were stingy with PPE, and Fran knew this was only partly that it was not available; she knew people were hoarding it, and she suspected the upper administration of hoarding it for themselves and their families. Regardless, Fran had gone to work every day without fail and slogged through the heavy assignments, with the needy, scared patients and the endless phone calls from their worried families. Now she was sick, and who would care for her? Who would take care of her children?

I have to figure out how to quarantine from the kids and Mom in this small apartment. Her biggest worry was Robby. If he got sick, she could never forgive herself. Since there were enough places to sleep in the apartment, she decided to take the bedroom as it was the only place that was enclosed. She would have to come out and use the one bathroom in the apartment. Luckily, she had saved one N95 mask, and she had a few pairs of gloves and some Purell she had snuck out of the hospital in a hand lotion bottle.

Fran called her cousin to drive her to employee health to get the COVID PCR testing done. She had to wait days for the results. She knew it was going to be positive. When she found out it was positive, she started to get furious. Afterward, she realized there was no point in anger; it would change nothing.

Fran knew she had to concentrate on getting better. She needed to quarantine herself for fourteen days. Fortunately, she did not have any shortness of breath. She had the worst body aches she could imagine. Fran felt like her head was in a vise grip. She took Tylenol when she was awake.

One day, during her illness, she went to bed at eleven o'clock in the morning and woke the next day at 6:00 a.m. She was astonished that she had slept so long—nineteen hours! She felt disoriented and dizzy. She had not had anything to drink for hours. She was afraid to go out into the apartment to the kitchen—afraid she would be spreading the illness to her mom and kids.

She called her mom on the cell phone to leave her some bottled water outside the door. Fran had no appetite; she had no taste or smell. She remembered those symptoms from some of her patients.

Fran felt so afraid. She started to obsess about her own impending mortality. She had no will, no provisions made for Robby and Lilly.

Why the fuck didn't I take care of this stuff? she thought as she lay in bed, confined to her room. But she couldn't focus enough to even make a telephone call or look on her laptop to find a lawyer. She was so tired. Day after day, she thought, *Is this the day that I'll have to go to the hospital? Is this the day I will be short of breath?* She had her own pulse ox which she kept by her bedside and monitored herself whenever she was awake enough. She was relieved every time the oxygen saturation level was normal.

She was so grateful for her family. Her mother would knock on the door and leave food for her when she felt she could eat. Her cousin would go shopping and bring them supplies. Robby and Lilly had a lot of Happy Meals. Fran FaceTimed with the kids and her mom whenever she felt like she would not burst into tears. She often thought about what would happen if she died. Her mother would not be able to keep Robby, and he would be institutionalized. She knew only too well what those places were like. She had heard the most horrible stories of abuse and neglect, and Robby was not cute or endearing. He was frustrating and demanding, and Fran knew he would never be treated well. She despaired about leaving him. She also worried about poor Lilly. Lilly was always getting the leftovers when it came to attention. She hoped Lilly would forgive her when she grew up.

Fran started to feel better about day nine of her quarantine. She was amazed to be improving. She became able to think clearly. She knew she was going to go crazy for another five days in isolation. She thought about her patients and how many of them had died from this. *Why am I so lucky?* She burst into tears.

Later, when she was stronger, she looked at her bank statements on her computer. *Not enough saved for my upstate house.* She was restless and started to think about the future again. She thought of going back to work and then about getting a second job, as though there were enough hours in the day.

Fran knew since she was almost on the other side of this illness that she had built up antibodies against COVID.

She felt that she would be able to go back to work with a renewed sense of optimism. Fran had only seen death from this illness. Now she had seen endurance.

I survived this. That means others will survive this too.

Epilogue

By the end of this story, over six hundred health-care workers have lost their lives to COVID-19. Many more have died without having been tested, so it is likely that the death toll is higher.

No nurse, doctor, lab tech, radiology tech, nursing assistant, housekeeper, or dietary worker thought showing up to work in 2020 would mean exposure to a virus that could and did kill them. So many faced delays in obtaining the personal protective equipment that could have saved countless lives.

Multiple challenges have faced frontline workers, including having to reuse masks and other PPE countless times, not being aware of the need to even use PPE, no early testing of patients, overcrowded emergency rooms, lack of adequate staffing, and lack of social distancing early on. Some of the treatments of COVID-19 have changed over the course of the year, such as the addition of anticoagulation, the addition of Decadron, the novel treatment remdesivir, avoiding intubation instead of jumping right on it, and using pronation to help aerate the posterior portion of the lungs. Few things were tried and found not effective, such as hydroxychloroquine and azithromycin. At the time of this writing, the use of convalescent plasma obtained from people who recovered from COVID-19 was being used under an emergency authorization by the FDA, briefly rescinded as it was interfering with the methodical study of that approach in a controlled clinical trial. It was later reauthorized with the study ongoing—which might help individuals if it really is an effective strategy. It will most certainly complicate the study. As of December 2020, there are two soon-to-be approved vaccines in the United States, and vaccinations are starting in the UK using the

Pfizer vaccine (one of the two early candidate vaccines). There is still no armamentarium of treatments although studies are underway.

Importantly, people, including health-care workers, continue to get infected, and many are still dying. Over 245,000 Americans have died from COVID-19 as of August 2020.

This chronicle is not at all meant to be political in nature. Therefore, the authors have not expressed their own political views. A new administration has been elected with the promise to make the control of COVID-19 a priority. Mask mandates are in place in many states coming from local legislators instead of the current federal government.

However, the authors, just as noted in their previous work *Nurses on the Inside*, can see the factors having an impact on the pandemic. Discrimination, stigma, ignorance, and different access to care once again are driving the spread and lethality of this illness. A lack of nationally coordinated policy, including a sloppy rollout of testing, has hampered any chance of a unified approach to treatment. Mixed messages have confused people about the need to wear masks and practice social distancing, and the absurd notion of COVID as a conspiracy has divided the country yet again, pitting people against each other instead of coming together as a country to fight the virus.

About the Authors

Valery Hughes is a family nurse practitioner who has focused most of her career on the care of people with HIV infection. She has worked in HIV research for the past twenty-one years. During the COVID pandemic, her research group at Weill Cornell Medicine/Cornell Clinical Trials Unit changed their focus from HIV to COVID-19 therapeutics and prevention as one of the sites for the remdesivir study, the Moderna mRNA vaccine trial, the Novavax vaccine trial, and the ACTG A5401 "Adaptive Platform Treatment Trial for Outpatients with COVID-19 (Adapt Out COVID)."

Valery lives with her wife, Mary Arzilli, of thirty-nine years in Manhattan.

Ellen Matzer has been a registered nurse since 1978. Her clinical focus was HIV until 2000 when the need for in-patient care for people with HIV was diminishing. At that time, Ellen returned to her first clinical interest, intensive care nursing, at an intensive care unit of a Long Island hospital for the next seventeen years. She is certified in critical care nursing (CCRN).

Currently she works as an educator in another Long Island hospital as well as a member of the clinical faculty of a Long Island LPN school. Ellen is working on getting the next generation of nurses prepared for whatever awaits them in the world.

Ellen has also worked clinically in the COVID pandemic by accepting assignments of screening and education in corporate settings.

She has two children, age thirty-two and thirty, and currently lives with her husband of twelve years, Kenneth, in Long Island.

Ellen and Valery are the authors of *Nurses on the Inside: Stories of the HIV/AIDS Epidemic in NYC,* winner of the 2019 POZ Award for literature. The book was featured in *A&U magazine and the Gay Star News.*

CPSIA information can be obtained
at www.ICGtesting.com
Printed in the USA
BVHW031831280222
630257BV00005B/48

9 781638 607151